In Ben Schrank's vividly realized debut novel, Martin Kelly Minter yearns for a meaningful relationship with his beautiful Puerto Rican neighbor, Luz, and a place in history as a modern-day Robin Hood. A college dropout, self-exiled from his middle-class family, he works as a moving man in Manhattan. When Kelly decides that the wealthy New Yorkers he moves don't appreciate what they have, he steals from them and plots to give to the poor. And on a cold winter day he bakes bread, counting on its warmth to seduce Luz. Kelly tries to do right, but when he gets the chance to make big-time money as a bigger-time thief, he calls this his destiny.

"Incisive Ben Schrank conjures love as disconnection, an ache that feels filling, as a young man swallows an attraction, knowing that romance makes everything okay and also becomes an opportunity to hate closeness."   —*The Village Voice*

"What's most refreshing about Schrank: He infuses his main character with pure, unbridled longing, which few writers in this aloof age allow themselves to do."   —*Detour*

"In this rough-and-tumble coming-of-age novel, Kelly Minter must reconcile the idealism he has been raised with and the harsh realities of street-level New York City. A stylish and intriguing first novel."
—Blake Nelson, author of *Girl*

MIRACLE
MAN

Ben Schrank

MIRACLE
MAN

a novel

Quill

William Morrow

New York

Chapter 4 appeared in a slightly different form as "The Good Chance Chicken" in
The KGB Bar Reader, published in 1998 by William Morrow and Company, Inc.

It is the policy of William Morrow and Company, Inc., and its imprints and affiliates,
recognizing the importance of preserving what has been written, to print the books we
publish on acid-free paper, and we exert our best efforts to that end.

Library of Congress Cataloging-in-Publication Data

Schrank, Ben.
    Miracle man : a novel / Ben Schrank. — 1st ed.
        p. cm.
    ISBN 0-688-16771-3
    I. Title.
PS3569.C52913m57   1999
813'.54—DC21   98-47671
                                                              CIP

Printed in the United States of America

First Edition

1 2 3 4 5 6 7 8 9 10

BOOK DESIGN BY CHRIS WELCH

www.williammorrow.com

The Lord said to Cain, "Why are you angry and why has your countenance fallen? If you do well will you not be accepted? And if you do not do well, sin is lurking at the door; its desire is for you, but you must master it."

—Genesis 4:6

There ain't no clean way to make a hundred million bucks.

—Raymond Chandler, The Long Goodbye

THE MIRACLE MAN WORKS

part one

1

We'd just finished a job, and I leaned against the side of
the International. Our truck was old and pretty busted up. It was
covered with a hippie-style painting of a massive pale hand (God's)
bursting through fat white clouds with a glowing cardboard box in
its palm. The rest of the truck was sky blue. The painting was old,
and it was peeling and torn in places where Teddy and the other
drivers had knocked the truck against cars, buses, trees, buildings,
and other trucks.

My brother Felix came up and stood with me.

"You take?" I asked.

"Nah, she said to come by later for a visit."

"Yeah, right. Ugly bastard like you—" I reached over and tickled his
chin. He pushed me away. Felix wasn't pretty, with his acne-scarred
face and two weeks of stubble on his skull, the bruises that all the

movers shared so evident on his neck and arms. We were built nearly the same, me just under six feet and Felix a little shorter than that. We were both thick—not fat, but solid. I didn't have my hair shaved like Felix, though. I wore mine shaggy and parted on one side, so I was always brushing it back. Felix liked to rag on me about that, how I'd brush my light brown hair back when I talked to women, try to look at them all careful with my brown eyes. And he wasn't wrong. Since I couldn't afford to dress well, all I could do was look right, smile, try to be dense in my face, and clear, be real present.

Felix was not my real brother.

He was a Puerto Rican foster child brought up in The Bronx, and I was Jewish and Irish and a true rural export, from Rantipole Farms, in Hawley County, Pennsylvania. Felix and I were Fresh Air Fund brothers from back when we were nine and my parents had him brought out to the country. They did it for him, because it was the right thing to do for an underprivileged kid, and for me, too, because I needed a friend. We got real close. We cut our thumbs with my Swiss Army knife and made ourselves blood brothers. The Fresh Air Fund deal didn't work out too well, though. And I think that's why it was eleven years later and we'd ended up working as furniture movers. But at least we were together.

It was the Friday before Labor Day and most of the rich people were wherever they disappear to when it gets hot. Trees were drooped down. There was no wind, no traffic.

During the unload I'd been looking, setting down boxes and bits of furniture—so lightly—on flowery new carpet, looking for the easy object, looking for something to take. The crazy rich customer watched. All the time, she watched. I hadn't stolen anything yet. But I wanted to.

I pulled up my T-shirt and wiped my face. The shirt said MIRA-CLE MOVE in big red letters, along with the phone number. Our tag line was on the back, also in red: MIRACLE MOVE—WHEN YOU MOVE WITH US, YOU'LL SEE—WE ARE MIRACLE WORKERS.

"It's hard," I said. "Customer was obsessive."

"And then there's fuckin' Teddy." Felix nodded.

Teddy came out of the service entrance door. He was bald and five and a half feet tall, with forearms as thick as his tough little head. He was angry and mean, and sometimes he was stupid. He rarely got us a good tip. He cursed us when we made mistakes and he even told Isaac, our owner, when we broke something. Isaac would estimate the cost of what we broke and take it out of the money we got for our next job. But Teddy cared about us, I knew that. When I was drinking too much or getting upset over nothing, he'd mention it, warn me. That was enough. I loved him.

"Tip?" Felix asked.

"Tip?" I asked. Then we both started saying it, singing it, looking at each other and dancing to the words, again and again, "What . . . what is up with the tip?"

"Stop it! She didn't do us right, there was nothing I could do about it," Teddy said.

"Tip?" We kept whispering it.

"You should see yourselves, it's not cute at all," Teddy said. He climbed into the cab of the International. "So lemme pay you."

Felix got paid first because I'd been with Miracle for more than a year, but less than two, and Felix had been there one more year than that.

"I was kidding. She said she liked you both, she thought you were retarded. So I said she was right and she gave us twenty-five a man."

I opened my eyes wide and smiled. "Nice!" I said. It was always such a fine surprise when we got tipped right.

"Not bad," Felix said.

"We should go thank her," I said. Me and Felix headed back toward the building.

"Yeah right, she said she'd meet you both later at Hooligans. Anyway, she did you right, so no bitching. Which of you is coming downtown and unload with me?"

Me and Felix looked at each other. Teddy always needed an extra guy to ride with him down to the lot on Chrystie. There was nothing to unload, really. But he carried all the cash from the job and he'd been robbed coming out of the lot late one night, so now he always brought somebody extra with him. And if you rode down with him, he'd tell you the story about how he was robbed and about just how angry it made him. I didn't like to hear it anymore. Felix usually went with him, because Teddy paid out six bucks for the extra time. Felix had married a woman called Lynanne since we'd been apart, and they had a fantastic daughter called Anastasia. He needed more money than I did.

"I guess it's me," Felix said. He hopped in the cab.

"Good-bye, my brother, I love you," I said.

"Good-bye, my brother, I love you," Felix said.

And then the job was done and I was just a guy, no longer a Miracle worker, earnest employee of the Miracle Move company, Miracle man.

"Take care, Kelly—there's work tomorrow," Teddy said, "and say a Spanglish hello to the good old El fucking Barrio from me."

"Teddy . . ." Felix said. But he didn't finish.

Teddy did his spit-cackle laugh and they drove off. I believe he didn't mean anything by what he said—for some people that is only the way they talk.

At Third and Ninety-sixth there's a sudden slope that heads you down into Spanish Harlem. I concentrated on the downturn. My building was on 103rd and Second Avenue. I didn't stare around too much because I knew there were people watching. It was mostly the teenagers who gave me the vicious looks. They were just about to be back in school, so I guess maybe they were pissed off about that, and I was too close to their age, too white, dressed more like a crankhead than anything else—they really didn't like me. In the place where I kept fear, I believed they would be my demise. I kept going, fast, toward my little room, my shoe box in the sky.

Though I didn't know it when I moved in, my building was pure tenement, ungentrified and dirty. There was a ghost panel where the front door buzzers were supposed to be, burned-out hall lights, the usual bunch of bugs and vermin. I'd ended up there because a former Miracle employee—a guy who was fired for walking off jobs that had too many flights of stairs—this guy's mom died. She had an apartment with really intense rent control. This was because it was managed by Housing Preservation and Development and most people that lived there had paid somebody to move them up on the waiting list. When this guy's mom died he offered her place to me for a thousand-dollar fee. The rent was $287 and I figured the guy needed the grand to cover funeral costs, plus I felt bad for him, since he'd just lost his mother. So I gave him $1200. I still got mail for a Mrs. J. Davis, and I paid the rent with a money order that had her name on it. Also, when the housing inspectors came by and I was home I had to sound like an old black lady who was delusionary and too scared to answer the door. I thought I was lucky, with a real New York native–type deal. Plus there was a White Castle around the corner on 104th and First, and they were open twenty-four hours a day. I had a deep love for that Castle.

I'd been there a year and I was just realizing how much you can tell about a building by looking at its windows. If they're small, close together, dirty, with curtains made out of bedsheets hung up to blot out the sun, all kinds of illegal cable wires and space heaters jammed in the bottoms, and no air conditioners at all, then it's a tenement and no mistake. But I didn't know that when I handed off my twelve C's.

There were good things. Somebody mopped the tiny vestibule just often enough that it was a pleasant surprise when they did. Once in a while the roof door would fly open and a breeze would come down the stairs. Of course, there were only stairs. A steep six flights of dirt-veined yellow marble steps, worn so smooth that going up you had to make sure to absolutely plant your feet, toe to riser, and going down, well, you could slip right down—I'd taken that slip to a fresh new dimension and I was convinced I'd learned to fly. I lived on the top floor.

When I got home that day and opened the gray metal front door with its thousand dents and scuff marks, I saw the Queen.

She lived with her family on the third floor. She was not old, but she was heavy in front, in the chest and belly, and she went up stupefying slow, especially when she had groceries. A little boy called Alfredo, who I figured was her son, danced around her while she climbed. When I got caught behind them it was always an additional couple of minutes on the trip. And it wasn't like I wanted to spend extra time in the corridors and staircase either, with the smells of roach killer and cooking, the purple paint from the ground to four feet up the wall and the graffiti-laden gray that went up past that and onto the ceiling.

The Queen was just getting started on the steps and already she was puffing. She had a bag of food, with a bunch of plantains on top. I gave her a real smile and took the bag. It wasn't heavy and me and Alfredo left her and went up. I heard somebody else come into the building and start talking to the Queen in Spanish. At the next landing, Alfredo handed me his tiny super ball.

"Smack it hard," Alfredo said.

We'd played before. I would smack the ball as hard as I could and it would ricochet around and Alfredo would jump up and down and try to catch it. I bounced it hard and it went right up to the next floor and we ran up after it. We were on the third floor then, and Alfredo banged on his door just as I smacked the ball. I mean I was deep into that ball, into the physics of the bounce.

The door opened and the ball curved—probably from the wind— and it hit a young woman right in the middle of her chest. She stared at us and touched the spot where the ball had hit. Alfredo busted out laughing.

He yelled, "She's down on two, he's got our groceries, he's *carrying* them!"

Though the boy was maybe five, superbly young, he knew he had to explain me. The girl rubbed her chest. I kneeled and picked up the ball and handed it to Alfredo. He stared up at me.

"Again," he said.

"I'm sorry," I said.

The girl held out her arms—still silent—and I gave up the groceries. I reached in and smelled baby powder and makeup and something warm that made me want to touch her neck with my cheek, my lips. I got a little eye flutter then, when I smelled her, and I hoped like mad that she didn't see it. She had the groceries, but then she couldn't pull Alfredo inside and shut the door on me because we could both hear the Queen making her way toward us.

To stare hard you have to be bold. You have to allow yourself to trust, to fall. We stared for a solid four or five seconds while Alfredo bounced his superball. She had big black eyes and pouty lips. Her hair was back in a ponytail. She was beautiful. My mouth was open.

Maybe I was sweaty, and my jeans were maybe a little ratty. She might have looked down and seen my high-top Adidas from 1995 that had long ago turned the color of playground dirt. I remember trying to brush the hair out of my eyes.

Then the Queen came through and I got out of her way. She was huffing like she'd been punched, but she still bowed and I did the same and we smiled at each other like we always did in the way that made the favor feel so good. The girl in the doorway spoke.

"Thank you," she said. "I'm Luz." She had a thickness to her voice, the assured sexuality that comes with that kind of thick sound.

"Kelly," I said.

Alfredo threw the ball at me, it bounced off my chest, he caught it, he ran inside, and the door closed.

I stepped away and I was just old enough to realize that I had met the second great love of my life. Then I ran up the stairs like a jackrabbit. There was a feeling in me—I'd seen somebody and then, for a second, *I felt happy.* I'm not saying that feeling was alien, just that I felt lucky to have it. Who knew you were allowed to have that powerful crush feeling twice? And true happy. How often does that feeling ever hit?

I got up and into my room.

There was a message on my machine from Cass, calling from Vermont. There was a picture of her on my wall, too, with her dulled-out "Give me everything you have and I'll take it and you'll wish you had even more to give me" smile.

"I am calling. To say hello. We haven't talked. And I wanted . . . to make sure. You're still doing well. Okay."

That's how she talked, stunted, slow. I swear to God I don't think about her as much as people think about their first love, like all the time, and each morning upon waking, and like that. It had been much more than a year and only a bit less than two and that's time enough to get over somebody, plenty time enough by anybody's standards. That's the way it works. I know that. It hurts in a funny way, when you lose people. And it wasn't right, the way we were just supposed to say good-bye to each other without getting something, without taking something from each other that we could keep forever. I didn't get that. I didn't feel like I ever got enough from people, nothing that I could touch, that I could keep. When she started to pull away from me, I broke up with her. Because I understood that if you do it that way, there's so much less to lose. Even if I dropped her because I was scared she'd leave, because she did leave, because I dropped her. Even if it makes no sense and there was no resolve, I'd had enough time to get over her. There had been enough time. I bit hard on my thumb and told myself all over again about how I was finished with being sad about Cass. And now, there was a really pretty girl downstairs, called Luz.

I had two chairs, one steel, one wood. I preferred the wooden one, which was white and had a nice roll to the seat, where it nestled me. I clasped my hands behind my head, put my feet up on the radiator, and looked out at the city.

I was high enough that I could look across Spanish Harlem and then into the Upper East Side, in between tenements and then down to the new high-rise apartments named after English manors and castles that create the ragged barrier that is Ninety-sixth Street. Then, beyond that borderline, I could see just a few of the true rich buildings. I watched for quite a while, until the sun started to dip, far to my right, and the buildings showed rims of glowing red and gold.

I walked back and forth across the twelve-foot square that was my room. I thought about Luz and how I could get her to like me, and the very, very little I had to recommend me. It is true that when people stop me in the street to ask directions I tell them, and I make myself clear. Sometimes I keep them too long, handing out alternate routes to where they want to go, and I know I should let them be, but it is hard, sometimes, when you want to help. I have gone to the Empire State Building with a man from Paris. I have walked the length of the San Gennaro festival with an older couple from Japan.

I like to give my money away, too. I do! My parents—with them it was checks written out on weekday evenings, charity always, this weird activity that looked like little more than some obscure chore. Just keep on writing the checks. Well, I didn't have a checking account. So when I walked by a guy on the street who needed a dollar, and I had ten, I gave him five. And in my head, there was always the notion that all I was doing was getting it tighter, this big damn distance between what you do and how it makes things good for other people. I just wanted to get money fast and then give it away. Not like my mom and dad, who moved too slow.

I got out of that chair and down on the floor and did sit-ups till the stars in my eyes exploded. Running up and down stairs in buildings all over Manhattan with boxes strapped to my back had made my lungs grow strong. My hamstrings had begun to stretch out and thicken. I was my own evolving species—my legs would get longer, my trunk shorter. And from then on I planned to be on my stairs a lot, to see her. I would become a crazy love pogo stick, a shock absorber, an industrial-strength spring constricted into the shape of a big fat crush.

Later, I went downstairs to get Chinese food for dinner. Teenagers were hanging out in front of my building, like always. They parted for me to get through. I did the thing where I was blind to them. They were all in tons of sports apparel. Baseball clothes were way popular then.

A girl parted from the group and approached me. She had a great mass of black hair, all in beautiful tiny ringlets, and she was in a Yankees warm-up jacket and stretch pants.

"Yo, you met my sister, right?"

I looked at her. She had the same black eyes, only she had a scar over one eyebrow that made her look impish, curious. She had dimples, too, and she was smiling, maybe even smirking at me. She might have been fifteen.

"Your sister is Luz?"

"Yeah, you know."

"I met her. I know your mom, too."

The other teenagers were quiet, watching us, but then one of the boys grabbed a girl's Orioles cap and they swarmed away, screaming and laughing.

"You like her, right? You're Kelly, right? I'm Jahaira, her sister."

"Yeah," I said. I put my hands in my pockets. I didn't have anything but my keys and some bills. "Listen, I got a present for her—I don't have it now, though, I'm going to give it to her soon, okay? I'll find her soon."

"Ooh, you do like her!"

"Nice to meet you," I said.

"Oooh!" Jahaira ran away then, with her friends. And then I thought, now you have to go find some present to give Luz.

2

There was no work the next Thursday so I arranged to take an afternoon walk with my brother, Kevin. He wanted to do the godforsaken East Side jaunt that I hate, that he likes to do. Kevin was never nice, but by then he'd gone further and turned into a true nasty high-level goofball, an intern at St. Vincent's destined for private practice in plastic surgery where he wouldn't ever treat really sick people, just demented old ladies, concerned models, and rich teenagers.

I hadn't seen him since early June, when I'd gotten through less than half of one weekend at his Bridgehampton share with his med school buddies who did tequila slammers and goosed one another's asses between talk about the stock market. When I woke up Saturday morning some more people had already arrived and had begun to mix mimosas while they sang the *Gilligan's Island* theme song, in rounds. I threw my extra T-shirt and shorts in my duffel bag and hoofed it to the train station, and all I could think about was how far I was from my brother, from those people. I congratulated myself a little, I admit, on the values that kept me from enjoying his fun. My brother—who knew what it was that got to him when we were little and tore out all the benevolence that my parents had worked so hard to shove into us? So now he was all out for him. And I specifically remember my mother saying how that wasn't cool.

"No matter what you do," she said, "make sure you're always thinking about how you can help to take care of other people. Your father and I believe that's why we're all here, and that's what we want you to take from us. Remember to always give to others."

"Mom, the only thing I'm going to give to others is the bill," Kevin said and cracked up. He was thirteen when he said that, and I was eight, and I hadn't even met Felix yet and already I was way confused. I remember staring, thinking, Why's my brother making fun of the gospel my mother just sent down?

I found Kevin looking into the window of a store and I approached slow. My brother is one of those guys who is like a seal, with his nose turned up a little bit, skin that's real smooth and clean, and black hair slicked back. Where my eyes are kind of big and awkward looking, his are small and beady. When we were kids he used to tell me he looked like Matt Dillon, but after a while I decided he was deceiving himself very badly on that score.

I came up and stood next to him, tried hard to look at whatever he was looking at.

"How's things?"

"Kelly." He nodded at me, like we were business partners.

"I said, How's things?"

"Good, fine. Isn't that beautiful?" He pointed at a brown blazer. I wanted to scream! It was a coat. It looked like a coat. Nothing more, some fabric, a fucking coat!

"You wanna go in and feel the nap?" he asked.

"The nap? No, I don't want to go in and feel the fucking nap."

"Your loss, buddy, that's vicuna, special stuff, where they only use the hair that comes from the underside of the lamb's neck."

"Yeah, gross, I really missed out." But I did sort of know the feeling, and I even rubbed my fingers together as we walked away, imagining that softness. I thought, Maybe Luz likes that feeling, too.

We walked downtown on Madison and I was next to him, but a little behind. He was wearing a blue blazer and a pair of khakis, some soft little rat-colored loafers without socks. He looked like an actual rich person, which he wasn't since I knew he was living off hardly any money at all after he paid off his monthly bundle of school loans. But he was trying, and trying hard. I figured it was working, since if nothing else, he looked different than me. What I couldn't figure was why he made it such a high priority to look privileged.

I pulled the hood of my sweatshirt way over my head so I could barely see out of it, and I began to walk hunchbacked—pumping up and down on the balls of my feet, two steps behind my brother, like I was his servant, the creepy assistant in *Young Frankenstein*. At first, he didn't notice. Then he saw me and put even more steps between us. I kept up my hunchback routine, rushed up to him, started pulling at the back of his blazer and moaning.

"The master wants new clothes! The master needs silk boxers!"

Loud, loud and hoarse, and people looked. I did some passionate groans.

"Stop it, Kelly, damn it!" And he batted me away, slapped at me, even as he continued to check out display windows.

"The master feels the fabric in his blood!"

"Shut up now, please." He didn't yell, but only because we were outside. If people hadn't been around, he would have thrown me into traffic.

My father used to say that the reason Kevin was so into clothes was because of our grandfather, who was a merchant who came up with Barney Pressman of Barneys superexpensive clothing-store fame. But our grandfather took a different route, called his place Ezekiel's, which was his name, and his place went down long before Barneys got real hip and expensive. Old Ezekiel had died only a few years ago, bankrupt and miserable, still ranting about how his Fourteenth Street store was sold and turned into a discount electronics warehouse that did a steady business in unboxed floor models and pirated videotapes that they sold off tables on the sidewalk.

Ezekiel said he'd been swindled into selling, but my father said he had to, because he overcharged so much, he was going to go out of business anyway. Ezekiel never could understand why my dad became a teacher and moved to Rantipole when there was a perfectly good business to run in Manhattan. My dad couldn't explain that he didn't like business, and that all he wanted was to teach little kids. As the old man got even older, communication dropped down to nothing at all. I wondered if my father ever thought about how much Rantipole isolated all of us. What's ideal about a community that has gates around it, that doesn't let anything in? Nothing. Maybe Ezekiel's obsession with clothes and money had skipped a generation and landed in Kevin. I'm not sure what I inherited.

"How's work?" my brother asked.

"Good, can't complain, still socking away bits of cash."

"No bank account yet?"

"Haven't found the need."

"You should let me take care of your money. I could invest it for you," Kevin said. He'd been watching stocks while I watched cartoons. He was the founder of our high school investment club—got his picture in the *Rantipole Farms Community News* for turning eighty dollars into several hundred while he was still in tenth grade. My mom was always suggesting that Kevin donate a percentage of his profits to a charity, to UNICEF, or Amnesty International, or anywhere, any charity of his choice. She wanted desperately to get him in the habit before he was grown up and away from home. But Kevin pointed out that it was his money. He'd made it, hadn't he made it? He wasn't planning on giving shit away.

"I guess I don't have enough to make it worth your while," I said.

"You'd be surprised," but he was smiling. He probably figured I didn't have a dime. It was barely six, but we turned onto Seventy-second Street and headed down to get a drink at the Hi-Life, so my brother could ogle girls. The Hi-Life was on the corner and it glowed with a lot of red and blue neon. Inside there was all this black padded naugahyde on the walls, and it wasn't dark, but it was glowing, with yellow light shooting up from behind the bar. There were bunches of young guys in there, all well dressed, in polo shirts and jeans, with brown leather business shoes. Their cell phones were ringing and they were talking to women who had on little skirts or hip-hugger-type pants. Those women were laughing. It was a sexy place, I'm not trying to say otherwise, what with all the people that I'd be like if I'd gone that way, looking so incredibly comfortable with themselves, jostling up to one another, and knowing that they're in a place that was built just for them.

My brother was always going to a bar like that, making it his, and moving on. He decided he'd made it when the waitresses were finally willing to joke with him, when they saw that he really wasn't going away. Of course the joke was on them, because when they gave up on acting cold and accepted him, that's when he stopped coming back. If they knew his routine I'm sure they would have tongue-kissed him the moment they saw him, just so he'd only be in that one time.

It was warm inside, and even through the cigarette smoke, they'd made it smell fruity and clean. Kevin ordered us glasses of single-malt scotch—Laphroaig—and I was forced to nod at his talk. Yes this was good scotch, yes I could feel how smooth it was, yes it went down like pennies from heaven. My brother appreciated all that— when he dropped ten dollars for a glass of alcohol, he wanted a name brand and a bunch of conversation attached. I did feel it seep into me when I drank it, but Robitussin did the same thing to me when I was seven.

"You still see Felix?" my brother asked. He knew the answer.

"We work together, Kev, I see him most every day. He's such a good guy, you know, I asked him, he doesn't even hate you."

"Hasn't got the right, what with all we did for him. He's still looking at Riker's?"

"Funny, that's funny."

Felix mostly grew up on Locust Avenue and 140th Street in Mott Haven, The Bronx. When he lived there he could look across the water and see the gloomy jail buildings that make up Riker's Island. His foster parents used to tell him to get a good look, 'cause that's where he was going when the state stopped paying them to take care of him. One of his punishments was to stare at Riker's Island for two hours whenever he did something wrong, like if he looked funny at his foster father. Felix was Puerto Rican and hard to look at and nobody wanted him. So he aged out of the system. That's a really bone-dry way of saying that he never did get any real parents, ever.

"Lord, I sure did used to ride his ass," Kevin said.

Felix would come into the kitchen to take grapes from the bowl that was always next to the fridge in the summer. Kevin would groan, mumble about contamination and decency, and then take the bowl and empty the rest of the grapes into the trash can under the sink, while Felix watched.

During the good summer we had before the bad summer, Kevin loved to remind Felix that he was not one of us, that our parents had to give him new Puma Clydes and throw away the torn sneakers he'd brought with him. They gave him shorts (Jams because there was a sale on at Foot Locker), Hanes T-shirts, Jockey briefs, tube socks, toiletries, Judy Blume and Robert Cormier books chosen from the Hawley Community Bookstore—everything so Felix could fit in better, so he could look like me and Kevin. And Kevin spent that first summer making absolutely sure none of it worked.

Felix would be in my room, getting dressed for the day. He went down to the bathroom to wash his face, and Kevin was there.

"You're gonna crap up another towel, huh, Felix, get some skid marks on it? When are you going to stop mooching off us? Oh yeah,

I forgot, you don't have a choice." Then Kevin would head down to breakfast, leaving Felix alone in the bathroom with a cheap towel in his little hands and a burning red face.

"Mom, Felix used a towel of ours."

"Please stop, Kevin, you're a big boy so you can stop now, please."

"It's okay, Mom, I know you have to act like you don't mind. It's like in the contract or something, right?" We'd all stand there, stunned, and Kevin would leave the house, whistling, headed toward his lifeguard job.

"God, Kevin, you were such a jerk," I said. Why hadn't my mother grabbed him? I knew she thought he was going to learn by watching what she did, but man, that wasn't happening. Sometimes I think she was amused that she'd raised such a tough kid. She would say she hadn't meant to, but Kevin, boy, there was a kid who could sure take care of himself. Then my mom would turn to me, after Kevin walked out.

"Oh, Marty, you don't understand. Kevy's just being protective of us. I know he seems mean now, but he'll grow out of it. Don't get upset. You're nice like me. Sometimes it's hard to be so nice."

I'd just shake my head. My mother always called me Marty. That's my first name. Kelly is my middle name, which I like way better. Me and Felix would head out into the woods, and we'd talk about how we could still be us, but maybe we didn't always have to be so nice.

Kevin pushed at me. "All little kids are jerks—that's what makes them good at business when they grow up. You missed out."

The bar was rowdy by then, with bunches of guys who looked like my brother careening around and happy to see one another, all talking about how well they did that day, how much market share they'd increased. A couple of guys next to me pulled out cigars and stuffed them into their mouths. They lit the tips and sucked hard, till there was smoke. I blew their air away from me. Kevin was talking to me, but he was looking down the bar.

"Your life is funny, Kelly. You start with Felix, end up with Cass, where you could have turned into something—and now you're back to nowhere with Felix."

"Actually, I've got a crush on this girl, I'm probably gonna ask her out."

"Oh yeah, who's the lucky lady?"

"Somebody in my building."

"Whoa, buddy. You're not telling me you're dating the natives now, are you? That's all wrong—this is your crowd, right here, you live up there temporary, 'cause you're in transition, back to college is where you're headed. No more about crushes."

"Kevin—"

"Yeah?"

I wanted to talk to him, to tell him what I really thought of him, to unpeel all the layers of crap that forced him to say things like that. But he wouldn't look at me. A girl with light brown hair and sweet blue eyes was next to him. She was trying to order drinks for her friends and my brother was trying to help her and she was trying to ignore him. She had a high perfume smell that blew near me and prickled me up. My brother was agitated. In the bar mirror I could see him staring at her in a way that I'm sure he thought looked sexy but really only looked hostile. He wanted one of those women, the cool ones that he couldn't have, not for several more years, until he was a real doctor who could make real money. But I had moved those women, had seen the black balls of dust in their underwear drawer, the photographs of family and old boyfriends stored away, the hardcover copies of Emily Dickinson and Jane Austen left over from college that were still so obviously unread. She was just a pretty girl in a bar, but me and my brother came at her from such wholly opposite angles. If we couldn't agree on one pretty girl who was a stranger, we could really and truly never agree.

I said, "This girl I like, she has the biggest black eyes, dark pools to look deep into, I swear—"

"Yeah. She'll have some family. We see plenty of jealous rage beatings in emergency, so watch it or you'll get ripped up good."

"Thanks," I said.

"Sure. You want some chicken wings?"

I said nothing, but he ordered them, and then we had to enjoy some of that good old hearty silence between brothers.

"You know if you cleaned your ass up and dressed like an adult you'd be a perfectly decent-looking guy," he said. He said that every time I saw him.

The bartender gave us a plate of wings—nasty, shiny fat-dripping things with a side of creamy blue cheese sauce. I watched Kevin pull the meat off the bone, saw his tongue, magnified, as it reached out to search and pull off all that was left. I felt a twinge, panic, nausea. He gnawed.

"I gotta go," I said.

"What? Come on, I ordered all this, you at least have to stick around and eat with me!"

I looked at the wings, at the little plastic well filled with dressing. The huge noise of the bar was suddenly unbearable, all of those bastards lying to one another—it was so distressing, I had to get out of there.

"Nah, eat that crap up yourself, fat boy."

"Hey, these are good wings!" he said, hurt. That's what Kev was concerned about, the chicken wings. I'd like to think it bothered him when I walked out. I slapped his head once, not too hard, and he looked at me like he didn't understand me, his beady eyes trying to figure out, once again, why we couldn't meet halfway and say a lot of lies like "This is good, seeing you," when we both knew it wasn't. I just walked out of there, away from him. It was sad—damned sad—but at least I was honest.

I could hear him behind me, he half said my name, but not so loud, "Kelly—" and then, "Hey, Janine, I didn't know you were working tonight."

"Well, here I am!" The false hearty voice of a woman who would be saying friendly stuff to people she couldn't stand for at least the next seven hours.

My brother said, "Things are lookin' up!" And I shut the door behind me. You really don't need me, I thought. You can't help. I've got to get home and try to understand just how it is I got here, and I've got to do it all by myself.

I walked west on Seventy-second and then I turned uptown on Park Avenue. Park must be the quietest avenue in New York. I always felt real uncomfortable there, but I liked it just the same. It was like passing through a place that would rather not let you in, going down a street that would most definitely be private if it didn't have to be public. And I liked the slight looks of nervousness I got from the rich people who I passed, because they knew I wasn't one of them, and with me around, they had something to lose. I walked slow. It was cool out and I had two, maybe three thoughts in my head. The first was that I needed something, and I needed it bad. I knew I got nothing from my brother and that I really needed to feel better. The other thought was that I sure wasn't going to be able to head in any specific adult career-type direction until I started to feel good on a more frequent basis. And then also I was certainly upset with my brother for getting racist about Luz, my new crush. That was wrong. She was good. I could already tell.

Park Avenue was clean. The street felt rolled out in front of me like carpet that somebody was waiting to tug, where they'd pull hard and catch me unaware, so I'd flip off. I walked by a black iron service door that buzzed and shook in its frame. On the Upper East Side the service entrances are tucked away where nobody notices them, and they're controlled electrically by doormen. Those guys are old and they don't ask many questions—they just buzz when they hear the buzz.

I slowed way down and looked at that noise-making door, and I stopped and opened it. It kept making noise. I went down the out-side staircase, through a door that was propped open, and into a basement. The walls were their usual astonishing clean green and white and the room smelled of nothing but ammonia and mothballs, working hard to smother more human smells. There were two eleva-tors facing me. One was open and dark, broken. I watched the brass half-circle dial on the other one. The pointer was at the roof, and then it slowly made its way down. The street entrance door kept on buzzing loud. The elevator opened. A young woman in sweatpants came out with a dog that looked like a weeping willow painted white. I was hidden in shadow. She didn't look around. I figured she was probably a professional dog walker, so she wasn't allowed to use the front door. She followed the dog out of the basement, up the stairs, toward the door and the street. I went to the roof.

The roof vestibule had two doors. One was locked, and led to the penthouse, and the other one led out to the roof itself. An area had to be set aside so that workmen could fix the elevators and so that in case of a fire, all the rich people could be airlifted to safety. I'd spent months and months riding in those boxes, talking to unionized elevator operators who were more than happy to walk me through every detail of their buildings.

I climbed over a five-foot fence and dropped onto a redwood patio. I figured I'd just take a quick peek—if there was somebody inside, well, I was in the wrong place by mistake and I was sorry and they understood. And if the place was good and empty? Then, well, I'd see what I could get. It was cool up there, cold even. I slipped the hood of my sweatshirt over my head.

I circled around, saw four rooms, one incredibly large, a kitchen, two bedrooms. Very simple, very empty. I saw dog shit around me on the patio. So the weeping willow was definitely getting a park walk, not a quick "do your thing and back upstairs" walk, like I'd seen so many East Siders give their dogs. I stayed low, and I did not look out to see if I could find my own windows in the great mass of low

buildings that laid themselves out like shiny pebbles going north forever from where I stood.

A sliding glass door was open a few inches. I took off my Adidas
and pulled the door open a foot wider. I went in and headed across
the streaky wide-plank wood floor and went right into the bedroom,
where white streamlined closets ran along either wall. There were
little nightstands on both sides of the bed, with one spindly lamp on
each, like magnified spider's legs. The nightstands had bedside reading: on the man's side, a copy of a business book called *Getting to Yes*
and a video under that, which had the label torn off and must have
been porn. The woman was reading *Thin Thighs in Thirty Days* and
some paperback with abstract art on the cover.

I walked over to a side table. I opened a small bottle of prescription
pills. Percodans. I left them alone. I smelled a deodorant, twisted off
the tops of a few moisture creams, used a remote control to turn their
television on: "This is Kate Hampton reporting live from City Hall, for
New York One." And then off again.

I picked up a glass bottle half full of yellow perfume. The cap was
built around a little set of wings. I dripped some of the perfume on
my forearm. It smelled sweet, incredibly similar to country flowers
and my mother's hair. But I couldn't figure how I could give Luz a
used bottle of perfume. I rubbed my arm on my sweatshirt to get the
smell away, but I screwed up, because instead, it grew.

The drawer on his nightstand was full of quarters. I took a
pocket's worth. On her side, the drawer was more interesting, more
varied. I handled a fat pearl necklace that must have been important, since it was apart from wherever the rest of her jewelry was.
That necklace was so rich-looking. I didn't like it.

I opened a pink plastic case and found the woman's diaphragm. I
ran my fingers around the rim and pressed down in the middle, and
it felt strong. Sex would be so good in a room like that! Afterward
you could go outside and stand naked, all revealed and free and safe
in front of the city. I went over to his side of the bed and put the

diaphragm under his pillow. Then I lay down for just a second, but I didn't close my eyes.

In the kitchen, I found several hundred dollars in crisp ATM twenties placed flat in the bottom of a pyramid-shaped cookie jar. I took the money. There was another hundred in an envelope that was stuck to the fridge with a magnet that was painted to look like their dog. Dog walker money. I left it.

I stood in that kitchen and saw that couple, how they'd come home and she would have a little Styrofoam bowl of shucked green peas that cost her $3.89 at the Korean grocery on Third Avenue and he would have two bottles of Corona. They would eat and drink and stare at each other. And maybe, if they were at all introspective, one of them would suggest that if they hadn't been such greedy assholes all along they wouldn't be arguing now about how much more money they needed to keep all of this up. I was so sure that that's what happened when you got money, that you just needed more and more and you got to feel like a slave to it. That's what my mom told me. The woman of the house would throw the peas and the man would slam down his beer and then they'd just stare at each other. Peas, little drops of green paint, all over that blond floor.

"We've just got to have more money."

Their heads would be busting with this one thought. It was as if they were in the room with me, talking to me, and I knew them.

"You two could be nicer," I said. "You'd both feel better if you shared." Maybe it was me who felt a little better then, too, because my parents would have said that if they had found themselves in somebody else's penthouse at dusk. I listened to the wind knock against the massive windows. Then, after they'd spoken, my parents would leave. And I really didn't feel like just saying something would be doing enough.

"I'm not kidding," I said, "people like you need to learn a lesson. I just bet like crazy that you two are real assholes!"

There was a little gold figurine standing next to the phone. It was

Mexican, or Mayan, or—old, I don't know. A person playing a flute, with eyes raised to heaven. It was a fine little thing and I knew Luz would like it. I put it in my kangaroo pocket.

The fine slow glide that was me as I walked around their place. Like unhurried smooth sex between people underwater, sedated, the dream sequence in a movie that leans heavy on sexy shots created with a Vaseline-smeared lens.

I put my sneakers back on and found the staircase and waited for a second before going down. The sound of the elevator, right next to the stairwell, the dog walker and the dog, coming up. Suddenly that stupid weeping willow dog began to bark like mad, a screaming bark, paws banging against the elevator door.

"What, what?" the woman asked. I heard her her pull on the dog's leash, the dog going out of its head because of something that only dogs care about—a smell. I sniffed my arm and frowned. There I was wafting owner's scent—stupid move, painful stupid move.

Before the doors opened, I yelled, "You got a really cute dog!"

Then I sped, flew down those stairs fast as anything.

I saw an old woman in blue jeans and a Yankees windbreaker standing in front of a bodega on Park and Ninety-ninth. She was counting change so she'd know just how much money she had before she went in, so she didn't take too big a container of milk or too many cans of beer.

I said, "Here, I got you." I gave her one of their twenty-dollar bills. She looked up at me with that half-suspicious look I get all the time in my neighborhood.

"Hey, thanks," she said. "I'll get you back when I see you again."

"That's cool," I said. "Don't worry about it." I thought, that's what you do. That combo is sweet. That combo is tight.

And that's when I ran into Luz, coming up Second Avenue with Alfredo. By then it was dark, and probably Alfredo was just coming from his first day of school, or from day care. And she was taking care of him. I was so psyched to see them but I wanted to be cool about it, and to wait, to not make such a big thing out of us, until we were both a little more ready.

"Hey," she said. She had a schoolbag slung over one shoulder and Alfredo did, too. She was in blue jeans and a pink polo shirt. Alfredo's hair was bright and really curly and he had that popped-out look around the eyes that kids get after a full day.

"Yo, what's up, man," Alfredo said. He had this real high kidlike voice. I still wasn't able to talk. I thought, Now I have a present for her. But I can't give it up now, not so fast, not like this.

"Where are you coming from?" she asked.

"Oh, just from downtown. From walking around." We got in front of the C-Town supermarket and she stopped. I stood there, and I was all mute! She wasn't immediately going in but she wasn't really looking at me, either. I had to say something, but I had no idea what smart thing I was supposed to say that would somehow impress upon her that I was crushing on her very seriously, but that would make me appear mellow and relaxed at the same time. I was better in that penthouse, smoother, when I was walking around in there.

"Well, see you around," she said.

"Yeah, I mean—I really hope so," I said.

"Sure," she said. Alfredo was tugging on her. He looked up at me and pointed his finger, and did a little mock frown.

"Later," he said. "She'll see you later." Then Luz laughed and pushed at his hair.

"Cool it. Bye now, nice to see you again." And she went through the sliding doors. I felt so high and happy and good. When I walked away, my feet barely touched the ground.

3

My **parents' place** was just within the gates of Rantipole Farms. The house was a Swiss-style ski chalet on the main entrance road, past the black-and-white-striped wooden guardrail that got broken off and splintered to bits six or eight times a summer. We were tucked back maybe fifty feet from the road. Our house—it might not have been the very poorest in Rantipole, but it was certainly in the bottom ten. The development was still young, and we were surrounded by old-growth forest.

My parents: Minna and Samuel Minter. They fled New York in the middle of the seventies because they were junior high school teachers, and they could make so much more money outside the city. They had all these beliefs, like ten thousand beliefs, about the right way to live life, but they couldn't square all that with their fear that me and Kevin would get bad educations in Manhattan public schools. So they compromised and pulled out. That's why they got a Fresh Air Fund kid, to help the kid, and to bring a little bit of the city out to us. They're good people—I'm not saying they're not. But when Felix Lina arrived the summer that I was nine, we spent our time in the woods.

By the middle of my second summer with Felix, we had our own language. It was all stealth and rhythm, where we could walk far apart and still be together. Short taps for deer sightings, bears were low whistles, bird twitters for approaching men—when we saw women we'd do rabbit purrs.

One night in the beginning of August there was no moon and we were wolves and we were silent. Maybe it was two—certainly after midnight, and me and Felix had snuck out of the room we shared, gone downstairs and out of my house. We had a penlight and a bag of paper clips. We were in our darkest clothes and I wore a scarf over my face.

"You're sure?" Felix asked.

"'Course—you said you could do it and I want to know. I want to. I'm sure."

During that second summer, Felix always talked about burglary. He lived in a foster home with heavy turnover and he'd met an older boy who believed his real father was a master thief. Felix was fascinated. The boy gave Felix lessons and then Felix brought those lessons along with him, up to Pennsylvania. We'd plot late at night, but we needed a target. I'd decided that we needed to practice. Robbing my house was my idea.

"'Cause I wouldn't—I mean, it's your parents' house," Felix said.

"So what? We're gonna get in, steal the money in the kitchen, get some food, too, like some bread and salami, some cheese, come back out here, walk, I don't know! We'll eat, then we'll go back in, go to sleep. The money is ours and they had a robbery—we don't know anything about it. You swore you could get in."

Felix selected a paper clip and straightened it. He looked up at me, like he wanted to trust me.

"What if they catch us?" he asked.

"Is that the way you were taught? Is that the way a real thief thinks?" I had to show him that I was tough, as hard as his friends in New York, as unafraid. And I wanted to steal from my parents. I wanted to take so bad. I just knew that it would feel so good, to take what I wanted, to show them that if I had to steal to make things clear, and to feel good, then that was what I was going to do.

"You learn real well," he said. "What's different from me is how you don't hold it in so good."

Felix went back to his straightening. He was a tiny kid, all hard and muscle, and he already had the beginnings of the lousy skin he wouldn't be able to lose.

We snuck up to my front door, slow as anything, careful to plant our feet hard on the pine needles and underbrush so they wouldn't stir. The front door was opened—maybe we kind of knew that. We were ten and we made a show of picking the lock anyway. We got in and snuck through the living room on our bellies. We made no noise and I remember gripping the legs of the coffee table, sliding along, feeling the rugs, and then the cheap, buckled wood floor, as we headed toward the money in the kitchen.

Trespassing made noise different. We were no longer in the right place, protected from the cold and the night wind. No, we'd only be safe when we got back out, when we were back out in the dark forest with everything I'd been afraid of up till then. I lay on my belly with a dead-serious frown on my face and one eyebrow arched way up, and I was a smart little fucker and I felt real good. Felix reached the kitchen and signaled to me.

I imagine that Kevin woke up and started to watch us from the top of the stairs about then. Even as we crawled I can see him going in the opposite direction, headed toward our parents' bedroom, to tell them there were real burglars in the house. I am sure he knew it was us.

I flashed the penlight on the counter. Felix groped around and grabbed the money.

"My brother scores," I whispered.

"Oh yes," he said, and I knew he liked it. I liked it, too. I felt real hopeful, as if right then I was making a promise. You just keep on stealing what you need, you'll have a good life after all.

We were taking a planned moment of rest, before opening the refrigerator—my trick would be to open it and keep the light switch pressed down, so we'd find our food in the dark—when we heard sirens. They cops didn't have to travel more than a hundred yards. My parents had called the main entrance gate and woken up whatever Rantipole Farms Community cop was sleeping there—who must have been nothing but excited about the prospect of kicking some poor burglar in the ass. Two of them approached the house, even as Felix and I were squatted down, paralyzed in the kitchen. Like a fool I'd gotten the door open and I did have my finger pressed down on the light and I was stuck. Felix held the two twenty-dollar bills in his hand. I remember watching him as he looked at the money. Then all the lights went on and the front door flew open and the cops yelled.

"Nobody fucking moves!"

The kitchen was in an alcove off of the living room. We didn't move, but we looked at each other and I remember Felix's face, his expression, all wizened sadness, shaking his head. He made a gesture with his hands in front of his face. Say something so we don't get shot. Ten years old.

"Mom!"

"What?"

And then my mom running across our living room, so fast and around the corner even as the two cops yelled for her to stay put! Stay put!

"My God!"

She stood in front of us in her huge sleep T-shirt that said I'M A PEPPER TOO! across the front in red balloon letters. We were still crouched down, and Felix held out her grocery money and the paper clips scattered on the floor and I got up slow. I was so angry! How dare you catch me? How dare you?

"What the hell? What the hell are you doing?"

"Uh . . ."

My brother, Kevin, began to laugh. He was fifteen and the Rantipole Farms poster boy for success. He knew the cops, and they laughed, too, on his cue. My father mumbled apologies. The cops left. My father brought our bathrobes out and then all five of us had to sit down in the living room.

It was three o'clock in the morning.

"Kevin, why don't you make some tea?" my father said.

We had two couches, one cracked brown leather and one made out of a scratchy yellow material that felt like straw. I sat on the yellow couch with my mom, while Felix sat on the other with my dad. Kevin put the kettle on. He flipped the radio on, too, out of habit, and then turned it off. We listened to NPR so much that the drone of those reassuring voices was part of our house, ideas so ingrained that I could find them in the patterns in our abstract kitchen wallpaper, thoughts as comforting as the rhythm and quiet bang of our baseboard heaters. Without their voices, we were all a little lost, and it made the scene feel even stranger. Kevin came in and stretched out on the floor, propped his head up, dug the scene.

"Let's begin by asking ourselves a question. What happened here?" my mom asked. She was a fourth-grade teacher and a true matron, didn't care about her weight, or her gray and brown hair, sometimes wore a bit of lipstick, that's all. A decent liberal woman.

"We were just playing," Felix said. My mother looked at him, carefully, the way you look at somebody who is a stranger to you.

"Last summer was a success, wasn't it, Felix? The reports we wrote about you were so nice! Don't you like it here?" my mother asked.

"It's nice here, isn't it?" Kevin said. "No poor people."

"Kevin, stop it," my father said.

"I like it here okay," Felix said.

"Then why did you try to steal from us tonight?"

"I—"

"We did it, Mom."

"I know, Marty darling, but I asked Felix a question."

And then I saw Felix harden. He looked at my mother and his face and his hands did something that I have seen a thousand times since—which is anger, which is knowing that no, you will not win, you will not overcome this distrust, this is something so much larger than you, a tiny child, and you must make yourself far harder than you had ever conceived, than you ever before thought you would have to be.

"I don't know," Felix said.

"Do you think about this a lot, Felix? About stealing from us?"

No, I thought, he doesn't. I do. I turned and looked at my mother, at one of the three rings she wore, the one her friend the silversmith made her, that spelled out her name in tiny silver leaves. I thought, Can I please have that?

"Well?" my mother asked. She'd tucked her legs beneath her and she was a patient slow-breathing mountain.

Felix stood up. We watched him as he went into the kitchen. We listened to him get a glass. Water ran in the sink. My mother got up, quietly, and went after him. There was a smashing noise.

"Now this is too much!" she yelled.

And then the rest of us got up, my father, my brother, me, and we went to see what the problem was. Apparently she wasn't aware that we were headed in there, because just as we made it in, she was holding Felix by the top of his arm, and he was struggling, hitting her on the back, and she was holding him away from her. She was shaking him, not so lightly.

"Let go of me!" Felix yelled.

"Oh, I'll let go, but you'll clean all this up and that's it—it's enough! In the morning, you go!"

He'd peed on the floor and when she came in, he'd smashed the glass in the sink. She swore from that moment on that she'd grabbed him and started shaking him because she was afraid he would hurt himself on the glass.

He slept on the couch. I was not allowed to leave my room but I came out anyway and sat down near him, on the floor, while he lay there with one of our camp blankets over him, both of us blown-out sad and not moving.

"They never did trust me," he said.

"No," I said.

"But I didn't want anything from them." We looked across the living room at the fireplace, and it was so dark. I looked into the fireplace itself, and it was the darkest place I'd ever seen.

I said, "My brother, I don't know why, but if you were still here tomorrow night, I'd want to do it all again."

"Yeah? Listen, Kelly, the shit you want from them, you can't hold it in your hand, but you get her barrette, or her food, or her money, you hoard away a goddamn placemat . . . well . . . maybe that's all you can have."

"Maybe," I said. I didn't understand him then, and I'm not sure he knew what he meant, either. But that's what he said.

The next morning we packed the army-issue duffel bag that only arrived half full while my mother got on the phone and explained the situation to half a dozen different people—officials, her friends, the foster parents. We listened to her. I had expected her to change her mind. Felix had, too, a little. But in the morning she was more sure. And she was angry that the situation was taking time away from her summer-school duties. I remember wondering if any of them knew that Felix and I were brothers.

"We have to do what's best," my mom said, while we waved good-bye to Felix. "We have to do what's best for you and your brother."

She smiled her "meek shall inherit" smile and we drove the god-damned blue Volvo back into Rantipole. Kevin joked about how sad it was that my friend wasn't coming back, the one who had been bought just for me, who turned out to be a defective model. Kevin had a snicker like gunfire, like Poppers. He laughed in the car and I danced like he was shooting my feet. We went home and I wrote to Felix. I told him how much I missed him.

And Felix? Well, Felix was mostly stuck on being sorry that his summer was over so early, and then he was back on the old DeCamp bus that took him to the Port Authority terminal on Forty-second Street, where he had to catch a subway on his own that would take him back to Mott Haven and his four different foster sisters and brothers. His real parents had died when he was five. They were crackheads and they'd OD'd during the initial boom of the very early eighties. He'd never talked about them much, except to say that he hated them for leaving him.

Growing up, I went to New York maybe once a year, mostly on overorganized school trips where the teachers wouldn't let us use the phone, and on infrequent Broadway play trips with my parents. I saw Felix one time. I was fourteen and my whole class had come in to see David Copperfield at the Paramount Theater. Afterward, we had a ridiculously early dinner at the Friday's on Eighth Avenue. Felix cut out of school early and showed up. He'd grown, not much taller, but rougher, and he was smart enough to know that his rough texture was a badge—he didn't open his eyes all the way and he said that he'd had to fight in school, a lot.

"It's amazing that we're still friends, Kelly," he said. "'Cause now, where I am, we chase guys like you away."

"We're still friends 'cause we're brothers," I said.

"Brothers?" He smiled.

"What's it like here?" I asked.

"Rough," Felix said.

"Tell me."

"This place, the Bronx, Manhattan—where I walk is in the most feared places, like too many bears in the forest is what it is here.

That's how I treat it. Living here is like being inside a living breathing thing that crosses your signals and mangles everything—so what I learned with you in the woods, it's twisted now."

"I remember that we learned to walk quiet, and to listen," I said, "but I know it went wrong. I know it was my fault."

"What happened to me up there was nothing. Manhattan overwhelms you, wait and see," he said.

I'm not saying it was a big deal. It wasn't. It just sucked and it was sad, that's all. Watching Felix get all hard like that.

And then he disappeared and I didn't see him again for six years.

4

Each day at dawn, the lumps of vertebrae at the top of my
spine began to ache. Sleep forced my bones and muscles to try to
help themselves, to right the bent shape I made for them when I
moved boxes on my back, and when I awoke, I imagine my body
gave up and got ready for more punishment. And at that moment,
when my body and I fought, right then was when I was just beginning to convince myself that upon waking, I hadn't thought of Cass,
she was not my first conscious image, even if I had, even if she was.
My building was not a quiet place in the morning. Everybody was up
making breakfast and listening to weather reports, news, and soap
operas in Spanish. Luz's family was as loud as anybody's. They had
salsa music on and there was the sound of pots banging and water
running; then they'd yell to be heard over all of that. I slowed on their
landing. I stopped in front of their door and found myself sniffing air,

trying to suck in her scent. Their door opened. I didn't move. My heart sped a bit and my lungs crinkled up and I was sure I'd just made a noise like air getting sucked out of a paper bag. A man came out.

He was dark, with one of those funny haircuts that's just a little longer in the back. He had a gold necklace with OCIDES spelled out in shiny wide letters. The Tasmanian Devil from cartoons? Built with strong little legs and a huge chest that supports a thick head? That was Ocides, except human, and big, bigger.

He nodded at me. For all he knew I was coming to check the gas, or the cable—I was nobody in particular to him.

"Hey," he said. Then I knew I'd heard his voice before. When I left for work in the early early morning I could hear him singing in the shower, his deep voice coming through several walls.

"Eeuh ay," I said, which was all I could get out, then I followed him down. I thought, slow: it is nice of him to say hello to a stranger.

Outside I went over to White Castle and ate a quick breakfast in a bright orange booth. Seven of their little egg-and-cheese sandwiches, hash browns in the shape of a brick, coffee that burned even though it wasn't hot—and I was ready for my day. I thought, no doubt, That Ocides is an all-right guy.

We moved a sleepy couple from a loft down in Tribeca to a house in Riverdale. They were all packed. They didn't have much, and what they did have was light. Some people are like that: lightweights, with loads of furniture made of bent birch wood and spindly bits of steel, without books, with posters in thin frames that we have to hold close to our bodies, so that they won't blow away in the wind. They did have a whole bunch of change, and like all rich people, they made us pack it up. Rich people are funny that way. You'd think they'd donate change or give it to beggars, but they move it out to Riverdale.

We were all quiet during the move, because the lush grass of Riverdale was beautiful in early September, and I think we all knew enough not to mess it up by yapping. We came back into the city and I got Teddy to drop me at 110th and Broadway, where all the pretty Columbia kids are, and then I walked back home through the park. I had to walk slow, what with all the plastic bags of small change I had stuffed down into my socks and sneakers. When I got out of the park I leaked most of it, so there were little pools of it behind me. I looked back and the changed glittered in the street.

I stepped into my local Chinese take-out, Hong Fat. Shiny photos of different dishes covered the walls. The place was half full and boiling hot, with everybody waiting for their order and only one couple eating at a table, both of them slurping up their lo mein and drinking Snapple iced tea through straws. I looked at the wonderful pictures of snapping fresh lobster and crab, of carefully arranged slices of duck and eggplant, and wondered why the hell they didn't bother to imitate them, why there was always so much chicken and water chestnut and never enough bright-colored vegetables. But nobody complained, and I didn't get that, how they could show you one thing and give you another, and still everybody would accept that fat gap as a given.

Then Luz walked in. A vein in my neck throbbed for a second and popped my head up an inch. I asked myself, Do you think about God much? The answer was no, and I thought, Well, why don't you think about God now, 'cause it's time to give up some thanks.

She had on shiny black Adidas warm-up pants, a white short-sleeve T-shirt, and black mules. She looked like a young woman from the neighborhood, but also—she looked dressed up, like she was there to meet somebody. The place was loud with the sizzling noise of boiling oil tossed around in a battered aluminum wok.

Two cops walked in. They muttered something about an opportunity. A dish highlighted in gold was called Good Chance Chicken. A love song on the radio: if I could get just one chance with you. But I stank! I looked down at my sweatshirt, at my blue jeans stained with cooking grease that I'd wiped off a pan I'd packed that morning. A man in front of me ordered wontons and hot-and-sour soup, $3.95. I pulled my shirt away from my skin. It was my turn. I could feel my heart beat, the word *chance* chanted over and over till it felt like I was back in Pee Wee hockey and my brother and his friends were whispering "spaz" louder and louder until I dropped my stick. I shook it all off. She was right behind me.

The counter guy gave me the half smile that I deserved since he'd probably seen me a hundred times.

I said, "Hey, good to see you. Make me what's good, chicken and vegetables the way the cook likes them, maybe the Good Chance Chicken, and give me seven egg rolls."

I stepped aside, so that I was next to her. But she didn't order. She turned to me. She said nothing.

"I—we met the other day, with your brother, Alfredo—"

"Yes. Seven egg rolls? Why?"

"You say, why seven . . ."

I couldn't very well say the truth, that usually I gave them away on the walk home. I couldn't think straight. It was scary. I don't even like egg rolls.

"I save them?"

"Yeah," she said. "Maybe you'll have extra—you want to share them? I'll buy one from you, then I won't have to order." She gestured to the woman behind her, who went ahead.

"I'll give you them," I said.

We stood there, looking.

"I can't eat all seven," she said.

She turned and put her elbows behind her on the counter and faced the front of the store. I dared to take a split-second glance and I saw her breasts jut out, the slow rise and fall at the top of her chest as she breathed. She stared straight ahead. She had her hair down and loose, and she took it and pushed it around so it came down over her right shoulder. Her hair was shiny, smooth.

The counterman said, "Thirteen eighty-five."

I paid and we walked out, with her in front of me. Now that we were outside the restaurant, I had no idea where we would eat.

"Tell me your name again," she said.

"I'm Kelly, and you're Luz, right?"

We shook hands slowly. It was cool outside after all that food heat and her hand was firm and I got in that extra second of touch. The physical feeling of her was astonishing—I had not touched a woman in months. The truth flashed at me. I hadn't spent an evening with a woman for more than a year. I'd been sexless for fourteen months. The only woman I'd ever made love with was Cass. I wondered if Luz noticed, if my prickled desire moved with me, if it was something she could smell.

"Alfredo says you're nice to him," she said.

"Yeah, he's my favorite little man," I said.

Someone interrupted us, said, "You got egg rolls?"

He was on my right, a man in a dark coat, with an earless Mickey Mouse hat. I knew him. I reached in and found an egg roll, hot in its little paper sheath. I handed it to him and then he reached into the bag and grabbed a packet of duck sauce.

I said, "You making it okay?"

"Not bad, thanks."

He held the food and smelled it. Then he put his hand on my shoulder, gave me a deep nod, and left us.

"Listen, Luz—we could go back to my apartment if you want. I got something for you there. A present," I said. "I just remembered about it."

"Let's do that then. Now. Otherwise you'll give all the food away."

"Right, right. Yes," I said.

Luz walked along next to me and I turned to her and saw that I had not walked along the street with a woman in so long, the experience was almost new—but I did take care to walk on the curbside, and to make sure not to bump up to her too close, not to box her in.

Then someone yelled for me, "Hey hey! Kelly! Where you been?"

Jimmy Charny sat on a stoop a few houses before my building. He was smoking and his knee was going up and down, fast. He was so thin that you could see his bones jangling under his canvas jacket, his clavicle, the pointed ball of his elbow. Jimmy had been with Miracle when I started there. Now he lived with his mother in a building all too near mine.

"Hey, uh, Jimmy—"

"No, no! I see you're with a lady, don't let me bother you now— only, your bet came through the other night, at Hooligans? And the bartender asked me to tell you if I saw you, that's all, you can collect on Tuesday—and listen, maybe I'll see you down there soon, right?"

"Uh—"

"Say no more, we need to meet soon is all."

He got off the stoop and waved. His body was amazing, all thick ribbons of muscle around bone, dope-addict thin, but you could see the tension in him—ripples of strength showed through just below his ears and along his jaw. He'd been fired for petty theft and people said he had to support his mother's methadone addiction. He bopped down the street, away from us. I hadn't made any bet at Hooligans. I did not want him to be interested in meeting with me.

"That your friend?" Luz asked.

"No more than anybody else," I said.

We went upstairs, slow and polite. I tried to let her go first.

"No, you go," she said.

I went up. I guess she didn't want me behind her, looking at her body.

"Stairs are good for you, huh?" I asked. She said nothing, only kept her breathing even and matched my steps. When we both passed her floor and she was still with me, that's when my heart began to really beat.

Inside, we didn't bother to unpack the food. We weren't hungry. I put the bag in the fridge.

We sat in my two chairs. She had one of those twenty-five-cent packs of Big Red, and she took out two sticks, rolled them both, and gave me one. Big Red doesn't fix your breath. I don't know why, but it doesn't. I chewed madly in the hopes that it would help, but it was fruitless.

She said, "I once had a friend like that guy we just saw on the street, you know, a girlfriend, who was always hanging around, always wanting something, and finally I told her, Fuck off, you know? Don't come around me."

"Yeah?" I said.

She wove her accent in and out, so that she allowed her Spanish to crease her English. She caged out my space, paced it off, touched my few books while she spoke.

"So I'm in eighth grade and I'm coming home from school, two of her friends throw me up against a building, they've got me pinned and there she is, all huffed up and angry at me? Her friend gives her a scalpel, out of nowhere, a scalpel, little shining thing—she comes rushing up, bangs my head against the wall, cuts me here, see?"

She held up two fingers and showed me four cuts, on her jaw, the shadow of her neck, a nick on her collarbone. She had to push aside her shirt for me to see.

"They laughed at me. I went home and got my father's baseball bat and came back out, they were all on a stoop, and I came up and I hit her friends and they ran, then I hit her on her back and on her head and all these guys had to hold me back and I was hitting every-body in sight. That girl went into the hospital."

"Don't worry," I said. "I'm not going to try anything."

"I know. I'm just telling you a story." She smiled. "Sometimes you have to tell a story, just to keep things straight. 'Cause who knows who you are, and I'm in your apartment and all . . ."

"I just think you're so—" But she interrupted me. The energy in that room pulsed, wide waves of it coming off us. I believe in all that—pheromones, smell, stuff deep below talk. She kept talking, pushing, afraid, maybe, of our connection.

"You go to school?" she asked. She stretched and put her hands behind her head. But then she saw me watch her, catch the rise and fall in her chest, and she put her arms down, over her front.

"No, I quit a few years ago."

"Oh, so you—"

"I move furniture. Do you? Go to school?"

"Two classes a semester, at John Jay. I have to help my mom a lot, and I work, at Duane Reade, on Fifty-seventh and Broadway."

I imagined her there, behind the counter, ringing up toothpaste and quart bottles of Coke. She'd be there, beautiful, and when the customers came off the line and got in front of her, they would gasp. She wouldn't look back at their faces. She'd be thinking of other things. The managers probably gossiped about her. They probably spent a lot of time behind her, messing with her cash box.

"What's your mother's real name?"

She giggled.

"Migdalia."

"How'd it turn to Queen?"

"It didn't. The first time you saw her, she said 'Qui'en' and then you thought she was saying her name, so you called her that."

"No."

"Oh, yeah." She nodded.

We sat at the table and I heard my stomach make noise and so did she and then we just laughed together, with the radiator making its first bangs of fall, and the dirt on my clothes and her beauty and my idiocy.

"Now my father calls her Queen, my son does, Jahaira, we all do, now, 'cause of you."

"Your son?"

"You knew that right? Alfredo is my boy."

"I didn't know that. That's good. He's a beautiful boy."

I thought, When we get married, he can be the ring bearer. I didn't ask about a father. She must have been very young when she had Alfredo. Selfish, I hoped that the father was a stranger now.

"He is beautiful. And I love him, don't get me wrong about that. He's my responsibility and I bring him up right. I pay for his clothes, I do his schoolwork with him. He's going to be just fine."

"I didn't say—"

"I just don't want you to go thinking I don't care about my boy. Not that I care what you think or anything."

Then I saw what she needed from me, how she wanted me to be thick and solid in front of her and to talk slow, to make her feel safe. I knew because that's what I would've wanted. And we weren't so different. I stood in front of her, but I crouched a little, so I was looking up into her face.

"No. I know Alfredo. I like him. We have fun together sometimes, you know, the hallway."

She kept looking at me, searching my eyes.

"Okay," she said.

She was suddenly leaning forward, angled and serious.

"Why'd you move up here?"

"It wasn't a particular choice, it was money mostly."

"Everybody said drugs, but I didn't believe it. Who would move to a place just for drugs?"

Then she looked pleased. I got up and went to the window and she did, too, and the street below was not pleasant or beautiful, but our place there, above, was maybe legitimate, our tenement castle, spaceship, our first date. And we were near each other.

"Now, I have to go. But you said—"

"What?"

"You had something for me?"

"That's right, yeah, I do." I went over to my refrigerator and found the little golden man, wrapped up in paper and hidden in an empty egg box. I took him out and blew on him, warmed him with my hands. I gave him to her. She held him up for a second and looked at him, and then hid him away.

"Thank you," she said. "That's a nice present."

And I thought, This is the only thing that can make me happy, is me with her, is this.

"It's really good here with you," I said.

"Here? Yeah. But this neighborhood—I don't think I like it so much," she waved her hands out, over the street. "I hate it here, I always have."

I could say nothing. They were much more her streets than mine.

"I'm going down now. I promised I'd help Alfredo with his math and it's almost time for his bed."

"You have to go?"

Between us a half-doe-eyed look, like we were even younger together. Her looking up, me looking down.

"Yes, I have to go."

"Luz, listen, let me take you out on a date, soon."

"That would be nice," but she was already crossing the room.

"To Hanratty's, Friday night, maybe, at eight?"

"Yes, but we'll meet there, not here." She came back halfway and held out her hand and I was able to hold it again.

"The little golden man? I found him for you—I stole him. To give to you."

"Yes. It's good. Thank you," she said.

Then she moved away, closed the door behind her.

I will learn to hate it here, too, I thought. I will take her hate inside me and share that, too. I stole for her. She smiled when I said it, and that felt so good, to know that she liked what I did. I believed that before I met her, I knew only discontent. My heart rushed up and pounded inside me.

5

The only other woman I'd ever known was Cass. And she was all about college. And college was a short year that started in a bar. I went to Vassar, a former all-women's school outside New York City. My mother had gone there, and I'd gotten in, but barely, based on an essay I'd written about walking around in the woods with Felix.

High school hadn't been a lot of friends, or a lot of anything really, and college felt worse—a kind of supercharged version of everything I couldn't understand in high school. Everyone was buddying up, and Felix had been my only buddy. I didn't want another one and that seemed to be the point of everything—study groups, communal dining, intramural teams. None of it made sense for me. Mostly, I took long walks away from campus, to keep out of the way.

But I knew that drinking is important when you're in college, so I went looking for a bar. That's how I found Dane's.

Dane's had a happy hour with dollar-fifty drafts of Coors. There was ZZ Top to listen to and Lynyrd Skynyrd and all that other monster rock that nobody ever played in the dorms. The bar itself was concrete blocks and wood paneling on the inside. It wasn't much to look at, but as strong and safe as you could hope for. It had none of the bright sunlight and incoming Frisbees and hackey sacks of the Vassar Green, which had no cover and felt like nothing so much as a battlefield, what with all the different organizations and factions competing for domination.

That's what I was thinking when I first saw Cass. She was on my left. Of course later it turned out that I'd stumbled on the hep bar where all the seniors who were cool hung out, but just then Cass was nothing more than a real good-looking woman who was dressed kind of strange.

"Hey, boy," she said. But she said it slow—my first experience with the slowness of Cass.

"Yeah?"

She said nothing, and I looked at her. I mean, she was beautiful and a woman and all that, everything about which I didn't really know. I was utterly virgin, and eighteen. Late, yeah, but that's the truth. There's a lot more of us than anybody thinks—a ton more. She was very near me, in the personal space we'd been introduced to during freshman orientation.

I figured for sure that I was in her seat.

"Stoli, up?" the bartender said.

"Yeah." She paused. "Up."

Then I figured she was on something, barbiturates, downers, bennies, reds; she acted quite exactly like one of those characters in the old drug movies they showed us in high school.

She had a big mass of blondish hair with some other streaky colors mixed in and she wore it wrapped around a big tooth from a whale that was a whole lot bigger than the barrette with the fish on it that my mother had. I almost said that, but didn't. And I think that it wouldn't be wrong to mark a tiny blossoming of brain cells in my head from that very moment. Where I suddenly saw that I was physically just as big as her. Where I felt stealth—woods smarts—as I gave a low glance back and saw a table of people watching us, and she was with me, and I thought, this person could love me. This person could save my life.

"You go to the college?"

"To Vassar, yeah," I said, "I do."

Her drink came, and slowly she moved onto the stool next to me.

"Got a name?"

"Martin Kelly Minter. But I'm called Kelly. You?"

"Cass, not with a K." She laughed low in her throat.

We talked about who we were, who she was really, and her friends called to her a few times, but she didn't notice. She couldn't; she could only concentrate on one thing at a time. She liked to put her hand on my leg, rub the top of my thigh up and down. There were moments when we both gazed at what I now think of as the world record for an uninterrupted public erection. I remember that she talked about persona and radiant being and the mix of public and private self. I nodded a lot. I remember the fall all around us and everything that drops away when you are getting into somebody, the calm that comes from knowing that you are sitting with someone who doesn't dislike you.

Later I learned that even though there was hardly a hint of a good reason why she'd ever pick me for anything, it was typical of her that she'd make such a move. She was a senior then, quite bored with the place and stretching to get out. She'd spent her junior year at an art school in Alaska, where she'd learned to carve stone and drink freezing cold alcohol to keep her body warm. These were traits she brought back to campus along with a coat made of sealskin that some native people had given her. The coat made her really stick out when she walked on the Green in the fall. She didn't care.

"Come to the bathroom," she said.

"What?"

"Come on. I don't want to stop having this cool talk with you, but I have to pee."

So I followed her to the back of the bar, and we went into the women's bathroom. I leaned up against the sink and put my hands down on the porcelain, and it was wet there. I remember flashing on an image of my parents, thinking that in all those years of slow, thoughtful lessons I'd gotten from them, they had never bothered to talk about sex.

"You'll get that on the street," my father said, and laughed. There were no streets in Rantipole Farms. And I thought that I should have gotten it with Felix, but he was gone. I had to learn in bits and pieces, from kids in my high school who I didn't think of as friends.

I remember wishing I had a Polaroid camera. I could've taken a picture of myself sitting on Cass's lap on that toilet seat, both our pants down, smiling. I would've sent it to them with a note: "Things are great here at school! I won't be home for Thanksgiving!"

She pulled down her orange jeans and her panties—I still wonder if I saw a glimpse of dirty-blond pubic hair, maybe, maybe not; memory paces it in and out that way, saw, didn't, saw, didn't—I did hear her pee then, loud. Water poured into a bucket from a gallon jug. She kept talking. I thought of me and Felix, hashing out possibilities in the woods. If only Felix could hear this story! She wiped herself and we went out, still talking, about a book she was reading, something that got deep into all we don't know about the speech of seals.

I made what I hoped was a seal noise and she laughed, she said she loved that noise. I made it again. She grabbed an olive from a glass on the bar and held it up, high. I pushed at it with my dumb button nose and then ate it, licked her fingers. We were both clapping like maniacs.

I moved in with her a week later, out of the freshman quad, into an apartment off campus. We didn't have sex until I was completely unpacked. I believed it was good, the first sex I'd ever had. And then I had a day to myself and I saw the truth, that I'd holed up in that

big old apartment with some crazy senior just like I was a scared rabbit hiding from a hard fall rain.

I hung around Cass's house. I learned how to bake chicken and
steam wild rice. I read all the tales from her Feminist Myth class.
Cass's friends acted like I was doing a natural thing, like there was
precedence. It might have been a bigger deal if I was a freshman girl
and Cass was a guy, keeping a concubine in his room. But this was
the opposite, so maybe that's why nobody cared. She said that sometimes my smile was so big that I was like a cartoon character. So she
called me Mickey Mouse. Instead of calling her Minnie, I called her
Daffy Duck. She liked that a lot. We wore each other's clothes and
we walked around campus huddled together, leaning on each other,
and I believed we were taking care of each other in just the right
way. I called my parents once a week and lied to them about where I
was and what I was doing. Cass said that was the right thing to do.

That fall I felt really safe, but the feeling was cut with the sharp
pain of knowing that it'd all be over soon, and Cass would graduate. I
didn't want anything to change. I stayed in the apartment more and
more, all cocooned up, and Cass didn't mind. That's the sweetest feeling, when you think someone is never going to leave you. I failed all of
my classes. I experienced academic probation and reregistered for all
the same classes in the spring. Introduction to Marxism, Twentieth-
Century European Painting, Novels of the French Revolution, Chem-
istry for Freshmen and Poets. I still didn't go.

Cass had an easy time convincing me that too much education
was not a good thing. She said that I could work with what I'd gotten
in that double dose of the same classes for a lifetime. She was right.
Three years later I was still mulling over things those professors had
said about painting, about politics. After a while it got all mixed up
together, and then I'd sifted it all down to one collective thought
about how power beats everything else. This wasn't so different from
the stuff my parents were always saying about rich people, that they
didn't act fair and fucked everybody up. I mean, they didn't say that
exactly, but that's the best way to sum it up. Those college classes

just sat there! They didn't do anything! It pissed me off when I realized that, I swear to God. That's why it was so easy to leave school.
It was like Cass said, nothing real was happening there.

After her graduation, we went straight to New York City. Why
not, I thought, why not? My parents were angry. There would be no
money if I wasn't in college. But I kept pointing out that the longer I
stayed in college, the more loans there were going to be, anyway. My
mom and dad—between the charities they supported and the community work that they helped to fund, and all the money they had to
spend on their students, all way beyond what the state allotted, all
so important, because they needed to do right, so they could be
great teachers and decent people, always on the side of good—well,
there wasn't that much left over. So when I dropped out, they were
upset, but they were also real busy. There wasn't that much they
could say.

6

September turned into October, and I was a donkey. The ends and beginnings of months are our busy time. Jobs melted into each other, where it was hard to remember what we'd moved yesterday, what the tip had been, who was on the crew. Most days started the same, and the third of October was no different. At seven-thirty, I came off the street and walked under a steel roll-up door, into the Miracle warehouse, through the dark storage areas (filled with other people's couches and boxes of stuff that they wanted, but didn't need) around to a side room, which was really just a bigger storage area, with a little fridge, a table, and a few chairs. I stood in there with the other guys, the other Miracle men. I was a few minutes late, but we hadn't gotten assigned to a crew yet, and I sipped my coffee, and waited. There weren't enough chairs for all of us. So if you were the last in, Isaac knew it, because you were standing.

Isaac entered his office from the street (he had windows and a door) and then, when he was ready, he opened the back door to his office, which let him into our back room. He handed out assignments and we ran to the trucks. It was like every morning was the same fire drill.

The back room stank. Felix smoked and so did a few other guys, there were fried egg sandwiches, coffee, and guys who didn't shower; the one exception was Dennis, who was this black guy with a wandering eye and bad teeth, who smelled like something special that women like. There was a lot of yawning, too, a lot of open mouths.

At eight-twenty Isaac opened his door. He had a wild shock of gray hair and he looked exhausted. He left his house in Leonia, New Jersey, at five to get into the city before traffic. He invariably wore a purple sleeveless T-shirt and blue jeans. One time I asked Teddy why Isaac dressed so funny. Teddy looked all contemptuous at me and said it was because he owned the company, he could dress however the hell he wanted.

"How's things?" Isaac said. Everyone mumbled about how things were good, because what are you gonna tell the boss, that things are bad, that you're fucked up? Staying positive was especially important because Isaac was an old hippie and if you gave off bad vibes he didn't want you around. He'd named the company after an old Grateful Dead song, and he'd talk about that sometimes and we'd all nod, and sometimes, if the mood was right, we'd try to hum it for him.

Isaac handed three steel clipboards around to the three foremen. Teddy got his. He looked at it for a second, winced, which could have meant anything, and started to bark.

"It's me, Felix, and fuckin' Kelly, like always. Check the International and see how much shit is on it—then check the gas."

Me and Felix hustled out, counted dollies, straps, pads, and tape. All around us, businesspeople came out of their big old lofts and made their way to work. Some nodded hello. The ones who didn't like the noise we made under their windows, didn't. Instead they sneered in the special way used only by people in suits.

The fuel gauge on the instrument panel was broken so I had to check the gas level with a broomstick that's wedged behind the seats in the cab. The stick reeked of gasoline and I always had to measure twice to make sure I had it right. It was a real nice way to start the day. Everybody joked about setting that broomstick on fire, stuffing it up somebody's ass, killing them. Why did I laugh, too? The broomstick was so impregnated with gas it would burn from the inside out, a heat hotter than hell, and the joke around there was that if the customer doesn't tip, the burning broomstick goes right up their ass. Ha! Sometimes I think the blood inside of us is dark like marrow, that the more you talk ugly, the slower the blood moves, the bigger the clot on your heart.

We pulled out and got caught in the snarl of Canal Street traffic and immediately Teddy started in.

"So my brother-in-law calls me up last night and invites me for dinner this Sunday and I'm so pleased—you motherfucker! You asshole! Get out of my way, you little Paki son of a carpetbag shit! 'Cause I got a little smashed last time I was up there—you know, when I yelled at his kid, Spencer, they named their fucking kid Spencer, anyway the little faggot was drooling on my leg and I pushed him away and the fight we got in! I had to apologize about seven times. Look at this shitbag! Look at this tweeterhole! Hey you, ya fuck! I'm going now, me, I'm going!"

Teddy had this sad thing where he was obsessed with family. He loved them and he couldn't think about anything else, because he knew he fucked up when he decided to become a sculptor and not to ever get a career-type job. His brother-in-law sold computer software to the Egghead chain and his sister taught kindergarten at some school with Country Day in the name. They had a house in Nyack. Teddy thought they were happy and every morning he woke up and looked around his loft in Red Hook and no matter how hard he looked, there was no wife and no kid. So when a cabdriver cut him off—didn't even cut him off really, just pulled cab's rights and did an abrupt lane change—he would want to cut that driver's throat.

"Spencer, as if the kid had a chance, they don't even like me playing with him. I bring the kid a paint set and they don't want him to
touch it. Pussy parents, pussy kid, I'd like to give them all a smack in
the teeth."

"Tell them they're wrong," I said.

"Then where in all God's abysmal country am I going to eat Sunday dinner? Go it alone like you do? That's not bright, Kelly, you
ought to know better. Family's important, don't forget that."

Maybe, I thought, but isn't family what makes you scream obscen-
ities at strangers who are only trying to get off Hudson Street?

I checked the name on the contract and it turned out that we
were moving a guy we'd moved before, a playboy type who lived with
girlfriends until they asked to marry him, and then he got out. He'd
told us that he had money, but that he liked to live that way—the
transience agreed with him.

We pulled up on West Broadway, at Grand, where there's a new hotel
plunked down that looks more than anything like an overgrown version
of my high school. We went up to the building on the opposite corner.
The apartment was a few floors above a fake-looking French restaurant,
La Nuit de Temps, where the fashion models ate and got their picture
taken for the gossip columns in the *Post* and the *News*. But at eight-
thirty in the morning, West Broadway was shut up tight. The only people moving around were dog walkers and people like us, who worked.

I had the contract, because Teddy was with the truck. We knew
this guy so well we even knew what he had: enough clothes for five
wardrobe boxes, two leather armchairs, an old steel desk, blond
wooden dining room table and chairs from 1954, book boxes filled
with something much too light to be books, some pictures and other
chowder, and a television set that was five feet tall. The set was so
heavy we got a service charge for it. He'd gotten it as a gift from one
of his girlfriends, and I think that was part of why he was invited to
live with so many women—he had this ass-kicking state-of-the-art
TV. His name was Wytold Van something or other.

We got up there and of course there was this attractive woman moving around the kitchen, talking very fast and quiet into a cordless phone. She barely glanced at us.

"Hey hey, my moving friends!" He came forward and shook hands with me and Felix. Most of his stuff was in a huddle by the door. The woman spoke a little louder into the phone. She gasped a little and I could see how she was holding back tears.

"You all going to get me out of here quick, right?" He laughed and slapped Felix on the back. Felix was looking at the way his stuff had to go down, what needed to fill the truck first. He wasn't nearly as interested as I was in seeing the guy's life.

"Good, good." He slapped me on the back, too. Wytold was a pretty happy guy. He liked to touch people and he probably knew that was a gift—that he was unafraid of other people's bodies.

We had wardrobe boxes with us. I went to the closet he pointed out and began to stuff his clothes into the box. I watched him move around the apartment. His hair was messy and longish, brown, and he pushed it back as he walked. I could see how he kept his center up high, around his shoulders, and it was this trained walk that gave him the grace that probably got people to like him, and kept him from getting an American potbelly. My own solid midsection and thick neck were suddenly embarrassing.

Wyt stopped to look at a small framed drawing of a hairy black spider with a big grin. He looked like he was trying to remember if it was his. I turned away, but I thought, if I were him, I wouldn't take it; it was a scary picture.

He wore the standard outfit of his class: blue jeans, a really expensive button-down shirt with two colors of stripe and French cuffs, a blue blazer, and a pair of extremely narrow brown driving slippers, polished in a thoughtful way that gave depth to the leather.

"You ready to do the TV?" Felix asked.

We did a nice dance around the set, padding and taping, and we kept it upright and slid it onto the dolly, real careful, because something that heavy can snap a dolly into bits, break floorboards, and rupture itself.

But if you tip and push, tip more, push more, take it real easy and keep whispering to the piece about how you're in love with it, that it's your girlfriend and you care for it, that if it had nipples, you'd kiss them, it'll be okay. All the best movers purr at furniture. It's a good way to make heavy, dangerous objects love you back so they'll do what you want.

I opened a window and looked down to Teddy, who was looking right back up at me.

Teddy yelled, "Wardrobes first."

I nodded and turned back into the room. Wyt was hopping around singing "I love to love you baby" and mangling the words with his shitty accent. While he sang he put both his arms up in the air and swayed his hips from side to side. He didn't stop until he saw that the woman he was leaving was still crying, no doubt amazed at how inappropriate his actions were. He took her in his arms and she hit him a little bit, at the top of his chest, where she couldn't do too much damage. Wytold saw me looking and winked.

"I'll do the elevator," I said. We loaded and I began to go back and forth, apartment to elevator to truck and then again. The whole thing took less than an hour, and by the end the woman looked better, like she'd hopped herself up on some prescribed drugs.

"Meet you there!" Wytold said.

We arrived at Twelfth Street just west of Sixth Avenue. We slowed in front of a reddish-colored brownstone with only one buzzer.

"Back me in," Teddy said. I hopped out and tried to back Teddy into a tight space a few cars to the left of the house. There were some big trees there, and I kept banging on the side of the truck and trying to get him to slow down, but he went too fast and took out a big branch. The branch made the sound of a slow bend and then there was a rip, a prolonged crack, and it fell at my feet.

I stared down at it. It seemed really sad for a second, a nice block minus a nice branch. But Teddy came up and kicked it away. I popped the lock on the back of the truck. Wytold opened the brownstone door. I grabbed a box and went in.

"They are giving me a back bedroom, nice, huh? They're distant cousins—family, right? Family is the way to go."

We went up a flight of steps that had a row of ascending black-and-white photos. Then we stepped into what must have been a back parlor. There was a fireplace and a mantel with a mirror. It was warm there, with lots of wood paneling.

"Great place," I said.

"Yes, thanks, I am very happy with it." And he did look happy. We got the boxes up pretty quick, since it was only two flights, and Wytold talked on the phone. Going up with the wardrobes it seemed like I was going to knock all the pictures off the staircase wall, but I made it, even as I felt the cardboard slide against the pictures, as I dared them to drop. Teddy stopped us when we were ready to do the television. We had the thing on the street, but it had to go up two flights of stairs and because of the low brownstone ceiling in the staircase it had to go up at an angle.

"There's a good chance we'll damage the insides, if we don't just drop it," Teddy said. We stood there and looked at the thing. Me and Felix had turned our brains off—we'd have just dragged it up and made the best of it—but if it broke Teddy would have to deal with Isaac. Wytold came out and looked at us from the top of the stoop.

Teddy said, "Listen, ah, I'm just gonna walk to the corner and call the boss, 'cause there's gonna have to be a serious service charge on this and I also want to know about liability, okay? Be right back."

"Sure, no problem," Wytold said. Teddy waddled off down the street without looking at us.

Wytold moved down a few steps and sat on the stoop. He pulled out cigarettes and offered the pack around. Felix took one and sat down next to him.

"You're psyched," Felix said. "It's a nice location."

"Yeah, and now with relatives, maybe there won't be so many fights." We were all quiet. I thought about the TV going through the stairs, what a mess that would make of the day.

"So," Felix said, "what do you do anyway?"

"I sell art!" He laughed. He said it like we were supposed to be in on the joke.

"What does that mean?" I asked. I watched him, all of us appraising one another like kids before they choose teams for baseball.

"I do a kind of a freelance thing where I know people who want certain things and I know others who have them, and I go between, you know, I set a price, we all have dinner, I get my cut." He laughed again.

"We see art occasionally," Felix said. "That's where the big money is, huh? Unless you, unless you're into stocks and the market."

"If somebody wants to make lots of money in this town—like really a lot of money—he sells art. Nothing makes cash so quickly. Not making movies, or stocks, or real estate, nothing makes money like art can." Wyt stopped. He looked at Felix. "And I know you see things, you know? Like when you're on a job, sometimes you see things. I remember last time you moved me, afterwards I couldn't find—"

"Right, right," Felix said, quick. "You understand." I looked at Felix and he was looking away. Huh, I thought, you stole from this guy?

I said, "Sometimes somebody like, gives us a painting or we end up with one. Do you think, if that ever happens, we could let you— handle it for us?" I looked at Felix while I talked. He nodded at me, like, right, now we're headed somewhere! It made me happy, to have said something that might get us started in a way that Felix liked.

"Well, sure! If it's worth something, I can tell you how much in a minute. That's what I'm good at."

"These are the kinds of things though," I said. "that need to be kept quiet."

"In life, you never hear about the best deals," Wyt said. "I know exactly what you mean." He considered us both. He had perfect sideburns, just a little long, so they said that he was hip, but not too long.

Felix shot his cigarette into the street. He looked at me.

I said, "This is a good idea we're all having together. This is a solution to our little problem."

I kept staring at Wytold. Felix had stolen from him before, and he'd called us to move him again. Are we all so smart? I wondered. Can we all look at one another and see what we really are?

"Perhaps," he said, "if we can be more specific, if I need something, I'll call you." He handed me a silver pen and a small piece of paper. I wrote my number down and handed it back.

"I have this number now. Your number. Sometime, perhaps I will call you, tell you to run into me on a street corner, maybe give you some more information then. You act on the information I give you. Everything goes well. We make another exchange after that. You understand? A few nice exchanges? It's wonderful how you workers can walk into buildings, isn't it?"

"It really is," I said. Felix nodded. His lips were all pursed.

I looked up toward Sixth Avenue. Teddy was coming back. It felt like a lucky street, lots of trees, good brownstones. And at ten-thirty in the morning, there was a calm. I was blinking repeatedly because there was so much light in my eyes.

"Okay, we're going to take it in, but it'll be a sixty-dollar service charge plus fifteen for insurance. Does that sound fair to you?" Teddy asked.

"Sure, it's good." Wytold stood up and smiled. "I know it's quite a TV!"

I got behind the TV and Felix was at the top. We were moving up the staircase, where there was so little space, so there was no room for Teddy to help.

"Did that just happen?" I whispered.

"It did. That's what we've been waiting for, my brother, no?" Felix asked. He groaned a little, but we didn't stop moving.

"Oh yes," I said.

Me and Felix made sweet love to Wyt's TV all the way up those stairs.

7

When I dropped out of college and moved to New York with Cass, my mother got concerned enough to take the bus into the city so we could have a talk. I was stunned. She hated the city, hadn't visited in years.

"I just want to be free and think. Mom, isn't that what you and Dad were doing? When you left?"

We were at a diner on the Upper East Side. We'd wandered from Port Authority and ended up on Eighty-sixth and Lexington, for no reason at all. Our grilled cheese and tomato sandwiches were just finished and we were all ready to have the important part of our talk. I could tell because my mother had rolled her eyes up in her head for a second and gone over the day's lesson plan.

"We left New York for you and your brother."

"You left. You left because you and Dad are cowards. Here is where it's important to be. Leaving here is wrong."

"You're nineteen! What do you know about right and wrong?" The waiter delivered a cup of tea and she picked it up and banged it on the table. Amazing, I thought. She's so angry now, because I'm getting tough. She's going to be so proud of me when things start to go really well. I kept thinking about how, somehow, I was going to carry out all the things she talked about with my dad, except I was going to do them for real. I remember listening so carefully at the dinner table when she talked about reapportioning funds for education. Kevin wore earphones during dinner for a lot of those years. He listened to motivational tapes and Tom Clancy novels. They fought him on it, but he said he really didn't want to hear them, and they gave up on trying to make him. I listened, though. I understood that when my mother talked about the meaning of luxury taxes and nodded along with Linda Wertheimer on NPR, what she was really saying to me was that somebody ought to steal from the rich.

"I want to do something good. Here is where I'm going to do it." I couldn't say any more to my mother. That was all I knew.

The counterman leaned across and watched us. The old ladies who probably only made it out of their apartments once a day, for their lunch—they were engrossed in our argument, so happy to see some life going on.

I could never remember talking like that with my mother before, like grown-ups, where she wasn't condescending, but she was actually upset, and I thought I was being smart, making her treat me like an equal.

"Didn't we teach you anything? About education? About decision making, during all that time when you were growing up?"

"Yeah, I learned a lot. But you also said we have to do what's best for us, that's why Kevin ignored you and now he's going to be a plastic surgeon."

"I expect better from you than this."

She shook her head. She got out her Mexican beaded purse and began to count her money.

"I'll give you a few hundred dollars now, and you can think about what you're doing. You and your girlfriend, the two of you can decide if you can't manage to have a relationship where you stay in college and don't ruin your life and she lives happily, just a few hours away."

But then that horrible seepage came back into her voice, where she was talking to me as if I were a child, as if I were nothing but a student. I remember her coming back from school, seeing me, trying to refocus, but I was just another kid. I looked at her then and I felt this weird gap, where either I was just a kid, or I was a deposit for a bunch of ideas that she'd never squared. And then I wasn't a kid, but I wasn't an actual person, either. I felt real empty. It was a scary moment because for those few minutes, I didn't even want to take anything from her. Before that, forever, I'd always wanted to get something from her, to take something.

"No. I don't want any money. And it's not about Cass. I'm going to do good here, Mom, I swear."

"What good? What good is it, that you're going to do?"

But I didn't know. All I knew was that I was truly nowhere. I was nothing. I had no job, no plans. It was a perfect place to begin.

"This is not what we planned for you," she said.

In truth, was there anything in the world she hadn't given me? There was nothing. Was there enough love? Sure, probably. It felt way, way late to wonder if there could have been more of it. Maybe there'd been plenty, loads, and I hadn't noticed and so that was my fault. Why worry about it? I had work to do—and as soon as I figured out what that work was going to be, I needed to get started on it. Then, then I'd show my mom. She'd be really happy with me then.

She had her purse in the palm of her hand, but she did not move. She pushed at the Heinz ketchup bottle and the metal container of sugar, the Equal, the Sweet'n Low packets. She looked away, and I reached out fast, put my fingers on her purse, pressed against it. I was amazed because there I was, and yeah, I wanted something from her after all.

"What are you doing?" she asked. I got my hand away from her.

"You said you didn't want money, Marty, didn't you?" She gritted her teeth, and concentrated on my face.

"No. Look, if you're just going to give it to me, I don't want it." We watched each other and I put my hands down under the table. I had to sit on them to control myself.

"Fine. We both know I can't force you to stay in school. You'll make your own way."

"Yeah, same thing you said about Felix."

"Felix. Yes, I've told you it was a mistake. I've said it, your father has, too. We were . . . jumpy, that's all. Forgive us for that." When she said that, I didn't know what to say. I didn't understand why it was so important, why she needed to be forgiven. So I was quiet.

I looked around and saw the old ladies watching us. The counter-man wasn't moving at all. He didn't even blink. I wondered if he'd lost a daughter or a son this way, over some misunderstanding.

My mother looked across at me then, more carefully than she had before. Her dislike of New York was in all her actions, the way she gripped her money, and didn't let her hands or arms touch the table.

"Do you know why we were so jumpy with Felix?"

"Because—" But no. I didn't know why. I said, "I don't think jumpy is the right word to describe what you did."

Her face was turned up toward me, and hers was a face without makeup or artifice, so there was nothing hidden there, as is right for a good teacher. So she didn't look forlorn at all.

"We were going to adopt him. We were making the arrangements just then, so the summer became a kind of testing ground. I mean, we never actually said that, but I know it was—that's how I felt. So we were jittery, Marty, we were just jittery, that's all. And theft is not something that you can educate away from a child who's already into his adolescence. Good rearing must happen earlier. Your father and I know that. I am sorry, sincerely, and I want you to feel angry at me—it's healthy now, but not forever. Please."

I remember cocking my head to one side, looking at her. She had an exquisite ability to talk clearly, to pronounce. Again, she was all about being a good teacher. And she tended to say things that were not what she thought, but were what she believed. Nobody had ever told me that once theft is in you, you can't get it out. I figured, if she believed that, then me, too.

"But everything that happened that night was my idea. I told you that," I said.

"That isn't possible. The two of you did it together. I know that." And we had been through this part before, and I could not make her believe me. Then, I didn't think I could change any of it. I wasn't angry at her, really. I just wasn't listening to her anymore. She was going to change my brother Felix's life and then she decided not to. I never could make her or my father understand that they shouldn't have sent him away. And as I got older, I stopped trying to steal so much. I just took things now and then, that no one remembered once they were gone. And I waited.

"At least Kevin is here, too. If you have any real problems, you should go to him," she said.

"I don't need him."

"Well, I think we both know, if you do have a problem, the way you're so proud now, that will go away if there's a real problem, and he can help you. I've spoken to him, of course."

I watched her, sitting there in her brown smock dress. She had her great mass of brown and gray hair tied up in back with her fish barrette. There were some real lines around her mouth, and some of them were frown lines and some were smile lines. There were a lot of them. But to me, she wasn't not beautiful.

"You threw Felix out of the house and you thought that he was going to be your son."

"Martin Kelly Minter. We did what we thought was right. You

were not unhappy, were you? You got everything you needed. I won't apologize again, nor do I think you'd expect me to."

"I don't, no."

"We acted the way we did for you, because we love you. Don't you know that? Where were you the whole time?"

"Does Felix know?"

"It's in his file. He may know, yes," my mother said. She'd had a whole life around children's files.

"Where's my file, Mom?"

"Martin!" But even as she arched her eyes, I knew. I had a file, too. Case closed. I didn't speak to either of my parents again after that East Side lunch. My mother and I walked away from each other and I made it impossible for them to find me. What was the difference between me and Felix, anyway? Nothing at all.

What are they thinking when they plan for you? The Rite Aid drugstore at the corner of Route 9 and Starr Drive when I was five years old. Long before the summers of Felix. My mother paying for Robitussin, Tampax, Bufferin, some small packets of Kleenex for the car. At that age, I was eye level with the candy, which is intentional, I know that now, it's a sales thing and planned that way. My mother pays and talks to the lady behind the counter, who is clean and friendly, twenty years older than my mother, and considers her an invader, from the awful city.

Me, smoothly (how I found this talent, I do not know) removing a pack of Big Red gum from the rack and slipping it far up into the sleeve of my fuzzy anteater-hood nylon coat. The move is all surreptitious, sly. Like I was already a vacuum and at my base, there was only a pull of desire.

A short ride home in the station wagon, groceries on the back-seat, both of us belted in, calm. We are home, in the mudroom at the back of the house, removing our matching green galoshes, and I am so proud of myself, my stealth, a reed of gum a gift in my hand. I hold it up to my mother. And I remember this, the moment, my smile, her (of course towering over, being taller) looking down, the smile on her face suddenly turning quizzical.

"Where did you get that?"

"I—it was on the floor—I took it to give to you."

"Oh no," and she started to laugh. She put her jacket back on, her waterproof boots back on, my outfit also on.

"Crazy boy," she said. She sounded sweet and she kept smiling. "You are one crazy boy. You shouldn't steal things for me. That's wrong."

And all I could think on the slow ride back to that Rite-Aid was that I didn't understand. If she was happy and laughing, why were we going back?

"You must understand that what you did is stealing," she said. Like she didn't want to admit that she liked what I did. She couldn't even let her real personality touch the subject, because I was so positive that inside the part of who she really was, she loved the idea of what I was, her crazy boy, her thief.

Of course I cried, later, when we went in and she explained, said, "My son has something he needs to do." And I had to hand across the gum to the looming presence of the behind-the-counter woman, the benevolent look exchanged between them, not me, and the apology I made. But even then, and in subsequent years, the thought nagged at me, Why aren't you proud of me? I did something, after all, I got the gum. I got it for you. I think you did like it.

We drove right back home, after justice had been restored. I didn't feel so good, though, not nearly as good as I had before I had to give that gum back.

"That was crazy what you did. You are one crazy boy, and I love you," and then she stopped smiling. "But you can't steal. It's wrong, and even if you thought that was fun, you'll feel better now," she said, all confident, her hands calm on the wheel.

Me thinking, I don't feel better. I liked it when you thought I was a crazy boy. You should have kept what I stole for you. Because without that bond, what are we? What can we be to each other?

"It's not how you feel that matters, it's what you get," my brother, Kevin, said, when I told him what I did. Me, stroking the smooth skin on my cheeks, still a complete child. I listened to him while we played Monopoly in his room. I always lost. A few years later, Felix came and the three of us played together. Felix was always up close next to me, knees together, afraid of my brother, afraid of getting kicked, beaten.

In the woods at night, I turned to Felix. "We've got to trust each other. He screws us up, my brother, and I'm not so sure I trust my parents, either. Promise me you'll trust me."

"I promise. It's like you say, nobody else acts fair," he said.

"No, we're going to keep learning that," I said. And that's when me and Felix began to dream of robbing my house, our own house. I gave up on trying to understand my mother. I mean, shit is complicated, don't dumb it down to morals. If you do, if you leave it at morals and don't go further and you're family, then things won't ever get clear.

The afternoon I left my mother, I walked around the East Side and looked at all that cool limestone and thought, You can't trust anybody. Who the hell knows what anybody's up to? If you can't trust your own mother to show you who she is, to let you be who you are, well, you can't trust anybody.

8

In New York, I found and lost jobs pretty fast. I painted a whole lot of gallery space with an insane old guy who liked to pay me in cash, by the half day, and who eventually fired me because he thought I was stealing from him. He was nuts.

Cass and I lived in Brooklyn, in Fort Greene, not so far from Crown Heights, where my parents grew up. Two or three nights a week Cass would come home with tequila and cheap margarita mix and slowly, slowly, make drinks for the two of us. She'd suck down three mugs of the stuff, get sloshed, and cry. She had a job at the Marlborough Gallery, and the owner made her rub his Botero sculptures by hand for hours so they'd shine with a "human touch," and she thought she was losing her mind. Was this normal? I didn't know. I had no idea what we were doing and I didn't really have any reference points for Cass and her job. I thought that if she didn't like it, she should quit. It wasn't like

she didn't have loads of money. She did. I knew that she shouldn't be
drunk so much. She kept asking me if I thought it was okay for her to
give up, and I said that I didn't see it that way. But I didn't see it any
other way, either. I just didn't know.

And then Cass surprised me. She took a weekend and went to a
family house she had in Vermont. I called her there, and she said
that that was where she was going to stay. So I said that I would
move up there, too.

"I don't think that's the best possible idea," she said.

"Well, what is a good idea?" I asked. I was in the kitchen of our
little apartment. I was heating up some mushroom soup I'd made. It
was just beginning to get cold out.

"Listen," Cass said. "You don't have to come up here. You don't
have to move out. Just stay there."

"What?"

"I was just thinking, I'm going to live up here. I can't stand New
York. You can come and visit on weekends, maybe we'll still be in
love."

"But . . . no. That doesn't work for me," I said. There was terror
running through me, where all of a sudden I was caught in New York
with nothing. I started to shiver.

"It's what I want," she said. "It's not like I don't want to be
involved with you. I just want . . . less."

"Well, maybe I—maybe I can't. Maybe I'm breaking up with you
then," I said.

She kept saying she wasn't sure, not about anything, and she still
wanted to see me as much as possible, but she wasn't coming back.
So I was supposed to go and visit her, when I put together the
money to do that. It was frightening and I didn't know why I said I
was breaking up with her. But I did say it, right then, after she'd
moved out.

I didn't go up on weekends. I started to hurt real bad. I couldn't
do anything but work, put together the rent every month and lie
curled in a chair, wounded. I was too embarrassed to call my parents

and I was too disgusted with myself to make a move—say, back to college, or back home.

I found that I couldn't work in an office, couldn't renovate loft space, paint faux marble, or do telemarketing, except when I was selling alarm systems—but that work didn't come around often enough. Then one day I was going down the stairs in our building—worried that soon I was going to starve without ever having done anything good for anyone, even as I was stuck in an apartment I could not afford—and I almost knocked into a guy who was coming up with a bunch of boxes strapped on his back.

I knew the back of that neck, and I looked closer and it was Felix Lina, my savior, my brother. He looked up at me and it was like, yes, I've been looking for you, needing to find you for years. And now you're here. We said nothing, only hugged. He took me downstairs, introduced me to Teddy, called Isaac, and I had a job. So he never met Cass, and I didn't say much about her. A guy you loved once comes up your staircase and gets you a job that leads to a place to live and a whole new life—it's best not to talk about what brought you to the low place where he found you.

"The job is just like we wanted back then," he said.

"What do you have to do?" I asked.

"Just watch me—it's easy. Remember walking around in the woods, all the big rich houses that we used to stare at, how we used to talk about those people? Well, with this job, we get to go inside, look around, you'll love it."

His life had gone bad for a while, but just when we found each other, it was getting better. He'd hit a guy a few years before, who turned out to be a cop. He'd been trying to order a beer in a bar and the guy pushed him, so he pushed back. They cursed at each other. And then Felix hit him. A whole table of guys stood up and rushed at Felix. They broke two of his ribs and his nose, and they left him lying on the ground with a concussion. But they must still have been angry when they left. Because then, they came back into the bar and arrested him.

He spent two weeks at Bellevue and six months in jail for assault. Right after that he married a girl from high school who he'd always hungered after, Lynanne, who already had Anastasia, his baby. She's a really beautiful child. Felix has put all of his love into her. So my brother and I were going to be fine. He only had three months left on his parole.

9

I was dreaming. Luz waved her hands in the air around me and I grabbed at her fingers, like anyone would, a baby with a pacifier, yes, or a lover. I dreamed her face, the cool calculation, the measurements of half-closed eyes. We were talking about how it would feel to fall in love. We were talking about stealing not just a thing, but a place, about taking over the world. I felt the fight then, and a furious smoke came toward us. Luz and I were touching fingers, our hands were pressed against each other, and we were adulated, loved in turn, by crowds. We were naked and beautiful in front of them. The smoke rolled in, the clouds, and there was a banging on my door. I woke up.

I reached out and touched the bolt. I didn't sit up, but I gripped my baseball bat (Hank Aaron, Little League special) and angled up toward the door from my bed. That's how small my place was, everything damn near within arm's reach.

"Yeah?"

"Felix."

I popped the bolt and Felix came in and went to my window, took a last drag off his cigarette, and flipped it outside. I imagined it floating down, bright red cherry of light, all of that before I was fully awake. I laid the bat back down.

"Listen," Felix said, "I'm sorry for waking you. It's—there was all this noise from the drunk bitch next door and I started banging on the wall and then Anastasia woke up and started crying, too. Lynanne got pissed and then I put my fist through the closet door. She told me to quiet down and I started cursing. She told me to get out. Then I was clear for a second and I saw this white sheet of anger, and I knew it, man. I know that anger. I got on the train."

I could hear his breath. He'd scared himself.

"Good," I said. "That was a good move."

I listened to him sniff the air. He went to the closet and got out an old Hudson's Bay blanket that he knew from when we were ten. I gave him the pillow I didn't want and he lay down next to me. He was already near sleep, all wrapped up.

"Take your boots off," I said.

"Oh yeah. Thanks, my brother. I get these few hours of sleep, it won't be an all-sleepless night." He pushed his boots off and we both lay there. I was sad that my brother was with me, was forced away from Lynanne. I watched him for a second and then turned away.

When we woke up, a little after dawn, Felix's face showed gray folds from where he'd slept too hard. We dressed quietly.

"When you started fighting, were you drunk?"

"Nah, two beers maybe. I got to cut back to none, though."

"It's the only thing to do," I said.

"Lemme get a shirt?" I threw him a plaid shirt and he buttoned it over his T-shirt, which was also mine—a white shirt with a snake on the front that Cass had gotten from an art benefit. I watched a tremor go through Felix. He knew how close he'd come to doing wrong by Lynanne.

It was seven and we went down the stairs and out. We got into a train and it was still cold, air-conditioned from the summer. It was half full. The school kids made noise, but everybody else hung their heads and tried to believe that the half sleep they got while they waited for their stop was real rest.

"You hear from this Wyt guy?" Felix asked.

"No. We know where he lives, though, maybe we could stop by," I said. Felix nodded.

"You know we could go big with this?" I asked.

"Like what we've been waiting for, I think," Felix said.

"Maybe I was just waiting on you to be ready," I said.

"Maybe the opposite," he said, and he poked me in the arm, and I had to nod. He was right. He'd been waiting on me. We kept poking each other, pointer fingers in the belly, in the ribs. We were both giggling like crazy.

The day's job was big. It was going to take eight of us and two trucks to move a lady who had inherited a fashion magazine from one big-ass apartment with a view of the East River to another even bigger place on Park Avenue that had a view of nothing at all. She'd had a baby without a husband, or he was dead, or ran off, at least we didn't see any evidence of a husband, and having the baby meant she needed even more space.

The lady was tiny, five feet or less, frozen at some age around forty, with a body that was without a doubt papery and stiff as origami under the sky blue shirt, khakis, and pearls she wore for her moving day. She was a real little Martha Stewart package, with an eyeball intensity that kept everybody working hard. At one point, while I was in her bedroom stuffing clothes into wardrobe boxes, she came in and collapsed on her bed.

She lay there breathing hard, and I watched her. She was really small. I could have gotten down on top of her and smothered her in about a second. She rubbed her hands all up and down the front of her body and let out some moans. I kept putting her silk shirts and little black jackets in the wardrobe box. She sat up.

"There now, that's better," she said. "Sometimes a little self-rub works wonders."

"Oh yeah," I said.

"All this isn't easy, you know."

When I was in high school the cool kids used to sneeze and say bullshit really loud at the same time. That would have been a good moment to try it out, if I'd had that kind of balls.

"Nnnn," I said.

"Could you be very careful with those shirts, please?" she asked. She just kept rubbing her flat little tits in front of me.

"Nnnn," I said.

"Clothes are valuable possessions," she said.

"Ahh, I washed my hands before I touched your stuff."

"That's fine," she said. Then she was running her hands inside the waistband of her pants. I saw where her shirt was crinkled, where it edged up and I could see her panties. She caught me staring. I saw her eyeballs turn into something—kryptonite, maybe.

"You white boys who do stupid jobs and don't live up to your potential—you think the world owes you a favor, an apology. That's a crock, you know. The world doesn't owe you a damn thing."

She slapped me just above my ass and I could do nothing, could say nothing. My hands were full of exotic fabric. She went out.

"Nnnn."

I should have smothered her, I thought. She hit me first.

The baby spent its time in the television room with a nanny. I stepped in and checked the kid out when I needed a break. The room was painted a gloomy red and it showed on the kid's face. He (or she) was chubby and feverish—not quite as red as the room, but certainly complementary. I watched some of the *Barney* show with the maid and the kid. One kid on *Barney* had such a big smile that it looked like it hurt her little face. Felix came in and watched with me.

"Look at that kid," Felix whispered, "that kid knows it—play with the man in the bizarre costume, keep the fuckin' smile on, and play the game and get paid."

"Smart kid," I said.

"Five years old and sold her soul; my baby's not gonna be like that," Felix said.

"'Course not. Let's get the couch."

The maid nodded and picked up the little baby. They kept their eyes on the TV and we upended several hundred pounds of leather couch.

"Reach for the shiniest star," Barney sang, "reach up, reach out, way out, way into the sky." The kids sang back at him.

I sang, too.

The maid laughed and the baby looked around, like, What did I miss?

1 0

We went to lunch in one of the cheap, diners that Teddy
favored. It was as if Teddy had some map in his head with all these
diners on it, and we bore the brunt of his lobotomy-stupid choices.
We sat down in a booth that looked out on to the street. The place
was heavy with the hot smell of coffee and fried things: bread, eggs,
bacon, and lunchtime burgers. I watched some old folks who must
have been regular customers. They looked resigned, as if somebody
had walked them in and shoved them down into their seats. Above
us all were a few signed pictures of the kind of stars you'd catch in a
diner: Tony Randall, Mariette Hartley, Mark Hamill, local newscast-
ers, some faces you'd recognize from long-running commercials.

It was me, Teddy, Felix, and Dennis. Dennis was in his late thir-
ties and he went to engineering school at night, so he was always

sleepy. Women loved him. He had something about him that they just went mad for. None of us knew what it was—I'd even sniffed him a couple of times to see if I could find his secret, but it wasn't forthcoming. The four of us sat quiet. Teddy liked to take his time with the menu, and we couldn't order until he was ready.

I whispered to Felix, "I didn't tell you about Luz, I saw her again the other night—"

"What's Luz?" Teddy asked.

"Some fine girl who lives in my building. I ran into her at the Chinese takeout—"

"Puerto Rican?"

"Yeah."

"I think I'm having the gyro," Felix said.

Teddy started in: "Puerto Rican girls—Kelly, are you sure you know what you're doing? Those girls, man, they will tear your heart out and serve it back to you with rice and beans, and your brains are a dish on the side, scrambled, man, laced with their spit, they don't fuck around. Felix knows it, that's why he married an Irish girl."

"I like rice and beans," I said. I felt my hands and my ears heat up. Why did he like to fuck with me?

"The moment you see those big fucking earrings and a pair of lips painted all primary red, I'm not talking about lipstick, I'm talking about paint applied with a brush that makes the lips a whole different shape and size than they were originally, you can handle that action maybe one time, maybe, and then it's fucked, they tear you up, make you feel like shit inside. They put your dick"—Teddy lowered his voice—"they put your dick in their mouth and they bite down, they look into your eyes, and they're saying, 'You clear on this, you gonna mess with me? Ever?' They bite down, just a little bit, grind their jaw—"

"Bullshit, Teddy, that's bullshit," I said. I thought of Luz's hand, her fingers moving through my sleep.

"Motherfucking asshole," Felix whispered.

"Felix, honey, I don't mean you—you're the best Puerto Rican guy

I ever met, half the time I think you're Dominican, Colombian even."

"Fuck you, Ted, we're at lunch and your shit bores me."

"I'm really, really sorry, Felix," Teddy said. Those two, they didn't ever get along too well, but they didn't hate each other. It was more like they just took each other excessively serious.

The waiter came over and his eyes were downcast, like he didn't like to wait on people who made less money than he did.

"I'd like the roast chicken dinner and two Heinekens, one beer follows the other, slowly," Teddy said. The dinner special included Greek salad, soup, some appetizers, chicken with vegetable and potatoes, coffee, and a piece of pie. Teddy was crazy. It was disgusting every time. The rest of us ordered normal—cheeseburger, tuna melt, things that wouldn't turn on us later in the day.

"Well . . . what's her name again?" Teddy asked.

"Luz."

"That's Lucy, Lucy's a nice name, friendly."

"Yeah, but it's Luz."

"It means light," Felix said.

"And you pronounce it like that, like 'cuz'?" Teddy asked.

"Enough," Dennis said. "He says it that way, so that's all right. Stop fucking with the kid. A woman walks into his house and he's pretty happy, he's had no sex in forever. Kelly, Teddy's just jealous— he's had nothing for four months, and at his age it's hard to get going again."

Dennis opened up his *Daily News* then, as if to say, That's it, I've ended the conversation. He spread it out on his knees and began to read. Teddy watched him.

"Ha, ha, ha . . . ha," Teddy said.

"Yeah," I said, "and the only Puerto Rican woman you know is Rosie Perez, and that's from movies, and that's an act."

But Teddy started waving his hands. He had his fork out and his face was flecked with Feta cheese. Felix put his pointer finger up to his lips, blew out his cheeks, and went nausea red.

Teddy glared at all of us, his shiny bald head taking on its own blue palette. He said, "Nah, don't start that, the older I get the less I think that way, the more I'm fucking sure that bad movies tell us the truth about people, the cliché way somebody acts, that's all we are, bags of shit. Ah, there's my chicken."

By then we were mostly done eating. And we were all grumbling about just exactly who was a shitbag. Teddy's chicken was a burnt-out brown half bird on a plate with some rusty looking green beans and French fries. I could hear the cracking as he tore into that dried-out chicken. I took a fry off his plate and ate it and it was like chewing hot air.

"You take my advice, Kelly, you can't handle that action."

"Teddy . . ." But he looked up quick, like "Don't fuck with me more on this," and he was older and the foreman and . . . no. I wasn't going to.

"I'm happy for you, buddy, we'll double some time," Felix said. Teddy had made him queasy, and he'd given up on his food.

The waiter came and said, "A note for you, sir," and handed Dennis a little piece of paper. Dennis read it while we watched. Then he looked over at someone behind me.

"Lemme see?" I asked. I grabbed and got it before Felix did.

It said: "Maybe we can party some time if you could like me. I think you look real cute. Call me after five at—" and she gave a 718 number and her name, Fatisha. I turned around and there she was, sitting alone, smiling at Dennis, unabashed.

"A true fucking Miracle man. She's cute, too," I said.

"Women love me," he said, and he shook his head and gave a little self-satisfied shrug.

Dennis went over and squatted down next to the woman. He had a wandering eye and he didn't dress great, but there was something about him—women loved him.

Me and Felix paid up and went outside and left Teddy alone with his lunch. It still wasn't fall cool, but there was a breeze that blew some garbage around. An old drunk was slumped ten feet down from us, and I walked over and handed him a bagel that I'd bought on the way out of the diner. He smiled up at me. There was some shit on his pants leg.

"You want some orange juice?"

"Nah, I got wine." He showed me his bottle. I nodded, saluted him, and walked back to Felix.

"You see Jimmy Charny?" Felix asked.

"Yeah, recently actually. He looked like he was sticking his nose in his mom's stash."

"Well, he might be able to help us with this Wyt thing. Next time you see him, make a date for a drink. And listen, lemme get your keys? I'm gonna get over to that locksmith right there and make a set while there's time, so I don't wake you up at night, in case—because of Lynanne."

"Of course." I flipped him my key ring. "Listen, you ever think of Teddy as kind of like a dad?"

"Yeah," Felix said, "but it's the bad parts of him that make me think that."

"It's bullshit is why, he's an idiot."

Felix nodded and headed off with my keys. Like I'm waiting for my dad to finish lunch, I thought. And I looked in at Teddy, munching away, tiny and bald and deeply into the sports section of Dennis's paper. He looked like nothing, the kind of guy you would never, never look at twice.

Dennis came out.

"You make a date with your new friend?" I asked.

"Oh, maybe I'll see her around. Listen, be cool with Teddy, he just envies you is all."

"Fucking Teddy."

"Let him help you when he needs to, and just remember, he's older than you. He's looking out for you, is all he's doing, even if he doesn't know it."

"He doesn't know anything."

"Look—he cares about you, don't doubt that," Dennis said.

We tapped on the glass and made Teddy look up, quick. His mouth was full and his eyes were red. He looked a whole lot like the customer's little red baby.

We didn't finish until ten o'clock that night. The lady had so much stuff that it became fluid, a river of possessions streaming out of two trucks. By five we'd all gone quiet. We were all shadow, dragging her boxes and mirrors and side chairs down a dark service flight, through a basement corridor, onto a dolly, onto an elevator, into her new place. I felt like an ant.

Near enough to the end so that we were all counting trips, I had three boxes of books strapped to my back and I was crouched low, headed down the service-entrance stairs. I wasn't moving quick, and I could see the worn toes of my sneakers not ten inches from my eyes. I could feel all those books loaded down hard on my back, begging me, pleading with me to go down, to take a tumble, to just say fuck it—this was too hard, too much of a test, and for what? I held my balance and rested for one second on those steps.

"Felix," I said, "Felix." But it must have come out real low, because I had both my hands on the strap behind me and my chin was pressed into my chest, so I was talking to my gut.

I thought of me and Felix at the end of our first summer, on either side of a stream, way back in the woods. August had been rainy, and a tree had been cut and made into a bridge across the stream. Felix disappeared and came back with two branches, each as tall as us. He gave one to me. We were young enough so that it often felt like we were in a movie, so when we came across the stream the *Star Wars* score played in our heads. We walked across and gripped the tree through our sneakers. I hit Felix's branch and he hit mine.

"For real or not?" he yelled.

"For real?" I didn't understand. We tapped each other some more.

And then he hit me, hard. My staff broke into bits and I flopped into the stream, hit bottom, came up. The water was cold, terribly cold, and I looked up and there was Felix, looking down at me.

"Didn't you say 'For real'?"

"No, jerk-off, I didn't understand." We laughed and he pulled me out of the stream.

I teetered on the stairs, a sweet and painful walk on the plank, then the wait for the push.

"Felix," I said.

"Arch up and go down slow. I got the weight."

He was behind me, holding up the boxes. We went down and at the bottom I shifted back and let the weight rest on a step.

"Yeah," I said, "good."

"Next time, take two." Felix took the boxes and the strap and loaded up a dolly and went away, down the corridor.

"My brother," I said. "Thank you."

"My brother needs to think before he tries to carry too much weight!" Felix smiled back at me. In the corridor I could see his teeth and his ugly face, his back rounded down as he pushed the dolly in front of him. I went back up the stairs and thought about how good it was that we had the woods between us.

We finished up by going around and looking for tape and any garbage we'd left behind. I came around a corner and there was our little customer, screaming at a woman who was even smaller than she was, who wore a huge pair of glasses and might have been a personal assistant. There was a great mound of pocketbooks and purses piled up next to them, in front of the kitchen. Apparently someone had screwed up and there was no place for all those special little bags to go. The woman with the glasses burst into tears.

Our customer screamed, "I will not let you manipulate me like this!" That was the last I saw of her. I walked away from that job with one teardrop-shaped jade earring in my pocket that I'd found in one of her coats.

1 1

Teddy had put together a whole wardrobe over the years from what customers had given him on jobs. A single woman's closet would reveal a bunch of men's things and she'd be up to hand them out; the old memories were an unnecessary burden on a new apartment. Teddy demanded first pick when this happened. He was a strange size, small and stocky, but he'd been collecting for quite a while. Most of us followed his example. We filled our closets with castoffs, we sat on discarded chairs, read books somebody else had found dull, listened to outdated stereos that no longer performed in the high range. I had never worn any of the things I'd been given. On any average day I stuck with my sweatshirt, my blue jeans, and my Adidas. But the night of my date with Luz I went into the closet and put together an outfit.

I found some brown pants with cuffs and a blazer that seemed blue and had a kind of shadow pattern on it. I found a white shirt that had been ironed so many times I could see the outlines of the tabs showing through the collar. I watered down my hair and brushed it back. I looked at my face in the mirror after I washed it, and I smiled. I had to keep reminding myself that Luz had said yes when I asked her out. She didn't not want to go out with me.

When the sun went down I walked straight up to Madison. The street was full of a lulled quiet; the drug havens in the abandoned brownstones were still gearing up for the night. I whistled while I walked. I'd never had a date before. Nobody I knew dated in high school. And I didn't have any dates with Cass, since we were in bed together before we'd ever had any kind of real dinner at a table. So I was nervous as anything because this was new, and I was sure there were all sorts of rules, and I didn't know what they were. The loafers rubbed raw spots on my toes and I wished I'd stuck with my sneakers.

Hanratty's was a big dark rectangle with high ceilings and French posters that must have been the inspiration for the ShopRite can-can ads. I waited in a booth in the back. I asked the waitress, a fifty-ish Irish lady who put both hands flat down on the table, for water. She grunted, like she was making a special effort to let me know that I was only a child to her and if there was any way to ignore me, she'd find it.

When Luz got there she came and sat down next to me, on my side of the booth. Her hair was up and she wore a light red shirt that had a swirl of lace moving down and in between the buttons, and through that lace you could see the additional lace of her bra. The effect was more than sweet.

"You look so nice," I said.

"You do, too," she said.

The waitress threw down some menus. She slid the table setting that was across from me in front of Luz. We ordered little salads and steak, beers. It didn't matter what we got since we weren't going to eat any of it anyway.

We talked about the neighborhood, about how intense it got when the wind started howling down Third Avenue. We talked about her sister Jahaira.

"Those are little murderers she hangs out with," Luz said.

"That's good to know," I said.

"If she's not careful, there'll be a baby and she'll have some ex-boyfriend in prison, like me."

"What?"

"My first boyfriend, Andres, he's in prison now for stealing cars. He still writes me letters but we're broken up. When he gets out he's going to the army, to stay out of the neighborhood. Alfredo thinks he's dead."

"Dead?"

"Yeah, it's best that way. Alfredo has enough people to care for him. He doesn't need a father."

Her voice had gone dull for a second. She watched me.

"Well, a father—" I said.

"What are you saying?" she asked. I liked it when she looked at me and she kept from smiling. Those looks said better things to me, since when quiet moments got serious like that I felt like we were more for real.

"Nothing. My first girlfriend is staying out of New York, too. She's in Vermont."

"Same thing," Luz said. "Anyways . . ."

While we didn't touch our little salads I took up her arm and smelled her wrist. She held it up for me, light, so we could both feel that she wanted me to do what I was doing. I'm not saying we had some divine shit going on, just that she wanted to be there and so did I and we were conveying that we'd been thinking about each other, that we knew. Her wrist smelled like Dove soap and our building and the warmth from the metal of her watchband and underneath all that was whatever the true smell of her was, which I knew I liked.

Outside it was dark and eleven o'clock and Luz said she wanted to walk. So we didn't have to bother to work to find a cab that would be willing to take us farther uptown. We walked along Lexington and Luz said hello to guys hanging around in front of the corner stores. They were subdued with her. They were young, teenagers, the only people in the world who I could see any reason to be afraid of, and here they were, saying hello to us, waving.

We walked up our stairs to her floor and she turned down her corridor and I followed her.

"Come in, but only if you're going to be absolutely silent," she said.

So we went in and sat down in the kitchen. There was a night-light plugged into a wall socket that threw shadow around the room. Luz did not turn on any other light.

The blue-and-green patterned linoleum on the floor was worn and clean and that was how everything was there. You could see where all the dishes and pots and food were put away, how each cabinet was full, had been filled thousands of times. We sat on steel chairs with plastic padded seats. I could feel so many people asleep so close by.

"My parents have lived here since before I was born. Before that they lived in public housing, but then my father got into construction, so here we are."

I thought, At the beginning of something you can talk forever. I wondered if it was because we are more profound when we act out our beginnings, and then I was sorry for my internal thought, because any analysis or acknowledgment of the real, the past, the future, made me feel bone-creaking old. And I was not old. I felt real young and good and Luz was going to be my girlfriend, not somebody I needed to hide me away, but an equal, a lover.

I was able to lean forward and touch the hard surface of her skin just behind her ear. I think we both closed our eyes. At that point, we seemed so good that it was like we had an agreement, we had discovered a power thing between us, like superheroes who touch rings and get strong.

There was a grunting crash from the dark entranceway that led from the kitchen to the rest of the apartment. Luz moved away from me. We heard a yawn and then the movements of a man in the room next to us, and then the noise of him pissing in the bathroom, which sounded even closer. I imagined that he'd drunk a lot, from the noise and length. He flushed and came into the room.

"Luz," he said, pure greeting. And then, when he saw me, "Ah."

I stood up and we shook hands.

"Martin Kelly Minter," I whispered.

"Ocides Acevedo, her father," he whispered back. "I've seen you before, in the corridor."

He was naked except for white boxer shorts and he was built big, shorter than me, but powerful, without slack fat on him, but plenty of muscle. Now he looked like less of a Tasmanian Devil and more like Harvey Keitel, or a little Incredible Hulk. His dick popped out of the front of his boxers and we all saw. He pushed it back inside.

He said, "You go to eat?"

"To Hanratty's," Luz said.

"Ah, next time, you stay home, and you eat with us. Martin, tonight the Queen made a feast—you come and eat with us."

He tugged at his boxers, gave himself room. He yawned and nodded at us, then padded out of the kitchen.

"He's nice," I said.

"He's all right," Luz said. She looked around the apartment. I watched her face and saw how she was taking in where she lived, forgetting me for a second, and that was wonderful for me to see her there, so self-possessed. She ran her finger over her jaw.

"No. He's better than that. Truly, he's better than most," she said. "I have to go to sleep, but soon I'll come over again, like we did before, and we can eat together and maybe you can tell me who you are a little more."

"Yes," I said. I wondered if she would be disappointed. There was not so much to me. There was growing up, Felix, Cass, moving, and her. I even dared to see it all as a path to her, but I did not dare say that aloud.

I went out into the corridor. She stood in the doorway and put her hand on my chest, on my face.

"I do want to see you again," she said.

"Good, soon."

Her hand was cool and I took it and kissed it, and she was gone.

The phone rang when I opened my door. It was Cass, calling from Vermont.

"My calls," she said, "you don't return them."

I lay down on the bed, but within moments I stood up, leaned up against the door.

"You act like you dropped me," I said. "When, in fact, I dropped you; I broke up with you."

Silence. Then, "Right. I'm not denying that, Mickey, Kelly, I'm not. But we're still, you should come up here soon, I want you to visit, so that we can hang out, talk, you can see my work. It's fine that we're broken up. I'm only worried about you."

I thought, That's funny. I'm kind of busy right now. There's no reason for anybody to worry about me. And I really didn't understand how she could move away from me and still be worried.

"I had a date tonight, Cass, with this woman who lives downstairs from me."

"Yes?"

I could see Cass in her farmhouse, in her living room, up close to the fire, clean air not simply the dreamy idea it is in New York, but real and her in a house filled with it, and thinking, Hey, I wonder how Kelly is, how that crazy kid I dragged to the city is doing. Could that be it? Could it be that simple? Could that silence on her end of the phone have been filled only with that cool air, soft and comfortable, where all she felt was curiosity about me? If that was all, that didn't feel so good.

"You should come up soon, bring her."

"Oh, we're not, not near that."

"Push it, Kelly, you never push hard enough."

"I thought you were tired of saying that to me, that you didn't want to have to say that anymore. And I do push sometimes, so now it's different."

"You're not still at the same job, are you?"

"Yes, remember, I like what I do, I'm happy. I am a happy Miracle mover, who's always moving up the ladder."

"Ladder," she said, like that was alien.

I rubbed my back up and down against my door. I felt the peephole at the back of my neck and I let it scratch me, the little circle there, biting me. I would fucking well show her, too. I could push it.

"Cass, we'll speak soon, okay?"

My windows caught the moon wrong and I could suddenly see my own reflection, and I was surprised by my look, the clothes, the fact that I still had on a blazer and it was past midnight and I was thinking, I didn't notice and now I have on a blazer, and I'm in conversation, and my life is changing. I almost asked Cass how it felt to be so adult, was it like this?

"Kelly, I miss you, I really do want you to come up. We're friends. All I'm saying is that I want to make sure you're okay."

"Yeah. Don't do my mother's job," I said.

"I'm not—"

"You are. I'll come up, when I've pushed it, like you're talking about, then I'll come up."

I didn't hang up on her. We breathed for quite a while before saying good-bye. I still missed so much of what I was with her, where I waited till she got home, looked at her to see if she was happy. Kissed her while she slept. But she made it so that I couldn't do that anymore. And I wished I hadn't learned that part from her, the part about how to leave.

I went and checked in the freezer and that jade earring was there (inside a roll of cash that I kept in an empty pint container of Ben and Jerry's New York Super Fudge Chunk, so my money smelled like chocolate ice cream) and then the phone rang again, and it was Wyt.

"Hi," I said. "How are you?"

"What? How are you? What? Listen. What you do is, you run into me on the corner of Eighty-sixth Street and Lexington. I am making a phone call there, in front of the HMV record store. You arrive, and you stand near me. I impart to you some information. Do you understand?"

"When?"

"When? Now. Of course now."

So I ran down the stairs and got on the subway and got down there quick. He was on the phone, and what he did was, he talked into the phone, but in a way so I could hear him, too. It was a Park Avenue address. He gave me a time, too, and a day, the next Thursday. We were supposed to take one picture, one small picture, of an old man, which would probably be in an old brown frame, probably in a dark corridor, leading to a bedroom. I didn't ask him how he knew all of this.

"This is only one little picture, you understand? You walk in at just this time, you are the carpet cleaners, you see? You are expected. If this works, then there will be more."

"Of course," I said. "We're only getting started. And hey, listen— we moved this rich lady the other day, and she looked like she had some real expensive stuff. I'm sure she did, only I don't know what the really good stuff was, but I remember her address."

"What? No, no, with me, you only do these few things that I—I suggest to you. Nothing else. These are not random choices I am making. I do not know about anything else. We do not discuss anything else."

"I understand," I said. But I didn't really. It only seemed simpler to not disagree with him. He'd been nice enough to meet with me, after all. Then he smiled, and I thought how happy I was to be in business with somebody I liked.

THE MIRACLE MAN STEALS

part two

1 2

I met Felix on a park bench across from the Guggenheim. It was midmorning and quiet, and we were several days into October. We didn't even need to bother canceling work, because there were only jobs for the top four guys on the ladder. Felix smoked one long, slow cigarette. We were dressed in blue jeans and blue button-down work shirts. I thought we looked as much like carpet cleaners as anybody did. I had the address in my head, and the name. Felix hadn't asked for any information.

We walked over to Park Avenue and headed downtown, as slow as possible, but not recognizably slow. And I thought to myself, Truly, there is an art to everything. We passed the people, the women with their little black fall coats, bags, high shoes, tiny bobbing heads. I prayed that the thing would work, that there wouldn't be anybody at home when we came in. Because then what would we do? Then it was all a mistake. What were we doing there? Well, we just wouldn't know.

We passed professional dog walkers walking all sorts of special dogs: a Russian wolfhound, a regal retriever, boxers, dachshunds. The dogs seemed calm, happy, well fed. I turned to see if Felix had seen the dogs, but he was looking up at the perfect rows of windows. He had squinted his eyes and he was breathing through his open mouth. I wondered if he thought of his probation. Did he even go to his meetings? He never talked about it. I never asked. Below us, the concrete on the sidewalks was smoothly laid out. There were not even little black smudges of old gum on those streets.

We passed the building. The doorman stood outside, staring down into the perfect stretch of curb that had been marked out as his territory. He might have been forty, or sixty—his gray suit with blue piping knocked him away from any clear age. He clasped his hands behind his back. I watched him roll a penny over his fingers, and then hand to hand, a subconscious skill that must have taken years to perfect. I stopped in front of him.

Don't use your mind. Let him invite you into his building. Step back. Stay cool. Let him feel right. My eyes were half opened and only revealed the dull responsibility of showing up for work I didn't much want to do.

"We came to do the work . . ."

"The measuring? For the carpet? You walk over?"

I nodded.

"On eight?"

"Yeah." We both had the same idea in our head, simple as the workday itself. Maybe I willed it.

"The Sandersons?" he asked.

"Do you give us the keys, or is the door open?"

"It's open, service entrance and elevator is in the back, but what the hell—go ahead through the lobby and down to the basement." He looked away from us and we left him to his finger game.

The lobby was a little area with a marble bench and some mirrors, but—like when you put on a good pair of glasses and things shine brighter? The edges of objects radiate light? Like that.

An old white-haired guy in the basement took us up. The landing had two doors. I turned the knob on the first one; it opened. Good luck.

"I'm not going in," Felix said.

I looked into a little room with several different-colored garbage cans and some mops. It smelled fine in there, even good.

"Hello," I said in a normal voice. There was no answer.

I turned and grabbed Felix's shirt and pulled him inside. I closed the door behind us. He pushed away from me and we both looked around.

We were in a pantry: country wood cabinets and cans, with graphically pleasant labels, of fat red tomatoes, English country scenes, golden-colored broth. I reached out and touched the cans.

Felix stage-whispered, "Speed it up!"

I turned to say something, but there was no explanation—he was right. I put a box of German soda crackers back on the shelf. We passed through the kitchen with its two massive industrial stoves, lots of aluminum surfaces, plenty of copper pots and wooden boxes filled with flowers on the windowsills. We had visited such rich rooms before, but never in the course of their midlife. I felt so good and safe and warm there. My dick was hard. If somebody walked in on us that's what they would have seen, my hard dick. For a second, until Felix pushed me, I couldn't even recall why we were there.

We walked through a living room and down a small corridor.

"It's a picture of an old man," I said. "A little picture." We kept moving and there it was, hung up right where Wyt said it would be, with no other pictures for several feet around it. Felix slipped it off its hook and held it.

"That's it, let's go," he said.

But I kept walking. I passed other little rooms and looked in. Kids' rooms. I ignored them. At the end, I found the master bedroom. The windows reflected in other windows across Park Avenue.

I waved and saw my outline across the street. Then I slipped back behind the curtains. They were impossible thick, all yellow-and-blue stripes and tasseled. They must have weighed fifty pounds. The room smelled of flowers and fabric softener, from a quilt on the bed that was so soft it might have been floating. My eyelids went up. I felt a tremor, a soft bang of dangerous pleasure going off in my head.

Felix stood in the doorway, paralyzed.

"You know about something else?" he asked.

"Maybe, maybe there's some cash," I said, because I didn't want to lie to him. I just wanted some time to look around, to be there. I checked through a big wooden box on top of a chest of drawers that stood between the windows. The box was filled with photographs of smiling children. Then I understood. If there was money, it would be where the children wouldn't look. The mother's underwear drawer. Tons of underwear, lots of it filmy, pink, nice, but no money. I moved across the room to the closets and found a black lacquer box, high up on its own shelf. And there it was—a pile of bills, laid flat and looking clinical and fake under some cufflinks and what must have been silver collar stays. I took the cufflinks, too. I looked around for something for Luz, but Felix was waiting, and I was kept from doing so much that I wanted to do. I turned and he was already walking back down the corridor, his hands jutted out and shaking at his sides. He'd left the picture on the floor for me to take. I picked it up and it was so small, small enough so I could slip it under my shirt, nestle its bottom just under my belt, let it rest in the small of my back. We passed back through the living room.

"Sit down with me," I said.

"What?"

"I want to sit down."

They had gray velvet easy chairs. I touched one and then sat down, light, so I wouldn't hurt the picture. A softness, a cool fabric against my neck.

"Kelly, are you fucking nuts? Get up and let's go."

"Think about it, would you?" I asked. "Please?"

"About what?"

"Living here, like this. Just chill and experience it for a moment."

I remember sitting there, feeling that gargantuan comfort, as if a good living room was an answer to a question I'd begun asking years and years earlier. If I could have this life, then I would not want to tear it down. This tiny glint of desire, a piercing sensation, even as I felt Felix grab me, felt him pull me away from that chair.

"Let's make ourselves lunch," I said.

"We're gone now. You've forgotten where we are. Cut it out with the games." He pulled me up, so I was standing.

There was a blue glass bowl of mints on the table next to me. I put some in my mouth and dropped a few on the floor.

"You're missing out on all the fun," I said. But Felix would not look at me and he would not let go of me.

The mint had a sudden sharp cherry flavor. It exploded in my mouth.

"Fucking rich people," I said, "making us hurry up our day, I spit on you." And I tried to spit on the carpet in that room, but my mouth was gobbed up and dry.

"You don't do right!" I said.

"Shut up," Felix said. "I'll spit for you, and then we can go." And he did. We took the stairs down and were out on the street and walking uptown before Felix took his hand off my arm. We walked on Second Avenue. Everybody on Second looked uptight and nervous. Shaking, walking on tiptoes, me and Felix fit right in.

Felix said, "Next time, don't fuck around. You understand that? We got what we went in for; you're not helping anyone by playing a game in there."

"Yeah," I said. "You're right. Sorry." I had the roll of bills in my shirt pocket and I grabbed his hand and pressed it to them.

"Feel that, though," I said. "You're telling me that doesn't feel good? Like you always said. Now we got money for us, and the picture for Wyt. And who knows how much he's going to pay us for it? This is so good, man, just like we planned, right?"

"Yeah," he said. "Sure. When do we deliver the picture?"

"Oh, I'm sure he'll call," I said.

"Let's leave it at your house until then."

"Okay," I said.

13

We moved a hippie couple from a basement on Flatbush Avenue to a garden apartment in Chelsea. The guy had bagged the songwriting in favor of a job in marketing, because his best friend ran the company. The woman had found a job teaching yoga. They told us all of this and they looked happy. I want to say they had a pained look behind their eyes, or they were resigned to their upward-moving fate, but that would be crap. They were pleased. They smoked pot in the garden while we moved them in. They looked up at their very own patch of sky while we got the boxes up against a wall and fit the couch in the only possible couch space.

They were sloppy packers and little pieces of her jewelry kept falling out of their boxes. Whenever I saw something drop, I stuffed it back in. I couldn't figure a way that it made sense to take from them. They weren't greedy yet, what with the way they just sat in their garden and admired the clouds. But I didn't feel so good about them, either, since, well, there was all too good a chance that they'd get bad before too long. But they weren't there yet. The tip was twenty-five a man for a four-and-a-half-hour job, which was generous. And then I felt reassured that I hadn't taken anything from them.

At the end of the move, it was only lunchtime. Teddy drove off without saying good-bye to me or Felix and we stood on the street.

"Why's he acting mean?" I asked. I wondered, Can he feel it? Does what we're doing give off a smell that he knows?

"Maybe his sister told him his art sucked. Anyway, his problems aren't ours. Listen, I called Jimmy."

"Yeah?"

"I'm gonna beep him now and we'll meet at the Wicked Wolf, we'll have some late lunch, a business lunch. He wants to help us out."

"Felix—J.C., he's less than stable."

"Yeah," Felix said, "look who's talking. We can't wait on Wyt forever. Maybe J.C. knows what we should do with our picture."

We caught a 6 train and headed uptown. I was sure that Felix's new attitude was brought on by a nasty thing on the side of his face. He'd been arguing with Lynanne, and she'd slapped him open-handed with her cigarette pointed toward him. He had this thing that was half scratch, half burn on the side of his face. He planned to sleep at my house, which meant I couldn't see Luz. So I was a little cranky.

Up at the Wolf, I thought a lot about the pimp shuffle. The pimp shuffle started when drunk pimps would get up from the table all wobbly but they'd have to look cool anyway, so they maintained that the stagger was hip, which meant they had to show up with it the next afternoon. Teenagers saw them do it and took it on and that's how it earned its place in the world. Jimmy Charny had a pimp shuffle, a hard Irish jaw, plenty of knife scars, and stupid stone-cold blue eyes.

"Lemme show you something," he said. "Wait a second. Felix, what the hell happened to you?"

In the dark bar light Felix's face looked particularly bruised, like he'd been slapped with a burning log. Felix put his hand over his face.

"Christ, what'd you to deserve that?"

"Talked to Lynanne when we didn't need to be having a conversation."

"You hit her back?" Jimmy asked.

"Yeah," Felix whispered. I stirred a bit. It hadn't occurred to me to ask that question. I looked at my brother, but he wasn't looking back at me, or at anything.

We were in a booth and the only real light came from out in the street. I'd gone to the bar to get beers and while I was up there I watched a roach crawl on a whiskey bottle. It was attracted to where the cap was screwed on, to the tiny drips of alcohol. I wondered what it would do when it was drunk.

"You two need to work out a new arrangement," Jimmy said.

"I'm not kidding about Anastasia," I said. I wanted to get the kid away from Lynanne, to get her with me, or to just—I didn't know.

"She's okay with the kid, and I am, too," Felix said.

But it was easy to see how he wasn't so sure.

"Down to business," Jimmy said. He had a desperate tone to him. He was the kind of guy who liked to wear a little black fanny pack on top of his belt buckle, and he always had earphones around his neck. There were bracelets on his wrists along with a big garbage gold watch. He was like that, overly accessorized, where you wear what you have because you don't have much.

He bent forward, so we could see more than enough of his eyes.

"What do you have for me?" he asked.

"If we had something, what would you do with it?" Felix asked. Then it was quiet for a second. Jimmy put the tips of his fingers together.

"Fair enough. Listen, Isaac fired me because a customer caught me stealing—actually it was Teddy who suspected me, so you have to watch for him. They didn't say nothing 'cause it's lousy for morale and also, I mean I'd been stealing for a while, getting good stuff, too. But I never thought like a criminal, which was my trick, lemme show you."

I thought maybe he'd do something that would prove just how goofy he was, like he'd pull a quarter from behind my ear and say, "If I can do that, then . . ."

"Here we go," he said. He pulled a cellophane bag out of his fanny pack. The bag was rolled tight and he unrolled it slow on the table, till it was flat. There was a key in the bag and he pointed at it, tapped it. It was little, for a mailbox or a storage unit.

"So?" I asked.

"I got my own ministorage location. I won't say where, but what I'd do is take little stuff and stuff they left behind, and I store it for a while. Then I go to shops, and I show them Polaroids of what I got and they take the stuff on consignment and I make money that way, steady income, see?"

He smiled, like we were gonna be amazed. I thought, If we were looking for the definition of a small-time, big-risk operation, this was it. What Jimmy had was a lot of angry people and a storeroom full of useless junk. Nice. He thought we were all about stealing broken lamps and stained carpets. And I had a little drawing of an old man in my house, who was holding a book that might have been a Bible. That picture was worth, who knew? A hundred thousand dollars? Maybe so.

Felix said, "This is what we're here for? So we can steal garbage that people wouldn't even miss? Come on, Jimmy."

Felix touched his fingers to his face and I could see how he was getting annoyed with his life, how between waiting on Wyt and the problems with Lynanne he was getting stuck, and this was no good, no good. He wanted fat change, not the same old small-time money he'd been seeing since we were kids.

"I'm hungry," I said, and yawned.

Felix said, "We're getting near big money, you're talking bric-a-brac sale."

"You don't want to be involved with me?" Jimmy asked.

"No, we don't," Felix said. I looked at Felix. He was looking tired-eyed angry at Jimmy. I thought, Why'd you tell him about big money?

Jimmy started to roll up his plastic baggy.

"Any bigger crime than what I do ends you up in jail, and you've already been there," Jimmy said.

"Thanks," Felix said. "Now you've wasted our time and pissed me off." He got up and out of the booth.

"We gotta go," I said. "See you around, J.C., sorry this didn't work out."

"No! You two don't forget me! Kelly, I know where you live now, you know that, I know people who know you. You don't forget me when the time comes due." Felix had already walked out of the bar. I didn't move.

"What?"

"Just remember me is all, as somebody who's hearing that you're having thoughts, stealing thoughts, you got me?" Jimmy looked like he'd said that kind of thing before.

"I got you. So, yeah, we'll be in touch," I said. I hammered his shoulder a little bit on the way out, to show there were no hard feelings, but he shrugged me off. I looked back and he was playing with his baggy, shaking his head.

I got outside and walked with Felix.

"I think he just threatened me," I said.

"Look at him, he already forgot we saw him. He'll be OD'd before he remembers he said anything to you," Felix said.

"You promise? Do you promise me? Do you swear to God and everything for me? Felix, do you?" I tugged on Felix's sleeve.

But Felix ignored me and kept walking. He wasn't up for joking around, and I think he was pretty bothered that he'd made us go and talk to Jimmy Charny at all, since it hadn't gone well.

1 4

In the mornings, when I saw Luz, I would give her something, once a flower, once a picture I drew of a bunny (this is the intimate stuff, the stuff you do during the days when you're all into old-style courting), and once, and I think this was my high moment, a very thick slice of freshly cooked bread. I learned how to bake bread at college. A friend of Cass's taught me. I remember her saying that it would be good if I knew some skills, that bread baking was always in demand.

On the morning of the bread it was whipping cold, mid-October, only days after we took that picture. There was very bright sun so my place had a shine to it, where I closed my eyes for just a second, opened them, and my little hutch glowed. What I did was, I got fully dressed, I had the bread in the oven, cooking, timed. I held a bread knife. I stood at the window and waited until I saw her come out of the building. Then, the moment I saw her, I flew.

I whipped around and got out the bread, pulled off half the loaf, cut the end, tore the half apart until I had a perfect slice, two inches thick, pure wheat brown, dusted dark crust, jammed the remains into my coat pocket and ran out the door. I got down the steps by going from landing to landing, one leap at a time. She walked slow, headed down to the subway and school. I came up fast and got in front of her, and I was able to hand her the slice, hand to hand, steaming, beautiful bread. She kissed me then, slow, on the lips, with the heat from the bread coming up and warming our chins, our necks.

She said, "Let's pretend like we're in love."

We went back upstairs together. I had no curtains and it was incredibly bright in my apartment just then, with so much sunshine streaming in. We stood in front of each other and she motioned for me to put my hands up. I did. She pulled my shirt off. I could feel her hands on my back as she touched the cuts and welts from the straps, the big bruises from pushing sofas and stupid huge wooden cabinets up a thousand flights of stairs. We kissed and lay down on the bed.

"Don't you hurt?" she asked.

"It numbs up, after a while."

She made a clicking noise with her tongue and kissed the scratches on my chest, where the corners of boxes had dug in. It was like she was telling me I was somebody with worth, who was worth being wanted, even as she dropped the bread on the floor and I felt the heat from the pulsing oven, forgotten and still on. She lay down and I half crouched over her, pulled her shirt up, and her eyes were closed. It seemed so impossible and I was near tears.

"You and me," she said.

She lay back. On my knees in front of her, I came forward and kissed her neck, and kissed her jaw, and then I kissed her cheek, and then her lips.

Her in her sheer black pants, the metallic click as I undid the top button. The way I lowered myself, ever so slow, onto her. And then finally, as I felt the first few soft hairs, as they began in a tiny line below her belly button, as I felt her excitement and I watched as she undid her bra and revealed breasts that were so beautiful—nipples so brown, so soft, so hard—I touched her and it was as if all the pain in my back and chest went down. We undressed and she held me between her legs. I did not ask to make love to her. I came, hard, in the triangle of space where she fit me.

We lay on the bed. Her belly button was small and tight, and I put my finger there and felt the little suck of air, like a tiny safe haven we'd created together.

She said, "Now tell me what you want. All the other night, you couldn't say what you wanted, not me—what you want in the world."

We listened to the hard wind at the windows, to the city, as it began to wake up and bang away.

"Do you want to know what I am?" I asked. I stood up.

"Yes."

I stood naked in front of her, for just a moment. I had never stood naked in front of a woman before. Cass didn't like it.

"I think I'm getting really good at something, that maybe I'm not supposed to be good at. Stealing. That's what I am. I am a thief."

"All your moving then, that's what it's for? You could do so much of that, we could have so much money that way."

"Not for us, for people who need it."

"We need it," she said.

"Okay, for us, yes. And for other people, too."

She looked past me. If she had a morning class, she was late.

"Be a thief then, Kelly. A guy who steals—Kelly the thief. I like that." And so she said it, what I would be.

"But I want to be with you. I want to help you," she said.

I lay back down and she lay next to me with her eyes closed. I felt better in that moment than I ever had before.

"You're laid down next to your thief," I said.

"That's right," she said. She smiled, and kissed my chest.

15

I stood with Ocides in the kitchen of the Acevedo apartment. We were drinking a mix of Budweiser and Clamato juice he'd made while I waited for Luz to be ready. The mix was bitter and intense. I was taking Luz to the movies on Fifty-ninth Street. We were going to see *Love Amongst the Thorny Roses,* starring Jennifer Love Hewitt and Adrian Brody. Luz had chosen it. Me and Ocides were talking about our jobs. He worked on a construction crew that had steady work renovating little downtown apartments for a management company.

"You see they tip you in your job, where for me, they never have to tip, never, never, never—and hourly, man, we make the same fucking thing, maybe I make more—but man!"

"It isn't fair," I agreed, "but you get health insurance, we don't."

"Health insurance!" Ocides yelled out. "Hah! We get dick! We get the big dick for health insurance! You're a good guy, but what are you, naive? You think there's any fucking health insurance in my kind of construction? Not much!" He moved closer to me, "You know the only people who always get it? The women. You want to know why?"

"'Cause they do office work?"

"Right, right, 'cause I can't get a job as a secretary, and I'd do that work, too, who wouldn't? Cush job, inside all day . . ." He went on and I leaned against the counter. I liked Ocides. He still had his backbone, and he liked me, too, you could tell. We had real work between us.

"So when I work with a new guy I gotta move half of half speed, 'cause if he drops drywall sheets on me, or a pipe, it's over, broken bone and I'm fired, that's what I always have to deal with. You know the joke: Fall off a ladder, you know when you're fired—the moment right before you hit the floor—ah, Luz!"

She stood in the doorway. She was dressed up, and her T-shirt was tight. We were both quiet, breathing, watching her.

"Kelly, come back to my room, would you? It's taking me longer than I thought."

Ocides nodded. "Go with her, it's fine. I'm going to look at television anyway, *Law and Order*."

He grabbed my arm on the way out and made me flex some muscle. He liked that, I think, that I had muscle. I know he thought that all white people were soft and weak, and probably the ones he saw were, and he was pleased that I broke his stereotype.

"Oooh, now you got him coming in the room," Jahaira said.

"Quiet," Luz said. "Let me take your green shirt."

"Take whatever you want. You're the one with a date."

Jahaira's beeper went off and she immediately giggled.

"I got the men calling me though," she said, and went off to the phone in the kitchen.

"She's got the little pistol packers beeping her," Luz said. She sighed. I looked after Jahaira. She really did bounce, that girl. The

Queen passed through the room, checking to see if anybody needed anything, a snack, or a drink. She was always thinking of food, concerned lest her family want for something and not be able to have it. It was her habit to keep fifty-pound sacks of rice wrapped in plastic garbage bags in the kitchen. That way everybody knew that the family had enough.

We listened to her go into Alfredo's room and tell him to go to bed. He was supposed to be sleeping, but he had too much energy, and he whined.

"Wait," Luz said. She went in and quieted him down. She came out with her mother, and the Queen beamed at me before she left us.

"So much good spirit," I said.

She looked up at me. "It's too much. Anyway, I guess I don't need my box cutter if I'm with you."

I'd seen her little knife before, but it was always a fresh bother when I had to see it again. On the job a lot of guys carried box cutters and used them to cut packing tape, but I preferred my teeth, where I'd just close my jaws on the tape, get my molars in there, and tear. Box cutter opens in your pants, it'll cut you. I didn't like them. I preferred to put up with the bits of brown tape that I spat out at the end of the day.

"Right, leave it here."

"Nah, I'll take it."

When we got out in the hall, Luz shook herself out before we went down stairs.

"I can't believe you get along with my family."

"I like them. I want to do something for them sometime."

We slid down the marble steps.

"My family doesn't need your help," she said. "You're just my boyfriend, that's it, not the savior, and not the boss of me, either!"

"Who said—" but she was already out the door and down the street.

———————

The movie started when the rich good-for-nothing character played by Jennifer Love Hewitt said that all she ever wanted out of life was to be loved. Then the detective played by Adrian Brody, who's tired and cynical and doesn't sleep nights, said all he ever wanted was to solve one big crime case. At the end, when the serial killer who's after Jennifer gets caught by Brody, somehow Jennifer and Adrian castrate the killer *and* look at each other deep and loving at the same time—they hold the knife like they're cutting their wedding cake when really it's his package they're tearing up—well, they both get what they want. Then they meet at some uptown bullshit bar and have a drink together. They talk about what they learned—killing is bad but this time it ended in love which is good and like that. They kiss and she gets on his lap and they spin on the bar stool and that's how the movie ends, in a whirlwind of happiness. It was deep nasty. Sometimes the camera caught the two of them frowning and looking away. Luz watched with her mouth open. She held my hand and followed the characters with her eyes.

Afterward, Luz said, "Let's go there."

"Where?"

"That bar in the movie. I know where it is. I read about it in *Vogue*." She had a set look to her eyes. She had not made a suggestion—we were going to that bar. I saw how she was dressed up. She had planned.

"Well . . ."

"Come on!"

I stalled, said, "I would have so much preferred to see that Spike Lee movie."

"Why would I want to do that? Every time I go to one of those it's, like, yeah? I knew that and I knew that, with these rich people movies, you get to see something you wouldn't have seen before."

"I don't like seeing that," I said.

"But you look like them, in the movie."

"Baby, only to you."

And she was walking us down Madison, away from home, and she was baiting me to keep me walking. Maybe I was a little curious, too, about what kind of bar that was, where the couple in the movie looked so happy together and at home, like they'd been invited, were members of the place. I'd never felt like that about anywhere except for the woods, where there are no people.

"Come on, Kelly, come on."

I tucked in my shirt and buttoned my jacket and then unbuttoned it. Luz was moving fast, like if we didn't hurry the bar would disappear.

Americus Bar and Books was filled with a lot of fake books that nobody in there would ever read, stuff that people generally left in their apartments when they moved out, or recycled. There were outdated etiquette books and copies of all the Dick Francis horsey detective books that my mother had but without their cheeseball covers, so it was hard to tell just what they were. It was a place where the men and women were like my brother, pretending to be what they weren't, which was cultured. They did this by drinking eleven-dollar glasses of scotch that, after that first sip, just taste burning. I didn't even have to look carefully to see the cracks in the seams of that place—the people and their effort came apart right in front of my eyes.

We sat at this tiny little table that was painted up and shined so it looked like onyx. I thought of Felix, in the Bronx, fighting with Lynanne. After all we'd promised each other, he wouldn't like to see me like this at all, sipping at a heavy square tumbler half full of Glenlivet.

The guys at the bar were as young as me and they had these incredible broad backs that made their suits ripple against their shoulders and I stared at them for a while—when they laughed they all moved together like undertow—until Luz grabbed my hand and pressed it against the soft inside of her thigh, where her pants nestled up to her and I could feel warmth. I watched her face, the hot flares of thought and temper that passed over her as she watched the room. I tried to get her to look at me, but she looked around the room, stared down every inch of that space.

"There's a back room where we could have dinner. I want to go there," Luz said.

"I—"

"We can split it," she said, and she stood up, so I had to go, too. I looked around but people didn't even bother to stare at us; we were far below their radar. We stepped into a room with different music and older people, and we were even farther away from where we should be. It was deeply, deeply wrong. To say I had a nervous jiggle in my leg would be an understatement. I had a nervous jiggle in my mind. I would see Luz, across from me, and I'd be happy, but then any line of sight away from her was, was painful.

There were so many bright spots, the candles on the tables, wall sconces, the shiny silverware and glistening steaks.

A couple in their forties with hunched shoulders sat to our right and I stared at them and wondered if I'd been in their apartment, if they were the couple I'd robbed with Felix. The way they ate—the pasta on their plates that looked like it was painted with oil, that in turn made their lips shine. I would have followed them home and taken everything of value from their house. After all, they did look burdened by what they had, what with their inability to talk to each other and all of the opulence of their ugly, patterned clothes. I looked at his watch, as it went up and down from plate to mouth. I couldn't recognize the make, but I knew the color of gold. There were watches I'd seen advertised in the paper that cost ten thousand dollars, twenty, more. My brother had a hefty watch, but I knew his was an Electron, a pale imitation of a Goldscheider, which was itself probably only an imitation of something else. Then his wife caught me staring.

"The pasta is excellent, but I'm sure you'll get the steak," she said. Then she did a light laugh.

"How was yours?" Luz asked.

"Really nice, fettucine with shrimp and green peas, very good," she said. She smiled at Luz, and Luz smiled right back. The woman's husband looked away, or didn't notice, and I pretended to do the same thing. After a while they left, and we were still there, eating.

"We can't stay for dessert," I said.

"Sure we can," Luz said. "Put some chocolate in you, sweeten up!"

She'd gotten another scotch. I felt fuzzy and wondered where she'd ever learned how to drink scotch in the first place.

Some lilting French music came on and a happy group at a table in the back began to sing. Luz turned and smiled at them and I got a chance to look at her. She looked exotic among all those white faces, and she knew it. She was as happy as I'd ever seen her, not alienated at all. She was only nineteen, I thought. If she knew better than to enjoy herself at a place like this, she was doing a smart job of hiding it.

It went on for another half hour. Then we paid the check and got outside. Luz stopped and kissed me, and we began to walk up Madison. We held hands as we walked, and I kept swallowing. The street was silent except for the little bits of excitement at the doors of restaurants, bunches of people around the glowing windows like little swarms of drunken fireflies. I guess it must have been up to those bastards to keep any real darkness from the Madison Avenue night.

"Let's walk and look at the windows," she said. "It's so clean here and I want to see all this. I never get to look here, during the day there's too much—"

"Money?"

"No, Kelly, Jesus, it's too busy is all, and I want to, to keep the evening going." She reached out and pulled my hand and made it run up and down her back, smiling at me, letting me feel the ripple of her ribs.

"I just feel good is all, and I like it," she said.

There was something different in her, where she did a thing when she looked that was different from longing. I watched as she stared into the window at Givenchy, where the models all had on

suits with a short skirt in different colors, a lime green, a pink, a yellow, where I'd never seen anybody dress like that in my life with the
exception of customers on the days when we packed them and they
headed off to work. She looked at that stuff like she was sure it
would look good on her and she couldn't wait to dress like that.

"Motherfucker," she said. Sometimes a swear sounds much dirt-
ier and pointed than other times. She touched the window, her fingers pushed at the glass.

"Some funny-looking dresses," I said. "Imagine wearing them,
how funny you'd look."

"It's so far away from me, Kelly, I can't even imagine it, it's so far
away. I hate that." She was long on the *h* and the *a* in hate. I knew
what she meant.

We walked up slowly, and we only passed other couples. I should
have been happy, what with how well our date had gone. But instead
I felt a tiny bit sick, a bit oiled, as if I would only be allowed to love
her if I kept up with her desire. And though I had no lengthy history
of love, I knew what following felt like.

Luz stopped in front of the Prada store. I'd seen it before, when
we'd moved a talent agency into the building next door and the
Prada doorman watched our truck for us. The windows were
recessed, so we had to step toward them, out of the street. There
were two men's suits and two women's outfits in the window, on
headless models. The clothes were all in these taupe colors and
shiny at the same time and I'd never seen anyone in the whole world
dressed like that—and I was about to say that to Luz when I looked
over at her and saw how she was into it. I watched her press her
nose against the pane, and I saw the little cloud of steam form
where her breath hit the glass. She put her fingers up and pointed at
the woman's suit on the right, which was a sleepy algae color woven
in and out of a reflective check pattern.

Luz reached up closer to the window and her shirt stretched

tight, and it was her sister's shirt and it was small for her, though it had looked good in the restaurant, but now, now I could just hear the scratching rip sound as the material tore, under her arm.

Another couple came up and we saw them shy away a bit when they got a closer look at us, because of Luz's color, probably, and the way we just looked poor. Luz put her hands at her sides. I guess they figured we were trustworthy, two waifs who would only be in awe of them, or more probably, the allure of Prada was too much. They stepped forward and looked in the window. They were maybe two feet from us and they were both in big overcoats; his was yellowish and hers was black.

"Ridiculous, sure, but wild, huh?" the man said. He could not have heard Luz's tear. He wasn't any bigger than me. I heard Luz breathe the breaths someone takes when they need extra oxygen to develop an entirely new idea. I could already see how it was suddenly too much, how she had been pushed—how the borderline had bonded all up in her to create rage.

"Wild," Luz said. And her knife was out. One upheld hand like she was throwing a wave to people she knew, only the gesture stopped when it got up high, and she laid the blade of the knife on the woman's chest, and pressed a tiny bit, where you could see this little thing, the little stupid box cutter that they won't sell to teenagers anymore, as it pushed into and up against all that fabric.

"Money," Luz said, "and your ring, and don't fucking move."

She used a Spanish accent that was even stronger and deeper than the one I knew. She arched her head slightly, and spoke to me in Spanish, and I nodded, even though I couldn't understand her and the only place I'd ever heard her speak Spanish before was in my bed. The man was shaking quite a bit, without any control, and it was obvious that he was a whole lot more scared than the woman, who was calmly taking off her ring. Then he had his wallet in his hand and he was holding it out, and I made a noise in my throat, pulled the wallet from him, took out the cash, and handed him back the wallet.

"And your watch," I said. I also tried to use some accent, which came out sounding completely ridiculous. Inside me something asked, You want it? You want another man's watch? You do. It was in my hand. The woman had slipped off her ring, and Luz pointed to her watch, and the woman took that off, too, and then Luz pulled the blade away. She was shorter than the woman, so she had to pull it down, then away.

"See," Luz said, "nobody didn't have to cut you."

The woman said nothing, and she and her man rushed into the street and ran right down the middle of Madison, against traffic. They looked funny there, running scared in their long coats with their hands in the air, their whole image of the sanctity of their neighborhood torn in one violent moment. Luz and I turned onto the side street and hailed a cab.

"You're gonna take us uptown."

"To 135th and Lenox, the right corner," I said.

"What—" Luz asked, but I motioned for her to be quiet.

"We're meeting somebody there, we have to wait a few minutes, for a delivery—any chance of you waiting for us while we do our business?" The cabdriver used his mirror and looked back at us.

"Not a chance," he said.

Luz got ready to start talking in Spanish but I stopped her again. We nestled in the back of the cab. My heart was not beating fast— my heart was not beating.

"He doesn't need to know where we live," I whispered. She nodded, and of course then the intensity of what she'd done took over, and I watched her shake, so that her perfect eyelashes danced and the whole beauty of her face played out to make her look even younger than she was.

I remember gripping her arm through the whole ride, holding her tight through her shirt, where the rip was, and I remember her leaning over and biting at my hand, both of us pulling at each other's skin. She was quiet then, as we sped uptown, past our block and then over, along 125th, and then up.

"I just couldn't fucking stand it is all," she said.

The cabdriver looked at us again, and I could see his eyes and what he was thinking, something like "No shit, who can stand it? Nobody can."

We got out and she ran down the block, away from me. One of those theatrically poor streets, with a steel can full of fire at one end, where people were congregated, and two rows of abandoned brownstone stoops running along the block, and only a few cars parked, children still running around though it was past midnight, and only one streetlight working. Where there had been a shining limestone color to Madison Avenue, here the street was a dull off-slate brown.

Luz was running and I was running, too, after her. She turned into the next block and there was a gypsy cab there, a blue Continental with a sign that said LIVERY in the window. Luz was already inside, bargaining with the driver. I got in after her and we went down to our building and already Luz was somehow of that place, where she talked to the driver in Spanish and laughed with him, all the while pulling and gripping at me in a way that made the driver avert his eyes from his mirror, like we were only a queasy street couple, desperate to get to a place to fuck and then get high. Whatever—he didn't give a shit. And we were. We were that couple.

She had her clothes off before I was sure I had the door closed. She stood at the window and threw her sister's torn shirt out into the street. I took off my shirt and threw it out, too; someone out there could use it, and I could never be seen in it again. Now we had a pair of enemies in the city, a couple we'd robbed at knifepoint. I took the money from my pocket and counted out four hundred dollars. I held it out for her to see.

"What have you done?" I asked.

And then she was down on the bed and begging me to come to her. She turned over on her back and arched up toward me.

"Come on, Kelly, please—"

"I'm not ready—"

"Come on."

I could see how she'd been thinking that way for a long time, and all she wanted me to do was fuck, and I saw how our chasteness had been all about me not doing it. It wasn't her holding back, it was my puritanical streak. I wondered if Cass had the same frustration with me, but Cass was too often drunk, and it was difficult to tell if she cared.

It was four, and there was a clean, strict moonlight in the room, where everything had an outline. She got up then and stood in front of me, naked, and she pulled down my khakis and my boxers and held onto my dick like it was separate from me and she could pull it away, and she pulled forward and it was like she'd popped something in me, and she turned around and put her ass up high to me, and I fucked her then, that first time, with both of us turned toward the city, and the weird lavish yellow light of the Upper East Side was driving us both insane. I went in and out of her as hard as I could, and we both yelled out, and it was like a champagne bottle and a cherry bomb and that moment where you walk away from somebody and you've beat them and you're the winner—it all exploded in my brain at the same time. And I pulled out and shot—through the open window, out into the street, toward all of them.

She turned around and said, "Now you are—"

"What?" I said. Then I was afraid she was going to call me a monster, someone who was no longer special to her at all.

"Even more what I want," she said.

And we slept together and we made love until halfway through the next day when I went downstairs and used stolen money to buy food and water. Then I knew that before, I didn't really know sex. And it was still new and strange. Sex with Cass had been more measured, labored. I had not thought that it could be any other way.

Luz sat in one of my chairs in only her black panties and a white T-shirt of mine, which was worn thin from the armpits across the chest, so her nipples showed through. It was the afternoon and there was pale light. My room was that good-natured after-sex mess, where the cartons of food were strewn around, our good clothes were on the floor, there was decadence and even beyond it, there was a little shining pile of what we'd stolen in the middle of my table. I knew I would have to keep the watch—a simple Bund-shaft with a gold strap worth just a grand or so—because what else could I do? Pawn it? My room was a thieves' den, with none of the trappings of forced austerity I'd burrowed into just a few months before. I lay in bed and watched Luz in my chair and she was fool-ing with her toes, stroking them, preening. The room was even too hot, with the radiator blasting out a noisy steam that mixed with my little Panasonic portable, tuned to KISS FM, all soul favorites—just then playing "You Bring Me Joy."

"Now we don't have to pretend," she said.

"What?"

"That we're in love."

I said nothing then. Of course love could only live in a room like this, not someplace with the bed made and little framed pictures on the walls and the ritual of hard work all around, like a whitewash against the truth. That I was a thief, that I loved what I was becom-ing, and her, and we needed each other, not to do better, but to revel in each other and all that we could do wrong.

"Say it," she said. She got up and walked toward the bed. She took off my shirt and stood before me.

"I love you," I said.

We whispered it back and forth to each other and giggled about it and said it even kind of loud so it sounded ridiculous, and we did that for hours.

"We can't attack people like that again," I said. She was calm then, in the darkness, now that she knew I loved her.

"I know," she said. "But didn't it feel good?"

"No."

I felt empty then, for just a moment, because I'd lied.

She said, "I never did anything like that before, but I knew that we could do it together, and I did it 'cause you wanted me to."

I just stared at her. Every damned little comment was a high-stakes bet. Anything we said had to be dealt with, mattered like crazy—there was no longer any room for thoughtless talk.

"Now you better do right by me," she said.

I was more than a little afraid and excited, that she was concerned, that she wanted me to do right by her.

"I love you, thief," she said.

"I love you, thief," I said.

It felt good, like we were adults, like I was a man.

16

The Acevedo family invited me to dinner. The invitation was formal; the Queen slipped a note under my door.

It was a beautiful evening, dark, six o'clock, winter cold, and inside, the warmth of family. They sat around an oval table with the Queen at the kitchen end and Jahaira next to her, to help. Ocides sat at the other end of the table. He was quieter than when I'd last seen him and he kept looking at Alfredo. Lately Luz had been saying that there was something wrong with the boy. She said he must have eaten lead paint chips, only Ocides would never have allowed the paint in his house to chip, so . . . Alfredo's head looked oversized. It swayed above his body like a balloon. He ate fast and his little arms were thin and his hands were quick. He winked at me during the meal and did little tricks with his fork that bothered his family more than they seemed to want to admit. Finally, the Queen took his fork away and he brooded for a while.

"I promise to use it only for eating," he said, all determined and proud. She gave it back. It was like my appearance on the scene was no surprise to him at all. I thought about what it would be like to bring him up. Would I pay attention to things like a noisy fork? We kept looking at each other, appraising. Now that things had changed and I was with Luz, Alfredo and I were a lot more careful with each other. I guess we didn't want to offend, or make the other run away.

We had yellow rice and black beans and two roast chickens, with a salad of cucumbers and beets. The table was simple, plates, silverware, glasses of water, milk for Alfredo, Brazilian red wine from a jug poured into small glasses for Ocides, and the Queen, and me. Luz and Jahaira drank water.

"See? See how I'm using it only for eating?" All of us watched while Alfredo took rice from his plate and ate so slowly, so carefully.

The room was bright, with fluorescent light overhead, candles, and a desk lamp in one corner, on top of a little television that was not turned on. Luz and Jahaira wore their hair in wonderful cascades, piled high and then falling down and touching their shoulders.

"Listen, now I ate the dinner, I want to go downstairs, come on," Jahaira begged. She tried everything, batted her eyelashes at her father, gave mad, hateful looks at her mother. She wanted to be down in the street so bad.

"You'll go when we're done and you've eaten," the Queen said.

"I did eat the dinner," she mumbled.

I could see the danger in the set of Jahaira's eyebrows, the slight gleam in her teeth as she grinned, as she watched her family, silent, resigned, waiting to leave.

I said, "This is great. I really looked forward to this meal."

"Better than Hanratty's," Ocides said. He didn't look up often. He had a clinical way of dealing with his chicken that took up most of his attention.

"Oh, sure, much better than that," I said. I thought, What would he do if I reached across and hugged him right now, thanked him and just kept hugging him? I thought, I love Ocides. I thought, He is so much more of a man than my own father. Maybe he caught me staring at him and he gave me a nod, like, "We're happy to take you in here, just do right by Luz, you must do right by Luz." Or he might have been nodding for the salad. Jahaira passed it to him.

"I saw over at C-Town where chicken is down to thirty-nine cents a pound," Jahaira said.

"Not the oven-stuffer roaster?" the Queen asked. And she put a hand to her chest.

Jahaira said, "I don't think it was the roaster. I know a bag guy there, if the roaster comes up on sale I can get you an even bigger discount, so it's practically free."

"Hey! Don't go taking favors," Ocides said. "We don't need favors." Jahaira nodded at him, eyes down.

The Queen, it was not that she looked tired exactly, she just seemed overwrought. Luz had told me that there were votive candles in tall glass containers etched with signs in her closet and she burned them at night. I imagined her in a big nightgown, hunched over candles, praying for her family. She was not fat, but she did have an abundant chest, breasts that had to be reined in each morning by a big Playtex bra, but she was not heavy to the point that eating was hard, sweaty work. She had her dark hair cut short in a bob. I was happy that I was sane, that I did not have to fight to keep myself from saying, asking, "Won't you pray for me, too?"

There was a game of dominoes going on in the apartment next door, where an older man lived with his wife. We could hear the loud slap as the men slammed down the tiles. Alfredo pretended to get a shock whenever he heard a domino go down.

The Queen shrugged and said, "Go play if you want to play." Alfredo jumped out of his chair and left the kitchen. Immediately we heard him go and find his plastic plane. We listened to him make it fly, with realistic engine noises. He came back to the door and watched us, with his plane in hand.

"I ate nice and now it's okay for me to play," he said.

"Come here," Luz said. He went to her and she wiped his mouth and patted his hair down. He was trying so hard to be patient. We could all see it.

Then I gave him a crazy cocked-eyebrow look and he started laughing, hard, and ran back to his own room.

"Well, this was really good. I had a really good time," I said. And they all looked at me, as if to say, White boy, we don't care too much what you thought of the meal. The Queen smiled at me. Ocides finished off his wine and set the glass down, but he did not even look at the bottle. The three women at the table watched him. He did not meet their eyes. But they continued to stare, as if he were the answer to something, some quirk in their lives.

The women were quiet, quiet. But it wasn't like they were afraid of him—they were only glum, maybe from all the rice, weighing them down.

Ocides said, "Okay, it was good of you to come by, we had a good dinner, now, now I gotta—" And suddenly two beepers went off at once, his and Jahaira's, but he did not notice that there were two noises. He looked down into the face of his beeper, like people do, like the fact that the message has shown up there makes what would otherwise not matter, matter.

"I guess I gotta go fix something somewhere, actually," he said, and the table laughed, and relaxed. He got up and went back into the apartment. Jahaira checked the face of her own beeper, while her mother looked on.

"She gets beeped so she doesn't tie up the phone line," Luz said.

"Of course. I knew that," I said, and the three women laughed at me, at my awkwardness.

I went into the living room and found Alfredo. We read a book called *Freddy the Friendly Seal*. Ocides came back home about an hour later. We drank a beer together on the couch after Alfredo went to sleep. Me and Ocides beamed at each other. I couldn't figure out which of us liked the other better. Maybe this good feeling was what they meant on the television shows. I figured, add several hundred thousand dollars, an apartment three times as big, and you have the American ideal.

Luz was yawning when I finally left.

She would slip upstairs later, into my bed. We were sure her father knew. He was always getting up to piss late at night, and he had to go through Luz and Jahaira's room to get to the bathroom. He must have known. And if he must have known, then he must have trusted me.

When I got upstairs there was a message from Wytold. He left a beeper number, so I beeped him. I started doing a set of a hundred sit-ups. I was feeling kind of thick then, from too many days off in a row, and I knew that the only thing that was keeping me from gaining real weight was my own nervousness. The phone rang.

"So, you have the picture?"

"I sure do," I said. He wanted to meet up in my neighborhood, to make it quick. I suggested Hollywood Chicken and gave him the address. He said to go there immediately. So I said okay, and I went there to wait. Hollywood Chicken was a block up from my house. The guys who ran the place were all Afghani, and though we got along, they never seemed to recognize me, so that was good. Their place was not as bright as most of the fast-food outlets. They didn't use fluorescent tubes. The floor was the requisite orange tile though, and the booths were red.

What gave Hollywood Chicken its off-kilter feel was the methadone clinic across the street. People from the clinic hung out there. They bought one chicken leg at a time, ate it, and dropped the bones on the floor. This drove the Afghanis crazy but they never kicked anybody out, and they probably never made the connection with the place across the street. So people like me were always totally inconspicuous in there, what with the drooling groups of meth addicts pouring infinite sugar packets into tiny cups of coffee and dropping burning cigarettes onto the table, where they'd sizzle for a few seconds and then begin to stink.

Mostly the guys who ran the place stayed behind the Plexiglas wall that separated the eating area from the kitchen. They stood there under a huge green FREE AFGHANISTAN poster and watched everybody with a lot of contempt. I don't know where they got the chicken from, but it wasn't too bad. If you ordered a four-piece dinner they were happy, because that cost some money, and I did that every once in a while. As I say, it wasn't too bad, except for the coleslaw, which was always rancid.

I ordered a Coke and sat in a booth. I had the picture stuck down in the back of my pants and I had my sweatshirt on, so there was no doubt that picture was unseeable. I didn't even try to figure what he'd give me for it. I just didn't know what it was worth. I had to wipe the table pretty well before I could even put my elbows down.

Wytold came in and I wouldn't have recognized him. He looked at me and then went to the counter and ordered mashed potatoes and coleslaw and a Coke. He swung an empty shopping bag back and forth, a white bag that said GOURMET GARAGE on the side. He had to yell his order through the Plexiglas twice. I could see that they weren't too pleased with him. Just sides didn't cost much. He came and sat down across from me, and his skin was olive and smooth, like the skin on people from the warm parts of Europe. It was clear why women liked him: he had doe eyes, with long blinks and slow movements. He looked charming, like somebody you'd want to be seen with, even when he sucked on his straw.

"I am thinking," he said.

"Don't eat the slaw." He looked down at it. He was dressed differently than I remembered, in blue jeans and a blue jean jacket over a charcoal sweater. But there was no wear on his clothes. He put the shopping bag next to him on the seat.

"Of course I would not ever touch the food from here," he said. "Now. Under the table. You hand me the picture."

"You have money for me?"

"No. I will next time. Listen, there's something else that somebody has that I need."

"How can I give it to you if you don't give me any money?" I leaned back in the booth. He raised an eyebrow. I figured if I rounded my back, did it hard and fast, I'd break the glass and ruin the picture, easy.

"You want to keep it? Go ahead. See what you can get for it. To you, it's paper. Now, listen, you give it to me, I give you another address, you do that job, we meet again and then, then I'll pay you, say—fifty thousand in all? This other task, you'll go to a town house; you may run into a maid who is there often, but that is all. It's three paintings, actually, three little paintings. You take them out, bring them to me, I pay you for all four. If you're not interested, keep the picture you have now. Hang it. Hang it in your apartment." He smiled at me. Then he turned and looked around at the place, but he didn't lose his grin. I pulled away from the back of the booth, slipped the picture out, and handed it to him under the table. All I thought was that he had another address, and that I wanted it. I watched him put the painting into the bag.

"How did you know we'd be up for this?" I asked.

"A little thief is a big thief waiting to happen, like what they say about drugs? Anyway, is there any part of this that you don't understand? No, right? All of this sounds good to you."

I nodded. I could feel the sweat in that place, the shaking hearts in all those dusted-out bodies. He took out a piece of paper and laid it down, but he kept two fingers on it. I read it.

"You can remember the address?"

"Yes." It was easy, a low double-digit number in the east eighties.

"The three in the dining room, the dining room, ground level, big room with a table in the middle, chairs?" He smiled.

"Where people eat with company," I said.

"Good."

He got up and walked out. He kept swinging the white shopping bag and it didn't even look much heavier. He hadn't bothered to dump his tray and that annoyed me and reminded me that I was not, in fact, his friend. I gathered up both our trays and left them on a table next to three women who were sitting over empty cups. They got the food before I was out the door and yelled some thank-yous after me. I am sure the countermen were none too happy. But maybe they didn't care. Maybe the whole place was a front for a gun-smuggling operation. Who knew? Thieves, drug addicts, Afghani nationals, we were all in there, eating Hollywood Chicken. It was pretty funny when you thought about it.

1 7

Me, Felix, and Teddy finished a tiny job where a waitress was moving in with the guy who managed her restaurant, where having movers at all was more about the guy trying to look good than anything else. The apartment was on York Avenue and Eighty-first and it was nice enough, where the guy obviously had brains in his head and had decided to just hold onto the piece of property, which he'd probably gotten a ton of years ago, when he was young and rents were real.

Early November and it wasn't so nice out anymore. There was a gray cast to the sky and I wore a jean jacket over my sweatshirt. Probably, I thought, it would be the last good day of the fall. When we moved on days like that we hardly sweated at all and I, at least, felt clean. We'd just gotten paid and Teddy had hopped up into the cab, where he was checking through the contract one last time before driving downtown.

"You need one of us to go down with you?" I asked. I had my town house address, but we weren't supposed to go until later in the afternoon. So we had some time. And I was trying to act real casual.

"Nah," Teddy said. "Lately, I feel just as safe alone."

"What do you want to do?" Felix asked. I shrugged. It was so early.

"Maybe the two of you should go to the Met," Teddy said.

"You think so?" I asked. He refused to meet my eye. He didn't say a word. I watched him look around the cab, for the contract and the rest of his stuff.

"Yeah," I said. "Maybe we will do that. Anything there you think we ought to see?"

"Arms and armor, you two'll love it," Teddy said. "And you should probably have a look at pewter tea services and crap like that, so you'll know what to steal." Teddy yawned. He started the truck while I still had my hand on the wheel well. The thing got going with a grunt, and it shook itself for a while until it rumbled clean, like a diesel, which it wasn't.

"What? That's not even funny," I said.

"No. It's not. I know what the two of you are thinking. I can feel it. I'll catch you, or somebody will be missing something and they'll call Isaac, and it'll be on a job I do with you. I'll hate that. You been warned."

"Hey, enough with that!" I said. But Teddy just shrugged, like he was a referee and his call stood, no matter what. He put the truck into drive and rumbled off, and I couldn't help it, I cursed and punched the side of the truck. Teddy reached out once he was in traffic, and he banged his fist against the side of the truck and then held his own palm out, flat. And it was like he was saying, So what? Bang all you want, stupid, you still have to watch your ass. You been warned.

"What's he mean by all that?" I asked Felix. Felix was quiet for a second. I listened to the low whistle of traffic on York. Where we were standing, it was very quiet.

"He means that he's watching us and we're acting like Jimmy Charny did, before they let him go. It's nothing to worry about though, we're not dumb like that. It's just—no more stealing off jobs, no more of that, okay?"

"Sure," I said. "I can stop that. I never even did it, really."

We walked up to the museum. A teenage girl was talking when she passed us. She was saying "I hate you" over and over again, like a chant. Her parents trailed twenty feet behind her, muttering to each other. Other kids sat on the big single-family brownstone stoops and smoked cigarettes—they laughed hard, but to me they looked very soft. We passed all types of women from all the other parts of the city pushing strollers filled with white babies. They talked together and rocked and swayed their charges.

"I talked to Wyt," I said. "Maybe we'll do something that he suggested later this afternoon. The museum is a good place to be until then." I didn't mention that I'd given up the little picture. I knew Felix wouldn't understand.

"Sounds good," Felix said. And then we were quiet some more.

I wanted to tell him about the pleasure in the crime itself. The same feeling as moving people—of progress—but for our *own* purpose. Plus the heart racing, where suddenly the world doesn't feel like a place to tread water, but where you dive from high up, like cliff divers in ads for the pleasures of places like Aruba and Jamaica, all kinds of warm weather resort-type places where I'd never been. Soon that's how we'd feel, like good-time people. But Felix had an amazing ability to keep quiet and focus down. It might have been because he was thinking about his family, and how to make them good. But I could not do that. I could not think of Luz without thinking of crime—and even in our walk it was apparent, how I was nervous and exploding and excited, and how Felix was clear.

We walked along and the streets were lined with fortresses. I watched Felix and he was looking at nothing but ways in: fire escapes, second-story windows above canopies that were unprotected, interstices in stone walls that were saying they were easy, ready for us to climb, get past the doorman, come in. Come in. Come in.

We stood in line at the Met and I got out the eight dollars for admission, but when we got to the front of the line, the woman who was selling the tickets looked up at me. She had her hair in a Mary Tyler Moore cut and you could tell she was doing some internship deal, where the money that paid for her pretty little black blazer came from somewhere else entirely.

"That's only the suggested price," she said. "You can pay less if you wish." She waited. But I took the whole eight and put it down in front of her. She shrugged, her thin shoulders making very little movement, and rang up my sale.

"It's a nonprofit institution, right? The shows are for everybody."

"Okay, okay," she said. She held up her hand as if to say she was sorry she'd bothered. She gave me a button. I turned and watched Felix put down one dollar.

"Why didn't she give her talk to you?" I asked.

"I'm Puerto Rican, remember? She wasn't interested."

"Oh," I said. "That's right."

We walked up the stairs. There were the names of donors on the walls, etched into the marble and painted with gold leaf. I had always thought such things had been there forever, since before me or my parents or anyone I had ever known was born. But this gold leaf looked very . . . fresh. And I looked more carefully at the names, while Felix calmly sat down on the stairs (within seconds a guard came over and asked him to stand up, and immediately he was miserable, like any tough guy who is out of his element, like what he was, a poor boy in a rich museum)—I saw that they were people who lived now, people out of the newspapers, and here they were. You could touch them. I wedged my fingers into the marble cuts, until I could feel the cool surface of the gold leaf.

"This is gonna weird me out for my whole visit," I said.

"That's probably why those names are there, to let you know who's boss around here before you get to see the art," Felix said. He grabbed at my sleeve and pulled me up the stairs, and there were hundreds of those names there, going back through history. Maybe the gold leaf got a little duller, but I'd never seen it that way before, where these names were only the people we moved. The same people who were mean and difficult when we set down their furniture controlled what we saw in this great big public place.

For me, the paintings were ruined. I knew I was wrong, that they were great and stood on their own, but they felt so much like pawns! And then I thought, So does any kind of genius. Everything great is only a plaything for those in power. I know I would have felt so much better if I could have burned away that idea, but the place reeked of it, of greatness beholden to money.

We walked around. Felix liked the angry lines of El Greco, and we both got into looking at a Rembrandt self-portrait. He said it looked like that guy understood us, and what we were up to.

"Because we're just doing what we're good at," I said. And then I looked a little closer and I saw how the lines the guy used in his picture of himself, they looked a whole lot like the scratched-out black lines in the picture of the old man we'd stolen. I kept looking. The guy in the drawing—he was the same as the guy in that painting. Rembrandt.

"Oh shit," I said.

"What, what's up?" Felix said. We were motoring through the rooms pretty quick and Felix was finished with that one.

"Nothing, I guess I just like that painting is all," I said. I thought, Did I just have something in my house that belongs in a museum? And then I thought, Boy, I'm never going to think about that again. Not ever.

Teddy was right. We spent most of our time in arms and armor, looking at all the old-style guns and charging horses. They're pretty cool, those guys on those horses. Me and Felix stared up at them for a good while: we were transfixed, and who wouldn't be? There was a lot of thrust and righteousness there.

"Pretend you're Robin Hood! Jump out of the forest and knock one of the evil knights off his horse, then steal his shit!" Felix said. I looked around, fast, to see if anyone had heard him. Felix laughed.

"Be cool, Kelly, one thing we know about the world, nobody is paying attention." So I spun around and pretended to pull a big arrow out of the quiver on my back. I got it in my bow and kneeled a bit, and shot it toward a particularly evil-looking knight, one with his headgear down.

"I just stunned him, see, that's all I need to do, get him off his horse and get his bag of gold, give it to those in need."

"What if he shoots back? You'll need armor of your own."

"We both do," I said.

People walked around us in that great white hall. They were intent on the huge horses, on the armor, not on two ratty young guys who looked just like what they were, overgrown versions of the same teenagers we'd been only a very few years ago, and nobody looked at us then, either.

We looked some more at the stuff around the armor, the big knives with complicated designs on the handles and the intense Asian armor, all gleaming clean with the solemn celebration of death, and then we left. After all, we'd been in that museum for an hour, easy.

We did buy a bunch of postcards on the way out. I found one of an angry Buddha and put Cass's name on the back. I thought I'd write her a note, something like: I'm in your great big beautiful world now. Catch me.

"I want to show you something," I said. We stood at the top of the small mountain of steps outside the museum. I had a big air feeling, the exhilaration that came with being free of that stultifying bad place. Felix looked up at the sky and I saw his face in profile, the wide eyes, the grin. I spread my arms out and held all of the Upper East Side before us.

"We're partners in this," I said. "We're going to do something very special here."

"We were born and raised to do this," he said.

"And we raised each other."

We passed the Marymount school and looked in the windows at all the pretty little rich girls, hard at work on their lessons. Soon enough, I planned to put Alfredo in the boy's school version. I had the house number Wyt had given me in my head and I just felt along, looked at where it might be, and it was there. It was one of those one-buzzer houses; that is, I looked up at this big wooden door and next to it there was just one lonely buzzer with a little video eye and a speaker. Usually, with a house that size, there would be a dozen buzzers, at least, all with name tags stuck below them. Me and Felix stepped back and looked at the house, at the clean enormity of it.

"This is all I have, this address, and the word 'dining room.' We take the paintings that are in there. Ground-floor level, in the back." I thought how we could have been concerned about people looking at us, but around that area, there's lots of people who walk by and stop, and stare up at the buildings with awe.

The door was painted white wood, with a little brass mailbox opening in it and a couple of locks. It was set back from the street, but only a little. It was a majestic opening, really, daunting in its ability to flaunt that it was the entranceway to an entire private house, in the middle of Manhattan. We watched it, like it would tell us something, like the mail opening would spout out an answer. I felt like a sharp-focus picture of myself, all hackles up.

"Yes," I said. "You know why nothing bad is going to happen to us?" I asked.

"Because we don't mean anybody harm, and we're all for the good," he said. He snorted and spat down on the street.

"Right, you got your speech ready?" I said. After all that pumping up, I could see how I'd thrown him, and he did a visible quake.

"What fuckin' speech?"

We hadn't actually discussed what we were going to do, or how. It wasn't enough planning, but I was growing more and more sure that it was better to work with too little than too much.

"Chill, I'm only fooling with you. I got it all straight. Do two things, kill your scary look, keep your hands where the maid can see them, smile."

"Why?"

"'Cause," I said, "We're going to do this based on trust. Head for the back is all."

"All for the good," he said. The righteous tremor inside me—that amazing feeling that this was something I could do.

We went up and rang the bell.

Seconds later, we heard a "Hello?" through the intercom. It was a girl's voice.

I made a noise that sounded like a hello, only garbled.

More moments, the interminable wait, and behind us, the street was filled with afternoon routine—dog walkers and businessmen, hired drivers in idling sedans and museumgoers filled with an envy of these town houses they tried to ignore.

The door opened wide. She might have been our age, younger even, dressed in blue jeans and a light blue T-shirt, no shoes. She had grown her hair longer than the girl in the museum, and her eyes were round, lucid, where it felt like she'd seen very little that was ugly, hadn't had to squint after seeing someone hurt. The three of us breathed, revealed that this was not ordinary circumstance. I looked at Felix's boot, rubbing the concrete step. She could not have been the maid. She was the daughter.

"Hello?" she asked.

I thought of the girls at Vassar. She was like them, with some gall focused on her family. A liberal feeling that probably helped to mask a slow descent to the family's own tendency to oppress. This was her, the old blue jeans, a beautiful house, an inability to fairly link the several sides she knew of the world. Thus, for just a few years, these wide eyes. Not so different from me, excepting the money.

Felix said, "Come on," with his mouth barely open. I wished I could have given him my one year of college, so he could've better understood.

"Hi," I said. "I guess we were looking for the maid."

"We don't have a maid. There's Jessenia, who comes in and cleans four days a week, but that's it. I could give her a message?"

"Uh . . ."

"What do you want?" Her voice hit on a different register, sounded a little strange. I felt Felix look away and I could not lie to this girl.

"I—"

But Felix was past her, into the hall. And we were running. She chased after us. Felix pulled his hood way over his head and I did the same. She screamed and I didn't blame her. There was a yellow phone on a kitchen wall and she grabbed it, but I only turned and looked at her while Felix went rushing down the hall. She put the phone down. I thought, If I'd done better in school, if my brother had gotten in my mind instead of Felix . . . if . . . this girl and I could have been friends. I almost asked her if she knew my ex-girlfriend, Cass Meynell.

I kept my hands up, like she was going to rush me. "Don't move," I said. "Neither of us is gonna move."

So much wide-eyed look from her and I understood that it was that look—that no matter how much I wanted to see some crazed trust and intuitive excitement, there was nothing but fear. And then I wasn't so sure.

"Walk close to me," I said. "Slow."

To the right was more kitchen, a gleaming bastard of a Sub-Zero refrigerator next to a stove the size of a car, a beautiful old wood table that had one book on it, one nibbled blueberry muffin, one pink mug half filled with coffee. We stood in the hallway, the flower-patterned wallpaper thick and twisting on either side of us.

"Fucking good smells in here give me a headache," I said. And I gripped one hand to the side of my head while I put my other hand on her shoulder, felt her little bones, and did not feel her fear, but her amazement.

"You seem like a nice person," I said. "How are you ever going to live all this shit down?"

She was quiet.

We took the hallway and went back to the dining room.

The paintings were small, there were three of them, and they were all on the back wall, between two sets of French doors that went out to a garden.

The curtains were drawn back and we could see out. There was a lot of nice light, pale and golden and warm, and I took a second and felt it on my face. The girl and I watched Felix take the paintings off the wall and stack them. They weren't more than three feet square, each. The paintings looked like they went together—they were big dabs of bright color on wood. That's all they were. It was so easy.

She leaned against a wall and stared at us.

"Where do you go to school?" I asked.

"What? I . . . Sarah Lawrence."

"Why aren't you there?"

"I—"

"We'll be gone in a second, it's cool."

"I come here when they're not in town."

"Right, 'cause nobody else is in the house, right?"

"Nobody else."

I looked out the window. The garden wasn't too big, but I could see how when spring came, there were a lot of places for flowers to grow. We stood in front of a long shiny table, surrounded by eight chairs. A sideboard had pots of flowers and silver bowls on it. I pulled out the chair that was facing those windows and sat down. The chair had arms, and I splayed myself out.

"Been to the museum lately?" I asked. "I bet you go all the time, right? Art history major, I bet, where you intern there?"

She bit down on her lower lip and I know she didn't mean to look sexy but that was how she looked to me. I did not want to touch her. But I did. I reached out and touched her arm. Her pale skin was cold; each tiny white hair stood on end. I stroked them down, but it was no good.

"Sit down."

"What?" Felix whispered.

"Me?" she asked.

"Sure, near me. Museum girl. Tell me some stuff, you sit here with your parents, how does the talk go, how does the money talk?" I let my eyelids flicker, close.

"How does who?" The sharp quavers of an uncertain voice.

"I told you to sit down." And I was sure that I could feel that group in those chairs.

She sat down. I felt like she was my friend, like she loved me but we'd got into some argument. Like she wanted me there and it was too bad that I had to leave soon, but she'd invite me back. We'd stay in touch.

"Get up," Felix said. I heard him whisper part of my name. "Get the fuck up." But I was looking at the girl.

"Jessenia, did she clean your room before you came home, good enough for you?" I thumped my fist on the fine wood of that table, a soft knocking noise.

"Get up," Felix said. "Boy, get up!" He had the paintings by the door to the room and he came at me, I could feel him behind me.

"Is it time for us to go? Have we got a cab waiting? Why don't you go get us one?" I was using a whole different voice, working from a center buried deep below the weak part of me where I lived, all too much of the time.

The girl didn't move. She was two seats down from me, and it had been long enough, she was staring, trying to look in at the sides of the hood, to see my face.

"Fine," Felix said. "I'll have them honk once. And then you'll come out quick with the shit. Clear?"

"Clear as my reflection in this beautiful table, my friend."

Felix left and me and the girl stared at each other.

"You like school?"

"School is fine," she said, and her voice was small.

"Are you in love?"

"I'm with somebody." She began to blink very fast.

"Are you nice to him?"

"Yes."

"Do you want to marry him?"

"No."

"We should eat together here. You could probably find something in the kitchen, we could close the drapes, maybe you could show me the house, go for a nap somewhere upstairs."

I touched her arm again and it was still freezing and the same.

"I—"

"I just wish things were easier, not so unfair you know? I wish you didn't live here, and that—look, I'm not going to rape you. That's not what's in me."

I watched her and her eyelids were twitching. She had both her hands on the table and they did not move. I reached out and touched her fingers. They were bloodless and cold, as if her heart had begun to beat slower, had pulled all of her blood deep inside of her, where I could not reach it.

"I hope you're warmer when you're with your guy."

I watched her ire go up.

"Don't worry about it," she said. She sounded just a little mean, like even if I could scare her, it didn't matter. I was below her. Like fear lasted only a short while, but her superiority was forever. Like Cass when I knew that no good would come of us, and it was over and she had to go.

A horn sounded once. I felt air from outside come all the way down that corridor.

"I miss you already," I said.

And I stood up, fast enough for the chair to go down behind me, but I kept my head far back under that hood.

"Walk out with me, slow, happy, and you'll wave good-bye to me and my friend."

I gathered up the paintings and she walked out in front of me.

"Think of what I could have done to you," I said.

"I am."

"You know what I am? Guess." We were in the flowered hall and she was near me and I had my hand on the small of her back, guiding her.

"What are you?"

"I'm—I . . . not telling, just wave good-bye. I miss you." And I got into the cab with Felix and she did. She waved, but she was already far distant. I could feel how we were already only a story she'd tell, and somehow, she was still the winner. It pissed me off, it really did.

"Take us to Grand Central."

I turned to Felix, but he wouldn't look at me.

"She was just like Cass. It really pissed me off. I got stuck on it, that's all."

"Shut up," Felix said. He was slumped down in the seat and his eyes were closed.

"Just shut the fuck up," he said.

We drove down on Lexington, not too fast, and the driver was playing some salsa music, so it was impossible to think.

"When Cass and me were good it was always a waiting thing, to see when she was going to go. We both knew it. Sometimes I'd come in from a walk and there'd be another guy there, or she'd come home late and pass out. She said she needed so much, that I didn't have enough, that I wasn't focused on her—"

"Please, Kelly, it's enough, boy. I got to get my head through what just happened, you make nice plans, but then you pull some crazy nuts routine."

The cab pulled over at Forty-fourth and Lex and we got out.

Felix said, "Why do you do that shit?"

I was quiet.

"'Cause it's fun?"

"I saw you in there, Kelly, that didn't look like fun at all."

"I'm sorry. Listen, it's all about trust. We have to groove through these things. You have to trust me, like in the woods, imagine it like that, like I'm the one who knows just how close we can get to the bear. Trust is all it is. Don't ever betray me."

"Betray?" he asked, like he didn't know what the word meant.

We got on the 6 train. We got out farther uptown and found a gypsy cab and took it down to my apartment. The three little paintings went in my closet. Just like that, no problem at all.

"I got excited, you know, one meets new people so rarely," I said, and I tried to laugh. He only looked at me.

"I'm not saying it wasn't a good operation, only, Kelly, you got some issues to work out."

"Hey, who the fuck doesn't? You know, who the fuck doesn't?"

"Okay, okay, only next time . . . warn me first," he said.

"Listen, the knights are dead, man, we're all that's left."

There was a knock on the door and it was Luz, who always seemed to know when I was home. I introduced her to Felix. She was in a short blue dress and a perfect black shirt that shined. She sat down on my bed, put her hands out and behind her, crossed her legs. Felix opened the top of the window, leaned against the sill. He smoked.

"Did something big happen?" she asked. She and Felix would not look at each other.

"Something happened, yes," I said.

"Well, good," she said.

"Yes," I said. She came and sat on my lap and I put my face against her back. She stroked my hair.

"I hear you have a baby girl," Luz said.

"Oh yes, my girl is beautiful," Felix said.

"So is my boy," she said.

"The children should meet," I said.

"I don't think that's a good idea at all," Felix said.

18

I saw Jahaira on the street one afternoon when I was coming home from work. She was in front of Hollywood Chicken. She stood there with five or six other teenagers. Their bags were in a pile in front of the place, and they were running around, screaming and slapping each other the way kids like to do. Jahaira had a sort of dimpled grin, but with just a few hairs at the top of her nose and eyes that were quite black. The effect came off as cocky, and even though I liked her because she was Luz's little sister and all, she seemed a bit mischievous. Sometimes I thought about having her in bed. Maybe I shouldn't admit it, but it's the truth. She was sixteen, and built all friendly.

"Hey, Kelly, big brother, give me some money for chicken," she said. Her friends got quiet then. We'd just gotten paid for the day, so I had about a hundred dollars on me, and I turned and gave her a twenty. I wasn't hungry, otherwise I would have just gone in and bought chicken for all of them.

"More," she said.

"You want chicken, your mother cooks the best I've ever had."

"Ooh, he likes my mama's chicken!" Then all her friends were laughing. It's hard to impress a teenager, I thought. I gave her another twenty and kept going. Then I thought of something, and I went back.

"Jahaira, how much is your beeper a month?"

She stared up at me, with her fist still around the money. She had an old-style Mickey Mantle shirt on and her jacket was thrown back over her shoulders. I couldn't help looking at the top of the V of her shirt, but then I stopped. I snapped my neck up fast, like I had a tic. She knew I looked, though, I'll bet. Okay, I'll say it: She had this great pair of tits, big and young and she enjoyed having them; I could feel it.

"Why?"

"I need one, for a couple of weeks—for work. Let me borrow yours and I'll give you sixty bucks."

"Why don't you get your own?"

"You don't want the money?"

She reached down and got the beeper off her waist. A friend of hers came over and watched us. He had sunglasses on, even though it was five o'clock and near dark. The glasses were big and they were signed on both sides.

"Tell your friends not to call you on it and hey, you, are those Jerry Jones sunglasses?" I palmed the beeper and slipped it into my kangaroo pocket.

"Yeah, Jerry Jones, he's the motherfucker!" the guy said.

"See you later, Jahaira, say thank you," I said. But she didn't. Instead she wrote her beeper number on a piece of loose-leaf paper and gave it to me.

She said, "I'll get another beeper. When I get the number I'll beep it to you, okay?"

"Good, yes," I said.

"Jerry Jones owns the Cowboys! He's the greediest guy in the world!" Now the kid was pissed that I wasn't paying attention.

"You don't think there's better role models than that?" I asked.

"Who, you? Furniture mover? No health insurance?" The Jerry Jones guy came in close. I guess the term *role model* bothered him.

"The players who do the commercials, you know, 'Give to the United Way,'" I said.

"Fuck that. Last time I checked there is no 'United Way.'" He pronounced the words slow, so he could fill them with distaste. Yet again I was stuck, where I didn't know how to convince anyone—not even a teenager—about what I thought was right.

"There's lots of people who do good things," I said.

"Yeah, once they make a ton of fucking money they give away five dollars. Fuck all that. I want to own a football team."

"Yeah? That's your goal?" Maybe he was right. The addicts in the chicken place stared out at us, all placid, like they had never had the energy of teenagers.

"You got a problem with it? You think I'm wrong?"

"No. No, I guess I don't. Okay then, thanks, Jahaira." But I did think he was wrong. I could see how it would be tiring, though, watching the guys who owned football teams strutting around on the sidelines, week after week, acting like they were the winners and they'd beaten the world. I could see how he'd come to those wrong conclusions. Only—it didn't make me feel too good. I thought that maybe he'd change his attitude when he got older. Maybe.

As far as I could tell, Luz wasn't working anymore. I had never actually seen her do her job, and now she didn't seem to ever be doing it. When I asked her about it she just shrugged, in much the same way she shrugged when her plans for the future came up. She did say she wanted to be a cop, but I think that was just because she went to John Jay, and all the cops went there. She just seemed to be around a lot: in my apartment, on the staircase, like she was watching to see what I was gonna do. I didn't mind, really. I was just afraid she'd mug somebody else when I was with her, and we'd both get arrested. We were at the point where we'd look at each other, in my bed, at night, and she'd say "What?" And I'd say, "Nothing," and then we'd switch, so that I got to say "What?"

I remember a lot of silence then, in November. The quiet was often punctuated with Luz moaning about all the Christmas presents she needed to get, and how she had no money. I was stuck on the image of that box cutter on that coat. And I would watch Luz sleep and put my hand on her chest, feel her heart beat, and watch the movement of her perfect breast, and wonder what was in her.

"Make the meeting somewhere else," Wyt said.

"Fine, White Castle, 104th and First."

White Castle, aching clean and white. You had to go through two doors to get in and two to get out and everything was behind Plexiglas, so it felt like you were sitting in a spaceship that just happened to have landed in the neighborhood. I figured we were going to be doing a real exchange. I wanted to be safe. I hustled over there with Luz, but we sat in different booths.

Wyt came and slid in across from me. He had a rental car parked outside.

"You had no problems at all?"

"None at all," I said. I smiled. The pictures were wrapped up in paper towels and packed in a Gap shopping bag that Luz had given me. I had the bag between my legs.

"This is working out very well then," he said. "I am very pleased with your fine work."

"Me and my partner, we just keep cool is all."

I listened to Luz hum behind me.

Wyt pushed a thick white paper bag under the table, so it was touching my feet.

"There's forty thousand dollars in there, even. There isn't fifty because my quote went down. So yours went down, too. You understand." Of course I felt myself shake. Little spasms ran up and down my neck and inside my arms. Forty or fifty thousand? What difference did it make? That was huge money. Almost as much as my mother made in a year.

"So you're okay with this, aren't you? I'll have more work for you soon, if you're okay with how things are going now."

I nodded up and down, like an idiot. The idea of having that much cash, of possessing it, I couldn't quite take it in. It was getting so the only thing that would surprise me would be something like no surprise at all, like the history tests I used to get back with grades in the low seventies. I knew I'd have to explain the cut to Felix. He would have to trust me.

"So now you are paid. I will call soon, and we'll get together and do something else. If you move or if your number changes, I generally have a drink in the late afternoons at the Bar Boudoir, in the Alexander Hotel—you know? If you need to see me, run into me there, or if you don't feel quite appropriate in there, just wait around the entrance. But"—he patted the table, like the table knew how much money was underneath it—"you ought to be able to get a decent suit now, wouldn't you say?"

When he was gone Luz came around from the table behind me and sat down where he had been sitting.

"Neat," she said. "Not joke money no more." She chewed on the straw in her vanilla milkshake.

"I guess it's real now," I said.

"You got fifty cents for a cheeseburger?" She cracked up laughing.

She said, "I'm with you through the thing now, it's okay. Only . . . what happens now?"

"I don't know," I said.

Felix came over to my apartment and we showed him the money. He sat in one of my chairs and maybe my miserable little room made him think, because he was very quiet.

"We never figured out where to put the money," Felix said. I didn't say anything. Felix and Luz watched me.

"For now," I said, "for now, we'll just put it up in the ceiling and wait, we'll just have it there for a while, until we can come up with what to do. I stored the paintings here, I should store the money here, too." They nodded.

"I have to go home anyway," Felix said, "but I'm gonna take a couple, three grand."

"Sure, of course." I watched Luz chew the insides of her cheeks while I gave Felix the money. I gave him three thousand and I took three for myself, and I gave Luz one. So there was thirty-three left. Felix cocked his head then, but he kept his mouth closed, and I didn't say anything either. Beyond what me and Luz had between us was the fact that she knew what was going on, every bit of it. And she'd helped me pack the pictures. So I thought it was best to count her in.

I stood up on a chair and pressed the seam where the wall touched the ceiling. I'd been experimenting, and I'd opened the seam before. They handed me the money and I made it disappear. We'd wrapped it in a whole bunch of garbage bags so it wouldn't smell, and the rats wouldn't eat it.

"If we can do that," I said, when I was finished, "we can do anything."

1 9

Then it felt like the whole building knew about the thirty-three in the ceiling. The Queen beamed at me like mad when I carried her groceries. Alfredo was an angel. He would take my hand and hold it, and look at me. I felt as if I was carrying some peace in me, but I'd done nothing yet! I needed to make the next step.

In all that haze and good feeling I went and did a stupid thing. On an afternoon in early November I walked over to Poor Richard's Playground on 105th Street and Second Avenue and watched some kids in-line skate around and tag up on one another's notebooks. I sat down on a bench there and stuck my hands in my pockets, leaned back, and jutted out my legs. Nobody was looking for me. I was due at Luz's house for dinner in a few hours, so I couldn't go eat. Felix was home with Anastasia. He'd bought her a computer and they were learning to type together. Lynanne was taking night classes at Kingsborough and so she wasn't around much. Apparently, they were getting along a little better.

I admit I was pretty proud of myself, even though my plan was unfinished and I didn't quite know what the next move was, except, maybe, to do it again. I figured I would go and see Ocides at his club and talk to him, maybe even tell him what I was up to, and he would set things straight, though I didn't know exactly how. I just knew he was a father, and a big, good one. Fathers fixed things, or were supposed to. I guess I thought that once I showed him what I was up to, he would talk me through it, and then everything would be okay.

I stopped in front of his club. There was a doorway with windows on either side, one blacked out and one with the Puerto Rican flag hanging behind a rubber plant. I knocked on the door. There was silence. I was pretty sure he was there. It was late afternoon, and that was where he said he'd be, if I ever needed to talk. So I knocked again, and again. There was a cold wind and I shivered a bit, felt the skin on my chest and arms tighten up and prickle. I knocked again, hard, and then I went and tried to look under or around the flag.

Someone tapped me on the shoulder. There was a musk smell behind me, mixed with a clean smell of sweat, not the stink of the sweat of fear I sometimes smelled like.

"Ocides!" I said.

"Hey, hey, Kelly. You wanna come inside, long day for me, real tired, this fucking boss . . ." He got out a key and opened the door, and we went in. A couple of old guys materialized behind us, the kind who never seem to do anything but hang out at the club. They followed us in. One of them turned on the lights. The other got a broom and started sweeping the linoleum tiles. The place looked like the dining room in a low-grade retirement home. There were some pictures of people on the walls and some flags. There was a shiny wooden bar in one corner, but besides that, there were only card tables and folding chairs, six groupings, and no romance at all.

Ocides went to a table and sat down. He put his legs up on

another chair and he motioned to me to sit, not facing him, but on his left, even though he was swiveled toward his feet.

"S'happening," he said.

One of the older guys brought us over two little Buds, nips.

"Well, I was just thinking, Ocides, it's so tough up here, right?" I heard this weird thing come into my voice, a kind of wussy young person lilt.

"I wonder, about you, you work so hard, I'm thinking what if you had a lot of money, you know, what would you do, to help?"

"Ah, if I had a lot of money." He leaned back farther, and put his hand over his belly.

"First, I'd buy a fat Lexus, quit my job, and get a house outside San Juan and then—no, first, I'd throw a big party, like a block party, with a roast pig, and I'd pay some money out to a guy I know and have him come up and smack my boss in public—smack his fucking jaw so it's all broken and hanging, maybe hit him again in the knees, with a pipe, till you can hear that little noise. Pop! You ever hear kneecaps broken? It's a little pop, where, like, they can never be fixed again. Funny noise when you get to hear it. Do that, then maybe give the girls some jewelry . . . why, you got a winning lottery ticket you want to share, you got a stock market tip?" He started to laugh.

"No, I meant, I meant," and I stammered. I thought maybe if I had a bigger belly I wouldn't stammer like a child, and I kept going. "If you had a lot of money and you wanted to help people—"

"What? I give them the block party, in June, a Saturday, call it Ocides Day."

"No, if you want to help people like long-term."

He was quiet. I watched his eyes, how they searched me, how he looked for the part of me that he remembered he liked.

I said, "I sort of came into some money, and I want to give it to the community. I want to know the best thing to do."

"The best thing to do with money is you keep it! Ain't no fucking mystery, you get yourself a place to live, you make sure you're all right!" This got a big laugh from the elders. Ocides took his feet off the other chair and straightened himself. He puffed out his tremendous upper body, made himself all chest and belly, a massive Tasmanian Devil.

I got closer to him, I whispered, "You see, I stole something and I got paid for it."

"You what?"

His speech got slow and long. I never, never heard my dad talk that way to anybody.

"What the fuck—you're fooling with me, right?"

"No, I got this money and I want to help but I can't figure out where it ought to go—"

He held up his hand. He bulged his eyes. The two old guys began muttering to each other in Spanish. One of them reached down into the cooler. He pulled out a little Bud and sucked on it anxiously.

"I'm good at this thing, where I can steal. I thought we could talk about—"

"You're a fucking thief?" And he bit off the words, so they came faster than his usual speech, and then I knew that was because he hated them, hated to say them.

"It's for good . . ."

"I knew there was something the matter with you. I knew you were stupid for one, but—" He looked down toward his feet, as if he was confirming his disappointment, his lifelong experience with hoping things were as they seemed, but just a bit better, and the opposite always, finally, being true.

"I worked my whole life. And not for assholes like you to go bringing crime to my family! My kids are honest, I don't need nobody in jail!"

I mean he yelled: He had a real bellow, operatic, the kind of noise that made my thoughts go grimy, dim, and unclear.

"I don't believe I can get arrested." Why would I tell him that?

But I did. He gritted his lips together—half, I think, because he was going to cry, and half because he was so damn angry.

"You can't get arrested? I put the last motherfucker criminal that touched a daughter of mine in Bellevue for three months before he was good enough to go to prison. Luz didn't mention that, hah? If I got to do that again and again, I'll do it. Understand me. You disappoint me here."

I said, "No, it's all for good—"

"Now I got to get up. Now I'm tired and you said some shit and now I gotta get out of my chair. Thanks a lot, punk."

"Wait—"

"You white fool, you white-trash bastard . . . you—"

He went quiet and we stared at each other across the Formica table. His power filled the place and smacked me down with the same damn clarity as when any real friend who you trusted and cared for turns on you, lets your bond go bad.

"Get out of my place, you live in my building illegally, I know that, you disappear, you never see my daughter again, you never come here again, and if you know what's good for you you stop stealing. You understand? You steal and you go away forever. You're gonna help? You ain't gonna help shit."

This last part had him standing over me, delivering his sentence, with his fat pointer finger in my face. The two oldsters stood against the wall, nodding. The one with the broom chewed a little bit on the stem, like watching us argue was making him hot. The other one reached for another little beer.

"I never met you, I never saw you, and you never, never see my daughter again. Now silence and walk out the door."

"You don't understand—"

He turned to the oldsters. "Would I fuck him up? If I saw him near my daughter, ever, would I round up the men and fuck him up?" I mean, he didn't yell, he roared.

The oldsters nodded. Oh yes, they'd be right there when I got caught. No doubt they had their own burning broomstick and it was meant only for me.

"I would fuck you up. Now disappear, you don't exist."

"You don't understand—"

"You already said that, you want me to hit you now?" And he cocked his head to the side and looked at me. I stepped back, out of the room. I swear I heard laughter when I got out of there. I listened and one of the oldsters was imitating me, the "stupid faggot crazy." Then the laughter stopped and they started to mutter, and I couldn't hear any more.

I walked the few steps back to the apartment. In the woods, Felix said, "Some people don't understand how bad the world messes with them. They think their poverty is their fault and they're wrong." I nodded hard to myself, even as I was unsure of whether Felix had said that or my own dad. After all, Felix was only a child when we were in the woods together. The street outside was even colder than I remembered. I felt some grim shame.

Up in my room I tried to think of a plan, but I had nothing. The money sat up in the ceiling. I looked at where it was hidden and it asked me just what the hell I'd expected to happen. I beeped Jahaira, but she didn't call me back. And there was no other way to get in touch with Luz.

I thought, Okay. Now I've set me up. Now I can run. And if it's true love between me and Luz, she can come and get me. Just like I didn't do with Cass, when she ran. I thought, No doubt, what happened is just exactly what I wanted. This is how relationships are supposed to go. This is the test, right here. Now I have to run.

THE MIRACLE MAN IN EXILE

part three

2 0

I stood in Felix's doorway, jittery with fear at the twists I'd gotten into. There was the money I'd left on 102nd, and the chances, the possibilities that were opening up. I was terribly sorry to lose Ocides, but I was on to the next big thing, and Luz and I were suddenly in a challenge, where we would see if we could withstand being apart—all for some goal that I was not quite clear on yet but that did have to do with success. Felix's corridor was a terrible place: dank, with battered plaster walls painted a sloppy brown. The green tile floors looked like they came out of a men's room. There was the hard bitter smell of never enough heat, and all that stays away when your house is not warm.

I knocked and Felix opened the door. I put my hands up, held back, not quite ready to go in. He was even bulkier than normal; he must have been wearing three or four layers under his sweatshirt. It really was cold.

I had a little knapsack with me, with some clothes and a bunch of money in it. Felix looked down at it.

"I had a little problem with Luz's dad," I said.

"What?"

"I asked for his advice."

"You told him you did something?" He butted his fist against the bottom of his jaw. He looked like he'd just woken up and he hit himself hard.

"No specifics, but yeah."

"Didn't mention me?"

"No."

"Painful stupid, man, painful stupid."

"But about staying here, you think it's okay?"

"Well, where else could you go?" Felix sighed.

We went in. I said hello to Anastasia, who was all cute and clean and playing with the laces on her little baby Adidas. She was just three then, a toddler, with the happy expression of a child who gets hugged a lot. Felix was all into breaking patterns. He'd read a book on child rearing and he talked about that a lot, how he was going to go about it the right way.

"I was totally sure he'd be on my side," I said.

"You're funny that way," he said. "You're not a great judge of the human character."

"No, I suppose not." I thought I saw him smile, and there were lines around his eyes. I wondered if he hadn't slept because he was scared. And what he said was true. I'm not good at seeing into people, at judging their drives. I always figure it's lucky for me they give so many outward signals, things like ritzy clothes and deep frowns, wide eyes that mean youth, clenched pocketbooks that speak of insecurity and fear.

"Look what happened when you tried to show Luz a night on the town," he said.

We went into his living room. Anastasia came in and sat on the rug. She started drawing with crayons. She wasn't making anything really, just putting colors together. The room was clean, if a bit empty.

There were a few pictures on the walls that Felix had drawn during his jail days. The pictures were mostly of hands, the hardest things to draw, and Felix had done okay with them, but only okay. I could see where he'd just pressed hard, hoping that the lines would come, that his effort alone would make him good. Just then his own hands were tucked in under his arms, and he was watching his kid. I went on with the story, about how angry Ocides was, how I had to get my stuff out of there, and was he sure I could stay with him?

"Me and Lynanne are just getting good . . . but yeah, stay here for a week, Ana can sleep in our bedroom. You want to talk specifics, let's go out of the room. Ana, keep playing." We went and stood in the corridor.

"Listen, I think I'm going to get an apartment nearer to them, even, right where they live." I spoke quietly, so I wouldn't get him excited.

"Who?" Felix asked. He was letting his hair grow in, now that it was cold, and he scratched at it. He looked better with hair, darker and younger.

"Who we take from is who."

"'Cause?"

"It's easier to get a cup of sugar, if you live right next door. I'll get a little studio on First Avenue or something. It'll be good for both of us, for me to be so nearby."

"Well, that's up to you. If that's what you want, go ahead," He didn't have any tone in his voice at all.

We went and played some music for Ana. She liked Michael Jackson, the *Thriller* years. We played that for her and the three of us tried to moonwalk in the living room, on the rug. Of course she was the best. Kids learn so much better and faster than adults.

"I guess with you living down there, it could make things easier," Felix said.

"Sure it will, and you can use the place, too."

"Yeah, hey, Anastasia!" She'd taken a crayon and started to scribble on the TV screen. I could see the ghost marks there, where she'd done it before.

"Once the money gets real, you can send Anastasia to any school you want," I said.

"She's okay for now, in public school. But we do this right, get a little more money, we'll put her in Catholic school. When the money goes big, Lynanne can start her own school, like she's always wanted."

Then we heard keys in the door and it was Lynanne, home from work. She came in and kissed Felix and then ran over to Anastasia, picked her up and held her.

Lynanne was not tall, but she was strong-looking, with big breasts, a square jaw, and some tough play around the eyes. She was Irish, and Felix had met her in high school, at Evander Childs. Her family hated Felix because he was Puerto Rican and the tension that created had messed with Lynanne a bit, where she was edgier than she might have been if she'd married an Irish guy. But the two of them were determined to stay together, to prove everybody wrong, even if that occasionally meant one of them getting a little hurt. I was more than a little afraid of Lynanne, but Felix believed in his soul that she was for him, and who was I to say different?

"Kelly," she said. Her blond hair wasn't thick, and it was pulled back from her face with a purple clip.

"Lynanne."

"Kelly's gonna stay here for just a few days until he finds a place."

Lynanne kissed Anastasia's forehead and looked up at me. Enormous vitality of the young mother, like that.

"I'll be quiet and all, you know me," I said. She nodded and walked out of the room, all the while whispering to her daughter.

"We're like a bunch of Buddhas in here! Why can't we loosen up?" Felix asked. But he wasn't addressing me or his wife.

"I don't want to mess with what you have here," I said.

"George Thorogood song, you remember, he asks to stay at his buddy's house, buddy says the wife's funny about it, George says, 'Now you funny, too, everybody funny.' Kevin used to play that album every day, up at your house. I would never turn you out, Kelly, you're my brother."

Felix, all buzz-cut, hooded-eyelash ugly, was a good man, and I would have gone to jail forever before I let him down.

"So we're all set," I said. "That's fine. I'm good with you, my brother, I'm true with you."

"What you need to do is stay true to your damn self," he said.

"*You* stay true to my damned self," I said.

We slapped hands in the corridor. We'd already proved we could do crime and we were partners, and we were golden. I listened to the soft murmurs of Lynanne and Anastasia that came from the bedroom.

———————————

I called Kev at home a few days later.

"Kelly? Where've you been?"

"Around. Listen, I saved up a bunch of money and I want to look for a job. I want to become a real estate agent. But I want to work in a good place, for a rich firm, or at least an Upper East Side firm. So, this is where you come in: I need some clothes that will make me look right around there. Good stuff, and you know about things like that. I thought we could spend a day together?"

"You just warmed my heart, little brother! Yes, absolutely, put together as much money as you can and I'll help out with the rest— we will dress you! You didn't cut your hair yet?"

"No, it's short though."

"Yeah, but you need a haircut, where it looks tended to, cared for. This will be fun!"

We made plans for that Saturday. If it was going to be fun, it would not be a fun I'd ever known before.

I set the phone down in Felix's kitchen and very lightly touched my fingertips to my forehead. This would all come together, and better even than I'd hoped. Ocides's anger was the good thing that I needed. I hadn't been moving fast enough.

A real estate agent. I knew enough about apartments, about how people lived, that it made enough sense to be a good cover. I had some nice ideas, too, about just how a real estate agent pose would put me in some of the right places.

I thought, This is what happens when you go adrift. Possibilities open up, potential is realized, good things happen. I did not dare step back and look at myself, or detach, or any of those terrible things that keep us all from finding what we're good at. I only looked at my good chances, saw my new vocation the way a priest sees his. Our burglaries were going to be as honest as absolution, where we forgave the sins that had plagued our—not victims—our brothers who had been near irretrievably lost in the nasty thicket that is unearned wealth.

2 1

"How much did you bring?" Kevin darted his tongue out, licked his meaty lips. He knew I had no bank accounts, no credit cards, that I could deal in nothing but cash. I'd left twenty-five thousand in my ceiling, but I had taken the rest of it, and the money from the Sandersons, and my own moving savings, which was only a thousand. I carried some of it with me, and I hid the rest in Felix's house.

"Five thousand dollars—is that enough?"

"Five G's? Where in God's name did you get it?"

"I told you, I saved it up."

"You are one strange guy, little brother. Yeah, that's fine. I got a whole bunch of places where we need to go."

We were at this *insanely* expensive diner on Madison and Ninety-first. We got a table by the window and the waiter came over almost immediately, and I could see how my brother would have preferred to bask for a while, but I went ahead and ordered a Western omelet.

"Fried potatoes?" the waiter asked.

"Sure," I said. My brother looked at me when the waiter went away.

"You don't need all that food—you'll get big like me."

"I need it. How much was what I got?"

"With the orange juice . . . twelve, fourteen dollars."

"No shit."

And the place looked no different from any other diner, with its smoky rippled water glasses, encyclopedic menu, sheet of glass over oilcloth on the tables . . . it made no sense, but that was location for you. There was a line to get in and we'd waited patiently, though I could not see why, but I said nothing. I watched Kev watch the people. No one returned his gaze. His hair was particularly greased back, and he had a blue half-turtleneck under his green-and-white-striped shirt. The turtleneck was bunched up and it made him look like he was wearing an ascot.

"You see that guy, the bald one?" Kev asked.

I looked around. There was a guy in line who was bald, in jeans and a blue blazer, shiny black shoes with buckles on the front, and a yellow overcoat thrown over his shoulder. He was with a woman who looked like she was made out of sticks.

"Where's that guy live?" I asked.

"A big triplex on Fifth Avenue. He's got the whole place filled with expensive paintings and crap like that—"

"Where, though, where on Fifth?"

"Seventy something, Seventy-first, fourth? Like that anyway. The new barons, the media rich—I read where that guy makes so much money that it confuses him, where he said he doesn't even know where it all comes from. He's slumming now, eating at a place like this."

I watched my brother, the way he hungered after that guy like he was a star baseball player and my brother was in Little League, with a big collection of baseball cards. We ate.

"You in a football pool?" I asked.

"Nah, I don't have time to follow it, I just watch the owners: Wellington Mara, Al Davis, Jerry Jones. Those guys are the real entertainment."

"Some little kids around my neighborhood are the same way. They have this real hate/love thing with those owners."

"Well, I'm not surprised. That's where the action is. You can only leap up in the air for so many years. It's owning the team that matters. Maybe it's not fun like playing, but players live on borrowed time, with only so long to bask in the sun. Owning is better." He kept going and I listened and he sounded just like a teenager who wanted to get paid. What was the difference? There was none that I could find.

It was funny because I looked around, and there were other guys at other tables and they, too, were talking about where the real money was, and the action. Waiters rushed to tables with steaming plates of no-egg-white omelets, women checked their mascara, felt under the table for their purses, everybody was going to buy a new suede jacket later, they had specific goals for the day, and if they ran into friends who were just a bit richer, so much the better and beyond that, if they saw prospective clients for lord knew what business they were in, that would be really good—a winning Saturday! It was pure frenzy, like a baseball card swap meet, but here the commodity was . . . here was the commodity, this was it.

"What happens if you win here?" I asked. I wasn't quite sure what I meant, but Kevin knew. It was like he had a third eye in the middle of his head that was always focused on the absolute shallowest point in the pool.

"You kick enough ass here, you buy a big fucking place in Connecticut, with a pond on it, and a pool and a guest house, not just a house, any asshole can do that, but an estate. Twenty years, fifteen if I get really lucky, that's where I'm headed." Kevin nodded, his jaw was set, and I could see how he was straining to overhear bits of talk that might help him get over on somebody else sometime in the future, so he could get his estate that much quicker.

I looked out the window, across Madison. A service-entrance door opened and a janitor wheeled out a blue recycling bin. He stopped and looked up at the bright sky and then, since it was nicer out than he'd thought, he propped the door and headed down the street, probably to buy a Snapple and some cigarettes. I looked at that opened door and then up, at the building's limestone walls and casement windows, at floor upon floor of ritzy eight-room apartments. I thought, Damn, it is so nice of you all to invite me in.

"You ready?" My brother was impatient again. The place had lulled and he wanted out of there. The lack of noise bothered him.

"Yeah, sure," I said.

We walked down, past Prada on our left, and I looked across, but quick—as if that couple would have come back to the spot to wait. My brother saw me look.

"You don't want to go over there, blow all that money on some outfit where you wouldn't look right in it next fall."

"That's right. I don't. I want to go to—" I tried to place my envy, to figure out just exactly where it lived. "To Barneys," I said. And I felt a little crappy, but that's where I was thinking about, inside.

"Right, good choice. Ezekiel is muttering praise right now from the grave."

I looked at Kevin, at this sick thing he'd said, and he was just bopping along! He didn't think it was strange to suggest that our dead grandfather cared where we went shopping. But I only bounced along next to him, thinking, Two months ago if I was walking along and I saw into a head like mine, headed down to Barneys for some clothes, I would have ripped a parking meter out of the pavement and taken a swing at it—and now it was me. It's all a goof, I thought. This is just one way to get where me and Felix want to go. Also, I was a little curious about how I'd end up looking after I spent some money.

"Maybe you're right, we're doing right by the dead," I said. And Kevin clapped me on the back, like we were brothers.

We kept moving and perhaps our pace was quicker than the street required. My brother tried to covertly point to men who he thought I might like to imitate. He muttered the names of the designers of their jackets and shoes. He could see a flash of watch and tell what it was worth. I thought of how Luz's desire was the same way, the same intensity. I had not seen her in four days and I could only wonder at how high the anger level must have been at her house. I imagined her mother in her bedroom, burning candles and praying, her father storming around, everyone suspect, an all-too-real cleave through the fine day-to-day life of her family. I wanted her very badly right then, but I thought she'd probably be cool with what I was up to, and I'd bring her in too, soon.

Earlier, I'd beeped Jahaira. She'd called me back at Felix's and said that Luz was looking for me, and then she suggested I go to Blake Hobb's playground during dinnertime. Luz could look out of their kitchen window and see me there. But she said to wait a week, that there was tension around her house, what with all the loss of trust between Ocides and Luz, because of me.

I promised myself that when I had enough to really share it around, I'd give them a big chunk of money, to spend as they wished. I figured I'd rig it where the Queen thought she won the lottery.

"Listen, Kelly," Jahaira had said. "My dad doesn't believe you ever took anything, he thinks you're crazy, he thinks 'cause you're crazy that's why you ended up in our building in the first place, where you're not wanted. He says he thinks it's proof you're nuts, that he chased you away."

"What else?" I asked.

"Well, Luz says you're for real with the stealing, and not to listen to him. What are you going to do with the money anyway?"

"What would you do with it?"

"Me? I'd buy clothes first, then a kickin' stereo system and a big house in, in New Jersey, and a car, a couple of cars—"

"No, no, if you had the money and you wanted to make people's lives better with it, what would you do?"

I heard her breathe on the other end of the line, as if I were a teacher who'd asked a rhetorical question and she wasn't supposed to answer. Why would she ever have thought on such a question? But I wanted to know. Jahaira had teenage guts that allowed her to walk freely on the street at all hours and I knew she'd seen things and I wanted to know what she'd do, and maybe I'd follow her call.

"Come on, Jahaira, what would you do?"

"I don't know . . . maybe buy everybody, buy everybody . . . what they wanted? Stuff they need? Food and shit?"

It was a tough question, I had to admit. Nobody had come up with a good answer yet.

"Tell Luz I'll come to the park."

Jahaira was only sixteen. What did she know about benevolence?

I walked along next to my brother and thought over all the new tools I'd need to really kick some ass. A whole bunch of clothes, a place to live—I smiled to myself—somewhere to stash the winnings.

"Such beautiful things!" Kevin said.

We were on the ground floor of Barneys, men's shoes, with at least a hundred other guys, and they were like Kevin in that they were taking their shoe selections very, very seriously. Nobody seemed to notice the room at all, it was all about focusing on what was right in front of you, whatever object, whatever trinket you hoped to take home. I was just able to notice that the air was pretty thick, perfumed probably, with a real snuggle-fuck feel to it, so I found myself fighting against the hope that if I took something back to Felix's, maybe some of that hot sexy air would stick with me.

I looked at my brother. You're a doctor, I thought. If you'd ever been right in your head you would exist far above this, because you have the power to save lives. But he was right in there, acting nuts like the rest of them, and he was amazing to watch. He looked at all the shoes. He sniffed them, stroked the leather, held them up to the light. He placed them on a low table and on the ground and walked six or seven feet away and stared at them, apparently to see how they looked from *there* or just *there*. I was a little sad, because I knew he would never show this much concern for a patient.

I looked at dozens of styles and I could detect only the smallest differences among them. They were all leather, mostly, bound up with some rubber or more leather. I picked up a pair of brown shoes that didn't offend me, and they were $575. I put them down. Kev was across the room, at the tie tables, where he yanked one tie after another out of their arranged pattern. He put them against his shirt, and he kept stroking them. I went over and looked more carefully and saw that everybody was doing the same thing; they were all a bunch of tie-tuggers.

"How did you get like this, Kev?"

"Like what? This place, it's everything Ezekiel's for men could have been."

"You should've been a haberdasher."

Kevin was rubbing a tie with a white daisy pattern against his fleshy cheek. His eyebrows were raised, but not to me—it was like he was saluting the fabric. I bought the tie, and two more, one with stripes, one that had no pattern at all—and that one really impressed Kev.

A very tall bald man in a suit slid over to me. He whispered something about being able to help if I needed anything. His nose was long and thin and he had this pained look, like this was good, yes, but it would be better if we were all sitting down somewhere, having a cappuccino or something.

"Thanks for coming over," Kev said, and he wasn't kidding. He motioned to me, like I was supposed to really appreciate the sales guy.

I asked for a pair of shoes with very soft rubber soles.

"I want to be able to come into a room in absolute silence," I said. The man simply nodded, as if to say, shouldn't everybody want that?

"These are the Crockett and Jones," the man said when he came back, as if he were introducing me to a family he thought I should know.

When I got the shoes on—a tannish suede pair with a bottom that was as soft and supple as an overpriced sneaker—I tried to pad around the room. But the sensation was not just of walking quietly, it was of the fact that nobody heard me, nobody was looking. They were all much too intent on their own choices, and that was great, I thought. Because when I came in and tore through their closets, found their stacks of bills, I wanted them to be sitting far away, in stupid offices, thinking the same crap thoughts, of what new clothes they would buy the next day. I bought two pairs of those shoes, the tan and the black. The salesman blinked a few times, all elegant, and asked what else he could get for me.

"I believe I'm coming up with a real picture of what you need," he said. I stared at him. I didn't hate him, because he was making me feel a little bit loved and kind of good. But no. He didn't know what I needed.

Kev clapped his hands. I'd never seen him so happy. He'd found a tie that he liked, and I told the salesman to put it with the rest of the stuff I was getting.

"For me?" Kevin asked.

"For you, big brother," I said. Kevin smiled. I could tell that he really, really appreciated that.

We chose shirts for me and then we went upstairs and I bought two sports jackets—blazers—dark colored and not too offensive-looking. I got two pairs of pants. They wanted to alter and send them to me, but I forced them to let me pick them up. My brother went on and on with the guy about cuffs and breaks and crap, and I listened but it was hard to get too concerned. They were pants, if they did even half their job they would cover me up and they wouldn't be jeans. So that was good.

Afterward, Kevin said, "I'm a little disappointed that you won't go to the specialty shops, Cruxman, J. Handbuch, Soldini. This was fun, but in those places they really treat you right."

"Next time," I said, and surprised myself. As we were leaving I saw a sweater that had a nice color to it, a brownish red color that I'd never seen before, but that somehow reminded me of my own coloring. I stopped and touched the fabric, rubbed the backs of my fingers against it.

"See," Kev said—he was up close behind me, practically whispering in my ear—"You're getting into it."

"Off me, asshole," I said. He laughed. It did feel good though, even as we left, as the massive glass doors shut behind us and then opened again so more Asian and European tourists could rush in. I thought: I like it. I saw a nasty little greed bloom in me like some cheap flower that's really a weed. It felt a lot softer than stealing, but also not so different. I went ahead and gave that feeling a wink.

Me and Kev walked west for a while on Fifty-seventh Street and then he left me. I went to get the R train. We shook hands and said goodbye and I was only a little sad when I saw how that shopping trip was the closest me and my real brother had ever been. I thought about how maybe he wasn't such a horrible guy if you played with him only and exactly on his terms. I wondered if such friendships could exist.

I waited in line for a token and the guy in front of me, a short guy in a cheap suit carrying a duffel bag, asked the token lady what stop he should get off at if he wanted to get to Ninth and University. The token lady looked at him half cross-eyed, like help was not part of her job description. Slowly, she swiveled and started to look at a map. I tapped the guy on the shoulder and he whipped around.

"Eighth Street," I said. "That's your stop. Get off at Eighth and walk one block west to University and then one block north to Ninth." I smiled. The guy looked up at me, and then he turned back away, so I couldn't see his face.

I said, "Hey, I even know the bar you're going to—Knickerbocker, right? You're going to listen to live jazz?" He didn't turn back to me. He waited for the token clerk to answer him.

"I just told you," I said, but the guy only flexed his back at me. A few more people got in line. They jiggled change and made noise like New Yorkers do when they're made to wait. I stared at the stiff hair on the back of the little guy's head. What was his problem? The token lady turned to him.

"Eighth Street," she said.

"Thank you," the guy said.

"I guess you can't trust me, huh," I muttered. "You fucking piece of shit." The little goof hustled himself away. I thought, I have been giving directions since the moment I moved to this city, and this rat-faced shit doesn't want to listen. Did I look dishonest to him? I thought about how I was a still a very good person, and I was sick with the idea of him being anything like afraid of me. I put my dollar bills down, and of course everybody looked at me like I was less than rational, what with the cursing. I went to the uptown platform and looked at that guy, on the other side of the tracks.

Normally, I would have felt bad. Here was this out-of-town twit, and I would have sympathized with the fact that some idiot from wherever he was from told him not to talk to strangers out of uniform. Then I would have felt bad about me, that I didn't look trustworthy, because maybe I didn't make sense, in my cheap button-down shirt and the army jacket I'd borrowed from Felix, with bags from Barneys in my arms. I would have felt sorry that the whole world couldn't trust me. But just then I was pissed. Why wouldn't he let me help? I wanted to take a bat—no, not a bat, the broomstick from work, take that gas-soaked broomstick and smack that guy with it, make him smell it.

"You don't fucking believe me?" I'd say. Smack! Then I'd light it up. "I'll send you on a fucking ride!" Jam that thing right up his ass, deep, force him to trust me. Teach that motherfucker a lesson about people who want to do good, that if somebody wants to help, you take their help. Beat all fuck out of him. Little runty fuck. He was the problem in the world, not me.

I looked across and there he was, staring right at me, like I was a story, a few scary lines he'd tell the folks back home. I headed back toward the stairs. He started to move, but, being from wherever he was from, he didn't know which way to go. Nobody watched him and he was caught. A downtown train came in and I saw him, still trying to decide which way to run, and then I was upstairs, running, past the token clerk, past the newsstand.

I caught him just as the train doors opened and I grabbed him by his sleeve and pulled him, hard, and he looked back at me. All he'd ever want for the rest of his life was for me to let go. I know that my face looked very brutal. The doors started to close. He took the soft pounds that made him up and threw himself into the car. I watched as he flew in and went down, hit the floor. He turned and we looked at each other. Then the train was moving and the conductor passed by and only shook his head at me, just a little disappointed. I turned and walked back toward the steps and the uptown platform. I don't know what I would have done to that man, what I wanted from him. But I did know that I'd just been introduced to another hefty chunk of my own rage.

2 2

Lynanne did a little something with my hair, cut it a bit and styled it, so it wasn't all over my forehead. I can't say me and Lynanne were getting along. She kept asking me when I was leaving, when I was going to make up with my girlfriend. I didn't know what Felix had told her, and I didn't dare ask, so things were a little tense, even as Lynanne bent over my hair, as she snipped away at the long bits that hung over my ears.

"Now it'll be easier for you to find an apartment," she said. "Because this way you won't look so ragged around the edges." I nodded. Her fingers were small and they moved fast. Anastasia watched her from the living room floor. Felix had bought her a new coloring set and some red corduroy OshKosh overalls. Ana was happy as anything. She liked to bite on the corduroy. She walked over to us.

"Please don't touch anything over here, darling. Don't touch Kelly's hair," Lynanne said. I didn't move and waited for her to finish.

Later that day I headed down to the Bar Boudoir, to find Wytold and talk real business. What I did was, just to tempt danger, keep myself sharp, and screw with the powers that be, I got off the train down from Felix's at 116th and walked right down Madison. Of course I stood out, like the white limos that cruise Madison searching for crack dealers in the evenings, and even as I *thought* that, I was like, no, man, watch it, careful now. Don't get all wizened sad. You're going to do right, ultimately. I was in my new blue blazer, my charcoal pants, with a nice white shirt and the tie with no pattern, which looked funny when I put it on, and I wasn't too sure if it was right. I wore my steel-toes because I was saving my new beautiful silent shoes for a special moment.

I had cash in my pocket and I gave some away but there was no empathy happening between me and the people to whom I handed off my dollars. I was, I don't know what the fuck I was, but they were blind to me, and because I was not of the place, the dollars seemed somehow the same way, just passing through. I thought, Wait till I get huge! I stepped fast when I was in the low hundreds. Ocides had plenty of friends, and I didn't need to get slapped around on the way to an important business meeting! Yes! That's me! Important meetings!

The Bar Boudoir was way down in the forties and I just couldn't afford to blow the time getting there. Somehow I thought I could walk it in half an hour, like I could do anything. I had to get below Ninety-sixth Street before I could find a cab.

The famous Bar Boudoir is up a flight of steps in the back of the Alexander Hotel. The doors are guarded by a couple of guys in long black coats. What I did was I got in there, and rather than approach Wytold, whom I saw immediately surrounded by women who looked like models—I walked up and down in front of the bar and I scoped on him and his pretty buddies, who were thrown all over some dark red velvet couches. There was loud ambient music playing and it contributed to the haze so that the off-blue walls shimmered and looked wet in the light. It was weird in there, so sexy—it felt like a movie version of happiness.

I tried hard to catch Wyt's eye. They were having the best time, those people, laughing so loud, and nobody could see me. Finally one of the extremely tall women looked my way and I made desperate motions for her to tap Wytold on the shoulder. She did it, but not before making sure I understood that she was laughing at me. Of course it took Wytold a few seconds to figure out who I was. But then he got up pretty fast, with a slightly more sober expression. I thought, Great, now what I look like more than anything else is a drug dealer. I didn't stop looking, though. That scene was intense. My brother would have dug it, and Luz, too. It looked like everything they tell you you're supposed to want. And in that second, I could see why. Wyt came over and his smile was very public, crinkle-eyed and honest. He hugged me, and that cooled me down pretty well.

But I still said, "I don't think I like looking like your dope dealer."

"In fact, you could dream of no better cover," he said. "Besides, you don't look like a dealer, you look like a museum guard."

He had his arm on my shoulder and I could feel him lightly guide me forward. I watched him take a fast glance back at his friends.

"No, no, I'm sorry, perhaps I am out of line. You look great, buddy, I knew you'd get it together," he said. "Really handsome. A nice change."

The doors opened for us, the good noises of winners drinking disappeared in a sudden hush, a soundtrack all too quickly turned off. I felt one thing then, that I was sorry to see that door close, sorry to be away from all those people, those who were happy and admired, preening jungle cats in a dark blue and red velvet cave.

Why couldn't I stay in there with them? I hated them, sure, everything was wrong with them, but I could sense the same kind of comfort I'd seen at Barneys, the insulation, the material world doing its best to envelop, to hide the pain of the real world. So no, there was no love there. But there wasn't hatred, self-hatred or otherwise. Sink me down on a sweet couch. Let me rest. You are not burdened. Why won't you share that fine feeling with me?

We walked twenty feet or so down the street, and we shrunk to normal size, and became just two guys. It was an ordinary midtown street dotted with people who had worked late and were going home, their heads down. There were too few streetlights and a terrible feeling of shouldn't-you-be-someplace-else? in all the doorways and faces of the night watchmen who sat behind steel desks, staring at television monitors and fighting sleep. Wytold put his boot up against a limestone cut in a building and began to tie his shoelace. I had to look twice at his boot, because it was so different from my steel-toes. It was much more ritzy, low-slung over the ankle, mahogany-colored, with little decorative details along the cap of the toe. I'd seen boots like that in Barneys with Kev and wondered who could possibly have the mix of confidence and bravado to wear them. Now here was the answer: amoral art dealers.

"You have something you need to tell me?" he asked.

"No. I just came down because, you know, I was wondering if there was maybe a job that you have ready for us to do?"

He straightened up and looked at me. We were about the same height, and if it weren't for his square-framed glasses we probably didn't look so different.

"Well, I'm waiting on something," he said.

"Look, I'm moving to the East Side, to get close to targets, you know? I'm serious with the business. I don't want you to doubt me."

"Who doubts you, my friend? Not me. Christmastime, there's something then, it's all patience for you till then. You go ahead and move wherever you like."

"You got nothing else, even something small?"

"Hone your skills yourself for now. If you're broke, I can lend you a few hundred if you like."

"No . . ."

"Good. You're my good buddy! We'll speak soon!"

"I thought—"

"We'll speak soon. Thanks for coming to see me."

There was a beat when I didn't respond. But he didn't get it. He looked at me and tried to figure out what else I could possibly want from him. I was so bummed that he had no address for me, nowhere for me to go, I couldn't speak.

"You want to meet any of these nice ladies who are with me? Ah hah,"—a terrible laugh from him, no humor in it, just, like, cued, external laughter—"no, no, you're on your own, we don't know each other. But don't forget how much I love to love you baby!"

He went back down the street and up the steps into the Bar Boudoir, without me. So I didn't follow him. I didn't really want to anyway, since they were a bunch of jerks in there, a bunch of long-necked monsters—laughing hyenas.

I bought a *Daily News* and went to a near-empty Indian restaurant that was tucked into the next street. I had lamb with spinach and then when that didn't do it I ordered chicken tandoori and some potato bread. I was fucking hungry. So they were happy with me, and I ended up with a free beer, a Kingfisher. I had no one to call and in my fancy outfit I couldn't go up to Hooligans or to the Wicked Wolf. So I stumbled out of there, full and sleepy and as lonely as I'd ever been, worse, much worse than when me and Cass fell apart. Now, no one could know where I was.

I saw how it felt then, to become homeless and apart from the world. You drift and float and time drags terribly, but I couldn't go back to my house and I was determined not to get back to Felix and Lynanne's until after midnight, so they'd have the night together. It was like I was in large part forced into this new role of Manhattan thief, thoughtful burglar, lone man walking the streets of midtown after a meeting with his fence. I was trying on my new life, and I wasn't sure if it fit right or not, or was it supposed to feel this way: all tight and slinky and like a photo of a man in silhouette who walks past a steaming grate and pulls on his cigarette before walking deeper into the night. I belched a little then, from all that fat lamb and chicken and bread and beer.

I went down to Forty-second Street and sat through a movie that starred Demi Moore as a prostitute who kills her johns. The police catch her at it, but then she convinces the sergeant, Tom Hanks, that she should be allowed to do what she does. He sets her free and she ends up killing more clients, and two of them turn out to be the mayor and the chief of police, which bugs everybody out and makes her some kind of twisted hero. I dozed on and off through most of it, so maybe there was more to the plot than that. It ended when Demi throws away her knife and a gun bigger than her forearm and goes to bed with Tom Hanks, who ends the movie by saying "Maybe I could be your very first repeat customer?" She laughs and kisses him on the lips, so I guess he could assume he was no regular john.

Outside a guy begged me for the price of admission. He was younger than me, and with his backpack and Grizzlies baseball hat he looked more like a runaway than pure homeless.

"It's a lousy movie," I said.

"I don't want to watch the damn movie, I want to sleep in there."

"Oh, right, of course." I paid for his ticket and gave him ten dollars for popcorn and Raisinets.

"Hey, man, thank you."

"You'd do the same for me," I said.

"Yeah, sure I would." He didn't smile and he was gone.

I went and got the subway up to The Bronx and it was filled with people who worked the late shift, cleaning office buildings and running the physical plants that keep the city alive. There wasn't even a seat and the lights on the train were bright as morning. I thought about how hard the city fights you when you try to give it a little romance.

2 3

I went to Blake Hobb's playground and waited for Luz. It was cold out and dark. The playground was nothing but a stretch of asphalt with a fence around it and two netless basketball hoops. I'd forgotten to eat and I was very, very hungry, but I knew I'd stand there all night if I had to, waiting for her.

I was in my new outfit, and I looked rich, or like a rich museum guard. Fucking Wyt, I thought. If I didn't look cool, why wouldn't he help me to look better? Weren't we friends? Wasn't I good enough to be friends with him?

I leaned in, against the fence, and let it cradle me. I was still staying with Felix and Lynanne, but I'd taken to changing into my expensive clothes and walking around the Upper East Side when we finished our working day. The place had a real ebb and tide to it. Two o'clock in the afternoon was dead, but three was busy with kids, six to eight was all rush-hour trudge, with everybody streaming out of the 6 train stops and going up into their little apartments, all east of Lexington, then after nine there were a lot of young drunks on the numbered avenues. During that after-dinner time, the side streets were busy with a steady stream of dog walkers. Then, on Park Avenue, people even talked to one another. The really rich folks were different, though. I spent a lot of my time watching them get in and out of black Lincoln Town Cars that waited for them at curb-side. Those true rich never seemed to be actually on the street. Publicly, they always felt like little more than a shadowy presence.

Luz came off Second Avenue and into the park. She faced me and there she was, beautiful and all, but I hadn't seen her for almost two weeks, since the idiocy I'd gotten into with her father, and now, now, she did seem of her place, with her arms folded over her chest and her little shoes pointed out and hard, toward me. Still I wanted her, for her to push me into her.

I said I wanted to go over to the Castle, but she said she wasn't hungry.

"We're gonna stay here and work some things out," she said.

I folded my arms across my chest.

"It's pretty dark," I said.

"Yeah, because it's nighttime," she said. Then we were quiet, because I couldn't think of what to say that would cool her.

It was eight and hardly anyone was in the street. Instead there was only the occasional M15 bus that came to a big grinding, spitting stop just fifteen feet away from us. A girl pushed a baby carriage. An old man carried groceries. I saw the glumness, the beaten feeling. You go away even for a little while, you never want to go back, never want to live so close, so sidled up to all that pain. The twenty-story buildings that were the Abe Lincoln Homes blocked the moonlight.

"I've missed you," I said.

But neither of us unfolded our arms.

"You're such a puss, Kelly, you know? Listen, I'm not even gonna go into how stupid you were with my father where you win the fucking stupid prize there, but more to the point"—and she took a breath, came nearer to the fence, refolded her arms, and stood in front of me—"as you can probably guess, he has forbidden me to see you."

"Well, I'm going to get a place and you can move in with me."

"You don't understand, he has forbid—"

I held my hand up and closed my eyes.

"You simply break away," I said. I'd done it, was doing it. She could do it, too.

"Maybe that was easy for you with your family who you think double-crossed you and you don't trust, but my father and my mother, they mean something, I do not cross them! And there's Alfredo, so I'm not doing any breaking away."

She turned and walked toward the middle of the playground then, and the light was so bad that when she was a dozen feet away she was all in silhouette.

"Did you take the money when you left?" she asked.

When I left I'd taken ten. There was still twenty-five in the ceiling.

"You need money?" I pulled out my new wallet and counted bills.

"That's not what I asked."

"Well, no, it's still there. And now I'm waiting on this other job—"

"Forget the job for one second! I want to know if you planned on ever coming back. Do you not know the answer to that?"

"What?" I asked. "Of course I was coming back. I'm here, right?"

But I saw how meeting her in the playground wasn't really coming back and how I'd blown some good bit of the trust we had.

She came at me then and grabbed my head, hard, pulled me off the fence, her hands around the back of my head, pulling me. I held her forearms tight and we were stuck like that. We would not let each other go.

"What are you doing? What are you doing?" I asked.

"Don't you love me? Don't you? You come upstairs and tell my father, make him forget this stupid stealing—"

"No."

"You don't love me then."

"No." I pushed her off me and she staggered back. "You don't understand. Luz, there's a bigger plan here, you have to wait—"

"Why, why do I have to wait?"

But I didn't know why she had to wait. I just wanted to do a few more jobs, get a little more full, and I wasn't quite ready for her, not yet.

"I love you," she said.

"I love you, too, you have to understand. I need to do this thing, to make a little more money, and then lay low."

"You're a fucking coward," she said. She was right in front of me and she cried out and I could feel how she'd let down her guard and trusted me when she should have hit me, too, with a baseball bat.

"No—"

"You love me all wrong. You don't know how to behave," she said.

"Wait!"

But she turned and walked out of the park and back across the avenue. I looked after her. All I could do was swear to myself that she was wrong, that I would come back for her, that I was not doing what I was doing. The self-deception, like the suspension that happened in the midst of crime, was not an unfamiliar feeling.

I looked up at our building. I needed to get in there soon. To get her back and to get the rest of that money soon before somebody robbed the place. I needed that money. I needed a plan and I needed to show Luz that I loved her enough to have her be with me, apart from her family. I needed to know if I was afraid of what she'd done that night on Madison Avenue, and if when I'd said I loved her, if I'd fallen in love with her violence and the intensity of her desire—as I'd suspected a million times before—or if I really had fallen in love with her. And if there was no difference? I needed to know that, too. But all I could think was let me steal a little bit more, let me get a little more full. Then I will be okay and I will be ready.

———

I ended up at the Castle, where I ordered a huge meal and while I waited for my food, I clowned for the clear-as-life video cameras. It's amazing to see yourself on television, like watching a little movie starring you. I hadn't seen them before, and there was a whole bank of them that you could watch, stuck up behind the cash registers, as many as five of them. So that's why it was so safe there.

When it got late I hesitated to leave and head back up to Felix and Lynanne's. My money was in that neighborhood, my passion had sprung from there, and my skill, and, I thought, my love. I also knew that the phone was ringing in my apartment, Cass was calling, and she would want to know what was going on. I didn't even know her number in Vermont; I didn't even know the name of the town. I would have walked back there and tried to fix things with Luz, I really would have, but if Ocides had told the kids (not really kids I realized, but guys my age who simply had nothing to do) outside the building that I was bad, that I raped his daughter or something, they'd take me into the alley behind the building where the garbage cans were and kill me. So I didn't go back there.

2 4

I had to meet Wytold for lunch. I'd been up for hours. I walked down from Felix's house and had breakfast at a bakery on 116th, and then I continued downtown, stopping to crisscross the mid-seventies, to learn. Sure enough, ten-thirty in the morning on a weekday was a surprisingly good time to commit a robbery. If you were out then, you had a kind of see-no-evil passivity to you, probably you were blissed out on not working, if you were around.

We met at a French restaurant near his new apartment. He looked as if he'd just gotten up; his clothes were clean and pressed, but his face was still doughy. The place was thin and long, like a railroad apartment, and the waitress poured our coffee into big blue soup bowls. Music played, a man singing in French.

"Perhaps you would consider letting me create a place for you to store your cash, and some of my own," Wyt said.

"This is something we would share?" I asked.

"But of course," he whispered. "We would both have access to this place. Do you like that idea?"

I nodded. That was exactly what I wanted, to share. He always had an answer, always knew just what I needed. He was getting friendlier. He would lean in close across the table and whisper at me, tell me answers to questions I hadn't yet asked. I could tell it was what made him a good salesman, that he gave his full attention to whoever was in front of him. He didn't have my brother's problem where he had to always look around the room. With Wytold, you were the main priority.

He pulled out a brown leather appointment book and handed me a card.

"Go see this man. He will know you are coming. If there is any misunderstanding—don't worry about it, he works with me, but don't tell him anything he doesn't already know. Let him think what he likes."

The card was for a guy called Tucker F. Golden, who was a financial planner at something called the National Capital Investors. There was a phone number, a fax number, an address, an E-mail address, and a telex number. I stared back up at Wytold.

"Funny, all these ways to contact him, and I have to see him," I said.

"Yes. We are unique in this way, even in this modern world, we must talk in person. In any case, he is my dear friend and a client, and I love him. He'll create a nice account for me and you, and everything will appear clean and legal, backdated even, so it looks like you've had the account for years, like your mother and father provided for you."

Since I had no idea what he was talking about, I only nodded. I had been thinking that the place we were talking about was going to be a locker, maybe at a gym, or a warehouse somewhere.

"Does this shirt work for you?" I asked. I was wearing a checked yellow-and-black shirt under a charcoal tweed jacket. I'd bought the shirt and jacket at Bloomingdale's, and even though it cost almost as much as the Barneys stuff, it didn't seem to work the same way. I couldn't figure out why.

"Well, what are you trying to say?"

"To say?" I asked.

The waitress came by with our tuna steak sandwiches. I'd ordered the same as Wyt. I bit into my sandwich and it tasted like a McDonald's fish filet, except with fresh tomato. There were homemade potato chips on the side and I ate one. They were terribly fresh-tasting. I left them alone.

"You see what I'm wearing?" Wyt asked.

I looked at him. He had on a suit.

"Yeah?"

"I am saying, trust me, because I wear a good Burberry houndstooth, you see? But with my tie, I am also saying how I am cool, and I'm okay with you knowing that." He turned his tie around, "Not Hermès, like you'd think, but Willington Mo, a brand-new designer. I'm hip, but classic."

"I'm not?"

"You are loud, but poorly thought out."

"Not smart, but unafraid to mix patterns?"

"More like clashing, but bad."

"Shit."

I looked down at my plate. The plate did a better job of matching the tablecloth than I did. For myself, I couldn't have cared less, but if I was going to make a dream happen, I didn't need to get tripped up because I couldn't wear patterns. And maybe I liked that. Maybe I was beginning to care, just a little. Really, what was wrong with looking good? I resolved to never wear the clothes I had on again. Instead, I saw myself in that Barneys stuff, but even better, stepping into a bar, not the Bar Boudoir, but somewhere like it. It had been raining and I was in a trench coat, Burberry, just finished working, stealing, pushing money in the right direction. Underneath would be me in a perfect suit, subtle, beige or whatever, like Wyt was into.

And Wyt would be there to check me out and nod the okay. He'd be standing with some women. They'd all greet me. How are you all? Let's get some drinks—on me, because today, today, I did good. Love me. I could tell them all hero tales and they'd listen, amazed at how brave I was. And in my future perfection, one of the women would be Luz. She would kiss me hard, rub at me, not angry, but happy with me. Wyt watched me finish my lunch. He'd eaten some potato chips and the parsley, and only taken a few bites of his sandwich.

"Listen, Kelly, do you recall when you told me about the shoes you bought? The Crockett and Jones? Silent shoes? Every aspect of your life must be like that. You are not the performer, remember, but the facilitator. You are a burglar, so, goodness and true love willing, only you will ever watch your show."

"Okay," I said.

I raised my Coke and he held up his water glass, and we toasted.

"I should introduce you to my brother," I said.

"You will introduce me to nobody."

I nodded, having forgotten for a moment that we might never be friends that way, that my brother would want to know why, exactly, I knew someone like Wyt.

"There's a party in a few weeks, where you will join me, stay twenty minutes and I show you the collection, we discuss what you need to take, and you meet the hosts. I'll introduce you as a . . . as a—"

"A real estate agent."

"Well, fine. In the meantime I have your beeper number. You should buy a cell phone, too. Get one where you prepay pieces of time, nothing permanent. And it's good that I haven't seen your partner lately. It is no racial thing for me, really, but the people I deal with . . ."

"I—"

A massive, deep brown waterbug wandered up the wall, just behind Wyt's shoulder so that it looked like it had crawled up from his chair. The wall was light yellow, and the bug was moving fast. I stared at it: it was big as a mouse and uglier than anything I'd ever seen uptown. Wyt turned, but when he saw the bug, he didn't flinch. Instead he tapped it with his fingernail, and it fell from the wall. Then he looked down, cocked his eyebrow, focused, and brought his chair up a few inches. He crushed the thing with his chair leg. It sounded just like the noise we'd made earlier, when we were eating chips.

"In New York, we learn to live with the vermin," he said. He smiled at me. So I pretended that I was not going to ask him anything about what he'd said. It was like, in the shock of the bug, I'd forgotten what we were talking about. I whispered these things to myself.

We had an espresso and got out of there. Wyt paid since he said it was a business lunch and he could deduct it. He was really being helpful and I was getting to like him.

Felix and I finished work early one afternoon and picked up Anastasia at school. She was enrolled in a prekindergarten class that she liked, but when we went there, we found that the class was being held in a windowless room that was really a shower. They'd pulled out the nozzles, so there were black holes, evenly spaced on the tile walls, and the drain covers had been removed, too.

Anastasia whispered, "Sometimes, if I have a crayon I don't like, I nudge it over there and push it in."

"You shouldn't do that," Felix said. "Next time pass that crayon to another little girl."

We looked and, sure enough, the drains were filled with bits of crayon and other crap. The teacher moved twice as fast as the kids. She was in a Gap outfit, khakis and a white button-down shirt, white Keds. Her jaw was set, like she was going to raise those kids up to her level no matter what, even if it killed her. I couldn't stop staring at her. She had this riveting quality to her, to her voice, and that and her determination made her freakish beautiful.

"Look," Anastasia said. She showed us a drawing she'd made, of me and Felix holding up a box that was twice as big as us. Of course Felix was bigger than me in the drawing, and had a bigger smile.

We bundled her up in her coat and took her home, and she slipped along on the ice on Saint Ann's Avenue. We stopped in at Pino's Pizza for slices. Anastasia had a Dr. Pepper and half of my slice. It was good pizza—they had those double-sized slices for a dollar and a half, like you never see on the island of Manhattan.

Felix gave her a quarter and she went off to watch the bigger kids play the video games. The kids knew her from school, and they were good with her. We both stretched out in our booth, and Felix put his feet up, so he'd be angled away from me and he wouldn't have to meet my eyes. He'd been growing a beard, and it seemed like it was getting even harder to really actually see him. So much of the time I was talking to the back of his head. I liked to watch him, though; his motionless quality was a good thing, a jutted-up rock formation in a storm at sea, like that.

"So I'm really going to get this new place," I said.

"It's a good thing. You'll walk among them, slip in and out, and we'll have a base right there. That's smart." Some guys our age came in and Felix nodded a hello. I was always forgetting that about him, about how he was from this neighborhood, how most of all his life had been there. He didn't tend to share that part of himself with me.

"How's work going?" I asked. I'd taken off some days and gotten knocked way low on the ladder. So even though it was getting busy again, since it was nearly the end of November, I wasn't working much.

"It's okay. I don't talk to Teddy. He ignores me right back. So no problem. They think you're working for Moishe's or Moving Man."

"Well—I did find other work," I said. I tried to laugh. Felix didn't laugh with me.

"It'll be nice when we start to see real money," he said.

"You're so sure, Felix. I mean I am, too, but you are so sure."

"Hey, I believe in us, in you, we got history."

"What does Lynanne say? Is she staying cool with me?"

"Well, she wouldn't mind if you didn't live with us anymore. But a few more days . . . it's okay. She doesn't know a thing. She may get a new job, at P.S. 107, secretarial job. That's what concerns her, not us. And I haven't shown her any of what we've done. We're getting along better, because I'm happier, and she is, too, and I don't want to fuck with that. I won't be taking any more than we need."

"That's a fine thing. That you don't want anything. But me—don't you want any, any luxury thing?"

Anastasia looked back to our table. Felix nodded to her. It's okay, darling. Keep playing.

"I got the kid, I don't need all that stuff, tugging at my heart, killing me. People and their things—nothing sadder. Just let me stop worrying about you, and I'll be fine."

"I'm good. You focus on your family, that's where you get your calm."

"Yes sir. You got it." But I looked and I could still not see his eyes. He would not show them to me.

Anastasia came back and sat with us. She'd given her quarter to some older boy. She didn't care, either, wanted others to be happy. I wondered how Felix had taught her so well.

"You want anything else?" Felix asked us.

Anastasia and I shook our heads in unison.

2 5

Tucker F. Golden's office was in the Lipstick Building on Third Avenue and Fifty-third. I got into my nice clothes and took the subway down there. To be among the rush of midtown office people was entirely different than to drive by them in a truck. I felt like I was in some kind of swim, and being invited in gave the whole thing a different, warmer feeling. The building really did look like a lipstick, all oval and reddish and twisted up. I took an elevator to the thirty-eighth floor and got out. A secretary greeted me by name and took the green army coat I'd borrowed from Felix because it was cold out and I didn't have a coat of my own. She pointed down a hall.

I could hear a murmur from the other offices, and the occasional trill of a fire engine far below, but above all that was a muted silence, created by carpet and thick glass and the whirring noise of artificially manipulated air. I stopped in front of an open door that said TUCKER F. GOLDEN next to it in raised steel letters.

Tucker F. Golden said, "Hullo!"

He was a shortish bald man in a white shirt and blue tie. He hopped up and came over and shook my hand. His sleeves were rolled up and the folds of fabric were rumpled, as if he'd spent the morning playing basketball in his work clothes.

"Well! Come on in, our little loves-to-love-you friend sent you over? Take a seat, call me Tuck, and you are?"

"Martin Kelly Minter."

"Ah."

I sat down across from him and crossed my leg at the ankle, like I'd seen Tom Hanks do in the movie when he wanted to look like he was cool, but paying attention.

"Listen, guy, it's close enough to twelve, you want lunch?"

"Sure, I'm always hungry."

He pressed a button on his desk and a man stood at the door.

"For me, my usual, and you?"

"A turkey on rye?" I pulled out my wallet.

"Hey, put that back!" Tucker laughed. The man disappeared.

The sandwiches showed up in two minutes. We'd barely talked, and Tucker made it clear that he preferred to eat first. They came on a tray with coffee. I'd forgotten to ask for anything on my turkey and the sandwich was awesome dry, like eating a T-shirt.

But, and this is important, now that I was walking around with cash, it seemed like I never had to pay for food. This was a kind of wonderful phenomenon and I made a mental note that this is what must have been meant by the law of inverse proportion. So, if I had to translate, I most probably would have noted something like: The more you have, the more you have. And, I thought, vice versa. While we munched, I had to sit there and wonder if what I would have to do would be to literally reverse this seemingly natural law. I say natural because while I watched Tuck Golden eat, small as he was, I thought of lions. This place, his office, his den, it was as if a massive appetite had retreated here, as if all the skyscraper people were predators, looking down on prey, and they used these anonymous sky-caves, glass nests, as places to rest and make strategy before descending yet again for the kill. So, where the rich hung out felt like caves, all safe and warm. And the homes of the poor felt more like lean-to huts, what me and Felix had made as kids, places that couldn't last forever; they weren't built for any long haul.

Tuck Golden finished his sandwich, crumpled the wax paper and tossed it into the chrome wastepaper basket next to his desk. He wiped his mouth with his hands and looked across at me.

"Ah," he said, then he looked beyond me, out to the hallway. "More coffee!" he yelled.

"So we're going to create an account for you, and Wyt. You'll see a lot of up and down movement in your portfolio, but, because of your youth, this is a good thing—you probably like technology and all that good stuff. I do, too, but maybe not so much, the volatile nature of techno stock now, with all that we don't understand about the Internet . . ."

I got a little exasperated when I heard all of that. I hadn't had a computer since I shared one with Kevin growing up. I hadn't typed on one since I'd lived with Cass. Luz didn't have one. Felix had that new one, but it was taking him forever to get hooked up to the Internet. He was getting frustrated. I'd never even seen the Internet, except when they showed it on television commercials.

"I don't know if I want to invest it—"

He held up a hand. He had a big, loose smile. He pulled some toothpicks from a drawer and offered me one. We picked our teeth.

"Don't worry yourself. In reality, you're just here to sign a form and to give me your social security number. Don't worry about how the money will work. If you like, we can have the fund pay you a little bit every month. Would you like that?"

"That sounds great."

By then the fact that I didn't know how to use the money for good had become humiliating. I was going to have to make something up, but anything I thought of had so many downsides, the whole thing was like committing to something—a dessert, say—and ordering chocolate cake when the pumpkin was completely different but just as good. And I kept thinking, There isn't time!

"And you said your business was what?"

"Me and Wytold are in business together, art dealing."

"That's what he told you to say to me?"

I stared at him. I didn't speak. Instead, I looked out the window. I thought, I've got nothing to say on this. I'm only a thief.

"Son, hypothetical question: What's to keep me from going to the police?"

"What?"

"Whatever you're doing, it's illegal, and most probably it has to do with drugs. Why should I feel right about this?"

He folded his arms and sat back, away from me. I sat forward in my chair. Was I going to have to hit him? Why was he being such a dick? I almost said that out loud, but Wyt said to say nothing.

"But Wyt—"

"I get nervous sometimes. I think maybe that it'd be better to do the right thing. The police are smarter than you think."

I prickled right up when I heard that. I started tapping on the wooden arms of my chair, and then I got clear.

I made my voice flat. I said, "You get nervous. Why should I care? You want to take five years out of your life to bust somebody who might even be helping people, who'll get maybe a year's probation, be my guest. While you're busy, perhaps you can recommend somebody else."

"That's funny."

"What is?"

"That you think your occupation is helping people."

I was silent then. People are so one-track-minded! You can tell them that you're different than they are a million times and it doesn't matter. They'll just keep on believing that you're a greedy bastard just like everybody else, and that you're not out to help others.

"Okay, just so you understand my trepidation. I'll have some statements made up and they'll be hand-delivered wherever you want. Wyt will have control over the account, too, as we discussed, so you'll see some major fluctuations."

Something sucked about that, but I said nothing.

"Great," I said. "This is great." He was smiling, sort of chuckling.

"You've been a real pleasure," I said.

"Oh," he said, "I pride myself on keeping the game amusing."

We didn't shake hands and I walked out. That's when I decided to keep my twenty-five-plus G's separate from the other money I made with Wyt. It would be quite something when I finally gave away all that money. I found the elevators on my own and I was thinking, Not since the 1300s and merry old England . . .

But I didn't think Tuck Golden would do wrong by me. He could fool with money, I thought, but he wouldn't betray me. After all, he thought I was a drug-running, machine-gun-toting criminal figure. Personas are okay, when they work for you like that. He probably was afraid I'd drive-by-shoot him—that it wouldn't be hard for me to figure out where he lived. Me and my crew would spill out of a big black van with the windows painted over, all of us in masks, and gun his rich white ass down. I wondered where I could get a crew, or a van, or even a gun. But then I shrugged and thought, Of course, I had the money to buy those things, if I wanted them.

26

I was on Eighty-third, between Lexington and Park, at just after nine in the evening. A couple who couldn't have been much older than me walked along and talked about which pasta shapes they liked best. An elderly businessman passed, with his chin up. I recognized a little corgi, walked by a fat chain-smoking man who looked nothing like his dog. Nobody looked at me.

I'd been watching a group of brownstones that had seemed impenetrable, but just then I saw a door open across the street, in a little garden that was gated and semihidden from view, and a girl who could have been a maid came out with some garbage. She was pretty and I wrote down the address. Wyt was compiling a list of a bunch of places that had things he could use, so sometime, when everything matched up, I'd walk into one of those buildings, and it would be good if I'd been there before, had seen the place, knew there might be a young daughter or maid hanging around even before we got there.

A woman walked up toward Park. She was young, tall, with long hair. She passed under a streetlight and I saw that she was carrying a fat leather briefcase, a duffel bag with CitiGroup written across the side in glowing white, a banana-shaped purse, and two shopping bags, one from Polo Sport, the other, E.A.T. She wasn't walking fast, and her big olive raincoat was slowing her down even more. I thought, How foolish.

And then two girls were behind her. They passed under the light, too, and they were Luz and Jahaira. The muscles in my neck jerked down. I couldn't breathe.

Luz and Jahaira, arguing, motioning to each other, getting ready.

Jahaira said, "Yo, miss, excuse me, miss—"

The woman walked faster, more awkward, with her coat and her bags and too much shit—too much shit on her, weighing her down.

"What the fuck, miss, I said excuse me—"

The woman whipped around, said, "What? What do you want?"

I was still watching, frozen up—but I could see the choice the woman made, that if she was going to be attacked, it would be better to at least see who attacked her.

"You got the time?" Jahaira asked. She was so incredible. In her puffed-out Yankees warm-up jacket with the NY emblem like a vicious slash across the chest, she came right up and at the woman, with Luz behind her. If Jahaira got *me* scared and excited just by talking, I'm sure that woman's heart was about to explode.

"I can't, my watch . . ." The woman shifted around. So much raincoat, laden down with so many fucking bags! She would never carry so much again.

"Lady . . ." Luz said. I watched Luz reach into her pocket. She was always slow with that moment, slow on the uptake.

It took about three steps to get across the street. I leaped between cars, over bumpers, and came down between all of them.

"Stop it!" I said.

"Oh, thank God!" The woman put her hands on my back, her bags knocked against me. But I didn't turn to her, didn't even bother.

"What are you doing?" I asked.

Before Luz had time to answer, before Jahaira could get her cool back and smirk, the woman saw that what she needed to do was get away. Suddenly there were no hands on my back. I turned and she was running from us, down the street toward Lexington. She wasn't calling out to anybody, only running, fast enough so her bags only flew behind her and did not even flail at her sides.

"Fuck you, Kelly," Luz said. "Fuck you! Why are you bothering us?"

By then, Jahaira was back to herself. She walked behind us. I saw her light up a Newport—a new habit.

"Luz, Luz, listen, you have to—"

"I don't have to listen! I know you're down here, walking around, well, me, too!"

"Luz, I want you to be with me—"

"I don't want to wait anymore. I love you! We were busy here, you know? And now I'm feeling scared, like you're not gonna make it."

"I'm not gonna make it? Look at the shit you're pulling!"

Then we heard the sirens. The police cars were not visible yet, but the noise was, and they were behind us, in front of us, the East Side sirens.

"Shit, goddamn. We should've at least got that Polo bag," Jahaira said. She giggled. Fifteen years old and so fucking nonchalant. She said, "Kelly, you'd best not be here."

I had not stopped looking at Luz.

"We need to stay away from each other for now," I said.

"I'm not going to wait on you forever—you need to get clear about us," she said.

I grabbed her and kissed her as quick as I could, and I felt her mouth, her whole body, push back at me. The sirens got louder and I could see the lights flash against the windows at the end of the street.

"Get under the Jeep," Jahaira said. "We'll say hello to them, so they won't get confused." Behind me, I heard something drop. Luz had tossed her knife. Two cars down, there was a new white Jeep. I walked over, fast, dropped and rolled. I disappeared.

I listened to police cars approach from both directions, to the woman jump out of one. There was muttering and the noise of police radios. Sighs from the police, since now they'd actually have to do some work.

I looked up at the gas tank on the Jeep. Far more shiny steel than black dirt. I felt a cold drop on my leg. Oil drip. But the street itself? Clean. I could breathe there. I didn't even have to be perfectly still. I was totally hidden.

The woman said, "There was a man here, who stopped them. I saw him—"

"Stopped us from what, bitch! He left out yo! Nothing happened here—I asked you the time! And you ran like a fucking bitch!" Jahaira would've kept going, no doubt, but I listened as a cop grabbed her, as she struggled exactly as much as she was allowed.

"The time, yeah. I'll tell it to you. Shut the fuck up. Get in the car." A cop's voice.

"I love you and you're acting wrong," Luz yelled.

It was quiet for a second. Luz and Jahaira must have gotten in the back of a car.

"Who was she talking to?" a cop asked.

Another cop said, "How should I know? Maybe you."

"Yeah, well, I love her, too. Anyway, uh, ma'am?"

"Yes?"

"We can charge them if you like, but did they do anything but ask you the time?"

"Listen, there was a man here, who got between us—you better listen!"

"We can charge them. I said we can charge them. It's just, asking the time . . ."

There was the clatter of the radios, of doors slammed shut. Snickers from the cops. There was no crime. This probably happened pretty often. Upper East Side people getting skittish around the poor.

The police drove off, but I waited half an hour before moving. No doubt there were loads of people at their windows. And I knew those people. They wouldn't turn away immediately. Watching would have made them thoughtful. They didn't need to see me emerge from nowhere, all greasy and involved. And I didn't want them to see me that way.

2 7

That Friday morning I went to the Sutherland Real Estate Company, on the parlor floor of a brownstone on Seventy-third, just east of Madison. I checked in with a secretary and waited in a room where the walls were covered with paintings of barn animals. Current magazines sat on a coffee table with curled wooden sides that were like sneering lips.

I was dressed up in a way that I thought for sure they'd appreciate: charcoal wool pants, the silent brown suede shoes, blue cashmere blazer, a striped shirt and tie. I'd been on the phone about it to my brother. He'd heard of Sutherland, and though I'd had a hard time making him believe I was there for a job interview, he recommended I dress conservative, but with rich fabrics. "Let them know you're one of them," he said, "not that you'd like to be, but that you already are. Tell them that where we grew up was a horse farm." I could imagine him on the other end of the line—his knee jiggling, his mind working over the idea that Rantipole Farms was our very own horse farm, not a second-home community for store owners and public school teachers from Queens, where my parents had illogically decided to set up sole residence.

I'd beeped Jahaira on and off for days. Nobody responded. And the beeper I'd gotten from her was dead, because she must have let it go unpaid. I'd called the police, but Luz and Jahaira hadn't been held. The cop on the phone had seen them come in. They were charged with a misdemeanor, for scaring a rich lady, basically.

The secretary came around her desk and handed me an envelope. Inside were the bunch of statements that made up my investment portfolio. Wyt had had it forwarded to Sutherland. There was even a handwritten note that must have been from Tuck Golden. He said that my account was now "up-to-date" and as of that moment I was worth $857,000. But there were also parentheses, where he said that, in fact, only a tiny bit of it was mine, and most of it didn't even exist at all.

But the account, he reassured me, had existed in one form or another since the year I was born, 1978. There was even a mention of the account's inception in a Pennsylvania bank, a bank that had shut down when I was in high school, that had become a Hardee's.

I wondered if I could do something like find a lawyer immediately, lie, claim that money was all mine, and take it all. I could only imagine what me and Felix could do with it all. And I smiled. I didn't know. I could only imagine. But that was okay. The money wasn't real.

"Dini is ready for you now."

"Great!—ouh, thanks you." I was sounding all slurred and fucked up! All up and down and nervous and I wanted to bolt out of there. I had that split-second sharp charge of backbone reality, where I should have gone and found some way to make peace with Ocides and burrow back into bed with Luz, but instead, I was pointed to an office in the back, and I went there.

I sat down with Dini Needmeyer, in a small room that was more like a cubicle. It was quiet there, but different than the chemical quiet of Tuck Golden's office. This was a garden-in-the-back quiet, a feeling you get in front of a window with a view of trees. Somebody came in and asked me if I wanted a drink.

"Coke," I mumbled.

"Mr. Minter, you tell me what you need."

No hello? I thought. No. No bullshit time-wasting at this level.

"Well, first you could maybe tell me how much I need."

She laughed. She wasn't young, but she batted her eyelashes like a girl. I looked across at all her jewelry, all that Elsa Peretti crap that I'd studied oh-so-carefully in Luz's copies of *Vogue* and *Elle*. I said nothing. She wasn't bad-looking—at least from what I could see through all the makeup and artifice. She was, like, between thirty and fifty.

"Let's assume I know nothing," I said.

"Come now! Everyone knows something."

We smiled at each other.

"Well, of course I'd like a doorman, and a location—you know— around here, and a high floor, just one bedroom, but a living room that's twenty-by-twenty at least, prewar—"

"We're talking high rental?"

"Oh yes," I said, breathy, like she'd asked if I wanted to fuck her. And she did look like she had.

"How high?"

"High," I said. All of a sudden, I felt like it was my birthday.

She held out her hand and I showed her my "investment port-folio"—minus the note.

I said, "I'd like an entrance area if possible; round is always cool."

Dini put down my statement. She watched me, she wrote little notes on a pad but she looked at me while she did it. I wondered whether she'd get me in to see the best places. Then I wondered, Where is all this puke nasty materialistic shit coming from? How could I possibly care this much about everything I hate? But I did not stop talking. All this desire, like I was a puppet for some sick inner monster, some true kin of my brother's, a desirer, a needer, like there was some desperate inner wind in me, some putrid-smelling want where my benevolence was supposed to be. I was thinking, What a load! But I was saying . . .

"What I also really would like is a window in the bathroom, good flooring—I'd practically die for wide plank, a Sub-Zero fridge—"

I stopped because Dini stood up. She had on a salmon-colored matching thing and no shirt underneath, and she smoothed her top and bottom halves before she said anything. Then she reached forward all the way to the front of her desk and grabbed a pocketbook. I caught a nice shot of big breasts, a lacy blue bra. I gaped. Who the fuck was I? I would give away every dollar, go direct, steal, walk uptown, give away. But not just then, just then I was going to get an apartment, just like the ones I'd been moving people in and out of for the past year. A place that others would envy.

"Martin?"

"No, Kelly. Everybody calls me Kelly."

"All right then. Kelly, let's go look at exactly seven places right now, all in your price range, all with nine out of ten of the things you're looking for. I have two in mind that you'll probably choose, but we'll wait to see if I'm correct. I've written them down on this piece of paper. Little game I play, keeps things fun."

I stood up and we walked toward the front door, and all around us were other Dinis on other phones making deals and other well-heeled clients sitting in chairs, except most of them seemed to have ordered waters instead of Coke. Small distinction. It was neat to see how well-heeled actually meant that you had a good pair of heels on your shoes. A black car was at the curb. We got in, Dini first, and she pulled my wrist, and even as I watched, she rubbed my hand down her back and I was able to feel her ass. I wondered if she'd wanted that to happen. With her other hand, she handed a sheet of addresses to the driver.

She said, "Numbers seven, eleven, nineteen, two, three, four, and twenty, in that order." And we were off.

The first place we looked at had so much damn molding in it you'd have thought you were in an English country house owned by an American who'd won the lottery.

"I want it in move-in condition," I said. "I'd have to tear all this gunk out." Dini tapped her teeth. She made a tiny mark on her list. Places two through four were good, damn near perfect, and we both knew it. They had everything I wanted plus some more: a sauna, a bar, a secret room behind paneling, a kitchen left behind by a professional chef. We had not yet talked about money, really, but she knew at least that I wasn't buying. I would rent, I figured I'd pay two thousand a month, maybe a few hundred more than that. It was outrageous, I knew, but I wanted to go through with my idea.

We got sandwiches at a bistro place that was painted pink. Instead of flowers, they had these huge displays of wheat, like wheat was God's food and should be blessed. I kept my eyes squinted because I was afraid that somebody would look at me and see that my eyeballs were doing irrational flipflops in my head. Dini knew people. And in my brain: Asshole! Get out of there, asshole! But I was hungry like a starving animal, a jackal, and I stayed right where I was.

"We're going to fast-forward to the last place," she said.

"Why?"

"Because I think I understand you."

We went two blocks away, to Sixty-third, between Park and Madison. We stopped in front of a town house building that was bigger than normal, but wasn't an apartment building, either.

"No doorman?"

"Sure there is." We went up to the little door and a doorman opened it from the inside. He bowed.

"The configurations here are very interesting, very special," Dini said. We got into a tiny elevator that was all in the inlaid paneling style I'd come to expect (it was my job to line such elevators with big green pads, and in the past I'd been concerned that we'd tear through and I'd get blamed), except here the proportions were smaller. We went to the fifth floor. There were doors on either side of the six square feet of carpet we stepped out on. Dini unlocked the door on the right. We stepped into a corridor. To our left was a staircase. There was a door straight ahead. Dini opened it. A bathroom was on the right, more corridor, and then an unbelievably big bedroom, simple, a twenty-by-twenty-foot square, with a wall of closets, a wall of windows overlooking the street and a small terrace, a ceiling that must have been eleven feet, and a sweet little teardrop chandelier. I laughed.

"Now, upstairs." Dini grabbed my hand and we went up the steps. There was a lot of natural light coming down on us. We stepped into a—it's hard to call it a room, it was more like the belly of a ship, in glass. It was twenty feet wide and forty feet long, with a triangle of skylight running down the length of the ceiling. There were windows on to the street, and windows on to the back, where there was another terrace. This one was shaped in a massive half circle, with a triangle that jutted out, and ended in a point. We went out there and leaned against the railing. It was too cold for birds and there was no other sound at all. In New York, that was the kind of silence you had to buy. We looked down on nothing but the gardens of the rich.

There was a kitchen in the big room, along one wall, European appliances, all white and a creamy shade of gray. Plank floors. Another bathroom on the left wall. Room for one massive ruling class-sized dining room table and at least three couches and plenty of chairs. A closet built to contain a stereo. A feeling, a very good, very unbelievable feeling. I thought, If I live here, I will feel good forever—no, I got myself right, I'll feel gross, but living here is the right thing to do.

I planned on filling that place, that giant glass belly, with stolen treasure and then, late at night, ship it up to those who need it. Me and Wyt and Felix would have huge parties, outlaw parties, where our status would be whispered and wondered over—we'd achieve infamy and our story would become true modern folklore, even as we made the world better, somehow, so much better. I looked at Dini, who was watching me, her eyes half closed, her head lolled a bit to one side. She tapped her lips with her pointer finger. Her lips were shiny.

"How much?" I asked.

She walked to the terrace windows. I saw how light came down through the skylights and dusted the room in colors. I held out my hand and my hand was clean. Dini was still quiet. I figured she'd say eighteen hundred, maybe two thousand, and I'd go that high—on Felix's advice, after all.

"Do you like it?"

"Yes."

"Of course it was the only one on my little piece of paper. To buy, the owners want seven hundred and fifty, but it's been on the market for a while, because of its odd configuration, so finally they decided to let it go for rent. But there's just been some additional interest. The heir to a southern newspaper fortune saw it just yesterday and liked it. But I hear prohibitive stories about him going around. We may not want to deal with him. He's a drug addict, and last year while he was still at Bennington he came down for vacation and attended a party in this very building and—"

"Well, so what's the rent?"

"Seven thousand."

"A month? My God!"

"Well, you can afford it!"

She looked indignant, like if I couldn't then how dare I waste her time?

"I can?"

"Of course, invested right, your portfolio earns you twice that in a year anyway, plus, once you rent for a year, there's an option to buy."

I guess I had spent a good part of our driving-around time lying, talking about how I stood to make a whole ton of money in the next year. I looked around that room, a storeroom designed for a superhero.

"Yeah," I said. "I'll take it."

"Thought you would." Dini smiled. "I'll take care of all the details. Our fee is fifteen percent, but if you like, I'll take care of everything, then it goes to eighteen, and no headaches for you."

She turned around when she said this. We were at the top of the stairs.

"Done. I want to do it the eighteen percent way," I said.

"Oh, good, that's good," she was almost whispering. "I'll close all the paperwork myself, cover up the rough spots about you . . . the place will be cleaned and ready in just a few days, say, the third of December. That's good, very good." She went down the stairs. At the bottom, she turned. We were suddenly very close, because I'd been looking up while I walked down, and I bumped into her. She put one arm around my back, to steady me, and then she let me go a bit forward so that I was rubbing up against her. Then, before I even had my balance right, she pushed me away. I watched her spray Binaca into her mouth.

"You're a nice boy," she said. "There is nothing you'd like to check on before we go down?" She was already out of the apartment, her hand on the elevator button. The elevator was there.

I introduced myself to the doorman, whose name was Todd. He was about my age, and he wore a massive overcoat that totally hid his body. He looked happy, like he was dealing drugs and had the perfect cover. We shook hands.

"It's the best bachelor pad in New York," Todd said. "We'll take care of you here."

"Oh, no," I said. "I'll have to introduce you to my girlfriend."

Dini shook hands with me on the street, got into that black car, and sped away. I walked up Madison, headed nowhere. I thought, Crazy shit like that never happened to me when I was poor.

Then I went and gave all the loose cash in my pockets to a cabdriver who had just broken down on Park Avenue, who was crying and cursing and whose pain I thought I could still feel, somewhere inside, perhaps slightly to the left of that horrible foul-smelling kinship I'd discovered I had with my brother Kevin. That is, when I checked my watch to see what time it was—though I only had places where it was best that I did not go—I was embarrassed that I was wearing a Bundshaft and I almost traded watches with the cabdriver, but then I didn't. After all, that Bundshaft was a good watch and I'd earned it.

2 8

I met Wyt at an Italian restaurant on Third Avenue, in the mid-
seventies. I'd seen the place before while I walked around. I knew
the price of dinner, what kind of people went there (families: The
men wore blazers even on the weekends and the women did not
look tired like normal mothers. The parents were happy to see their
kids, probably because mostly these kids were with their nannies
during the day. The place was run by real Italians, and deliveries
were made by the Tomcat Bakery in Brooklyn and a pasta store
down in Soho that was owned by a prominent family with connec-
tions in both real estate and government, but I didn't know where
they got their meat). Earlier, I'd told Felix that I didn't need to sleep
at his house anymore. I told him I'd found a place on First Avenue
for a thousand a month, and, though it wasn't ready, I was going to
stay in a hotel until it was. Lynanne was sick of having me around,

and now that I'd signed with Sutherland, it just felt like a bad idea to be too near Felix and his family, in case something went wrong.

I went into the Italian place and Wyt was sitting at the bar with one of the owners. They were laughing and not speaking English. Wyt drank his red wine from a water glass, which was probably something only friends of the owner got to do. I made a mental note to tell my brother. I sat at the bar and was not introduced. If I'd been naked and painted blue I could not have felt more watched, more checked out.

There were waiters in there who were twice as big and thick as me and they gave me stares like they knew what I really was, or worse, like I was the delivery guy who'd asked to use the phone, two times. I ordered a glass of red wine, drank it too fast, and Wyt sidled past me, nodded, all subtle. I paid out eleven dollars and walked out, and we met up again at the corner.

"Make that place the hangout for you, the owner imagines he could use you for a few things."

I put my shoulders up high.

"You really think it's such a hot idea for me to get involved with his organization? I mean, I felt like those guys were memorizing me, and it was not a cool feeling."

"They were just checking you out because that bar is not a bar. You cannot order drinks in there. You did not notice? There were only four seats? It looks like a bar, but it is only there for people waiting to eat. Perhaps you are the first person in history to have a drink there who didn't sit down and eat. But they're interested— you're prime right now, nothing is beyond you."

"What about you?"

"I ate with Gianni, the owner, at the bar, get it?"

"I get it."

"Remember now, you're in for fifteen minutes and a good look around, then you've got to go, just understand what you need and get out."

"Okay." With me along, Wyt must have been a little nervous. I could smell cologne coming off him, and it mixed with his fear and came out dank, like he was pushing, trespassing in territory where his passport could be revoked.

We walked into a Park Avenue building, Wyt said his name to a doorman who must have been seventy, and we went up in an elevator with another old guy. I watched Wyt do a deep-breathing exercise, where his eyes went up in his head and he sucked in all the air that was meant for the three of us.

When we got out, it was a cocktail party.

The place was lit deep and low, no ceiling light, just little precious lamps, tons of them, so that while some people got sidelit and looked good, there were plenty of men and women who got caught with light coming up from below them, and that made their faces look like death masks. Like when you're little and you put a flashlight up to your chin and scare your buddies, like me and Felix in our pup tent, when Kevin'd sneak up and scare all fuck out of us, way late at night.

"Hellooo," Wyt said, and it was on. I shook seven hands in a row, short people, tall, very old, clothes hanging off their bodies like they'd never been in anything else, like they'd popped out of their moms in blue blazers or choker pearls.

The first thing I overheard, spoken in whispers: "They don't have a billion dollars, they have nine hundred million, maybe, and that's all."

"It's not nothing."

"It's not a billion, either."

I nodded, as if they should include me in their analysis. But then there was a voice behind me.

"How do you know Wyt?"

"Old friend." I'd been told to say that and then move away, quick.

I looked around, understood where the two entrances to the living room were, saw into the dining room, where there was a buffet of what looked like everything in the world, but mostly from the underwater section, clams, oysters, caviar, a big platter of something that shined like blue jelly in half shells that were spiky and off-putting. There was a cover of little sprinkles of vegetables in a bunch of colors, big red lettuce leaves standing at attention, and next to this crazy setup were little stacks of gleaming plates. It was hard to listen in to conversation, since everybody was having one.

The painting I was supposed to take was located in the foyer. It was a small painting of a very thin naked man with dark hair. He was scratching his crotch, even though the act seemed to be causing him profound displeasure. I looked at it, put on an expression that was supposed to represent admiration, and turned around. Wyt was way far across the room, and the room was crowded. Not too crowded of course, too crowded was for high school beer parties. This room, I thought, was just crowded enough. No one talked to me. No one even looked at me. I made my way over to the buffet and put together a seafood salad. The other painting was in that room. That one was of some blackness, with a big messy red star at the top. I did not think about what pricelessness meant, about how much money had been assigned to that funny little picture. I only nodded at the image. Hello, new friend.

Wyt was in front of me. The way it looked, as far as anybody else was concerned, we'd just met.

"You're all set, no? I'll call when the date is fixed, now eat up and head out, okay?" He said all this with a big smile on his face. I nodded since I probably wanted out of there as bad as he wanted me out, what with the noise and the enemy all over the room. I didn't want to see their faces, didn't want to know how sad they'd be when I ripped them off. But then, as I was looking around at everybody's middles, while I was chewing on octopus, I saw someone beautiful. Cass. I put my plate down on a side table. I buttoned my blazer and got ready to run. It was an instinct, below thought.

"Mickey!" She spoke quite loudly, and a few people turned around. The only way to keep her from yelling again was to go to her immediately.

"Excuse me for a second, Wyt, I see somebody I have to talk to."

"Wha-at?"

Even as I walked toward her, as I felt how much I'd loved her, I wanted to be running, moving in the other direction.

She was on a blue-and-white silk couch and her head was rolled way, way back. Like she'd been lying there forever, since long before the party started, and now she couldn't be bothered to pull her damn head up. She was like that, Cass was, where she had the kind of smoothness that allowed her to really and actually forget where she was. She had on a pair of clinging white silk pants and a black turtleneck. She wore no jewelry. Her light brown hair was swept back and even when I was with her I never understood that, how she could be anywhere and still have this beautiful mane of hair that looked like it had just been blown back by a warm wind. I walked over and stood in front of her.

"Sit down with me, Mickey. I don't know. I don't know what you're doing here but I am pleased. Sit down."

"So it's true?" I said. "Sometimes the white wolves really do come down from Vermont and invade the city."

We used to joke about this, at the beginning of when we fell apart, that she'd gone up there to be with her wolf family.

"Wolves?" Some guy covered in a suit of pale blue velvet looked up and acted all annoyed. Cass liked to breathe through her mouth, and she raised her brackish eyes even as she kept her lids at half-mast, like a drugged Madonna, a sleepy god.

"Mickey. I have really missed you."

"That must be my cue," the velvet boy grunted, and got up.

"Sit down," she said to me.

I slid onto the couch next to her and she let her head flop back, so I flopped mine, too. It was like watching television while lying on your side.

"Love," she said, "I've tried to call you a lot."

"Moved out."

"Up?"

"Like you wouldn't believe."

We lay there, breathing, staring at each other. Wyt passed through my line of vision, gave me a real vicious look. He didn't like this at all.

"I can't stay here much longer," I said.

"For another moment, you can stay."

I think the room must have hit its peak, because the noise went up, and people laughed more. Cass and I had to speak—not louder, but more clearly.

"What is it you're doing exactly?"

"Can't say just now," I whispered.

"What?"

I felt a push on my knee, a kind of push against my pants leg. I thought: Take this as an order to get the hell away from her. The push again, more a hard jerk, and I had to look up. Some fuck was standing there. Some guy with dark black hair only on the sides of his head and a gray suit that looked like it might have had elastic in it and was most definitely ridiculous.

"Nice to see you," he said. But it clearly wasn't.

"I have to talk to this man. He could collect my art," Cass whispered. Then she giggled, as if the fact that she'd gotten a career was a kind of joke between us. The man still had not removed his leg from mine.

"I haven't had a chance to talk to you," he said, to Cass.

"Help me up," Cass said.

I grasped her hand and helped her up. She came forward and hugged me a little bit and it hurt. I didn't want to feel anything for her. And then I moved away and I didn't feel anything. Then, of course, Wyt was next to me.

"Time to go."

"You will come and visit me in Vermont," she said.

"Sometime," I said. "When I need to."

"No. Sooner, because you and me are not finished. And that bothers me."

"Okay," I said. "We'll discuss that."

Me and Wyt ended up leaving together, because in the end we'd both been there too long.

"That was my girlfriend," I said, when we got outside.

"I thought you loved a Puerto Rican. But don't tell me how you know this other one. Anyway, you got the feel of the place? The call should come in a few weeks, you'll do the job alone, without your friend."

But the job felt wrong. Somebody would put it all together. Seeing Cass had clued me in. The world was getting small and knowing that, recognizing it, was bad. The evening felt like an unpleasant introduction to the possibility of getting caught.

"Look, the job seems impossible to me. I don't think I can do it. I've never taken anything that big from a building before."

Wyt didn't flinch. Instead, he checked his watch.

"It's already done—you'll do it. It's amazing, you leave no trace of anything. As a thief, you are more like a mean feeling that comes over a place, and then there's some art gone. It's quite wonderful, really. We keep this up and you'll stop soon. A few more jobs, then it'll be over for a while, you'll just be a myth some people talk about at parties. The master criminal, the prince among thieves."

"And they've seen me. Your idea was wrong. It's a job I can't do."

Wyt studied me. We were at Sixty-eighth Street and it was nine, and he was probably late. Some model in a black dress was sitting in the Bar Boudoir, waiting for him. He frowned and I thought I saw a bit of his age. He might have been old enough so that when he felt tired of a conversation, it was a physical thing.

"You are going to do exactly as I say. You think I don't know how things work? I can find you. We know each other now, what we do, and we have an understanding."

"You can't make me do anything."

"Didn't you meet so many of my friends earlier? In that restaurant? You are known, and you will do just as I say."

Wyt had eased his accent while he spoke to me. He wanted me to understand. He was brilliant, Wyt was. If I didn't do what he wanted, his friends would find me and hurt me. Simple.

"You will leave me a phone number where I can reach you."

I gave him Felix's number. He put it in his breast pocket. Then he came forward and hugged me.

"Do you see how we are all vulnerable?" he asked.

"Yes," I said.

"I'll be in touch. And relax! Soon it will be the holidays!"

He hurried down the street and I looked after him. Even then I thought he was still a sort of friend. Though he had done an awfully good job of ordering me around. And he'd cut Felix out of the deal.

It took a few hours of walking around for me to decide to go back to The Bronx and surprise Felix and Lynanne. Even though I'd said I wasn't coming back, I wanted to thank them. They would understand and I'd stay with them for just a few more days, until my place really was ready.

I figured I'd get them a big basket of food. I went to one of those gourmet grocery stores on Lexington Avenue that stay open late. I got pounds of different salads, red potato, green bean and lime, couscous; two baked chickens; a couple of bottles of Martinelli's sparkling cider; a chocolate cake that the guy promised would get gooey in the middle if I heated it up just right in the microwave.

We'd have one of those happy homey parties, and Lynanne would forget that I'd come and gone from their house in the very late hours for nights on end, that I'd sat quiet and done nothing for whole days, for a month, and Felix would—but I didn't need Felix to do anything for me, since we were closer than brothers.

When I knocked Felix came to the door. He was pale and he did not move out of his door frame. I stood in that shit hallway looking in at his clean white space and I did not set down the bags, but held them tight in my hands. I swayed with the weight and I wondered, What's the problem?

"What are you doing here?" he asked.

"I—it's a surprise. A thank-you. I brought you all this food."

He didn't say anything. The apartment was totally silent behind him. I wondered where everybody was.

"Well . . . look, it's late. You can't come in."

"Why not?"

"Lynanne is upset. We had a fight."

"Well—"

"And it's enough, you know? You stayed here long enough."

"I know, I just—"

"Look, it's not me. Lynanne said she doesn't want you near here anymore."

We stared at each other, and the doorway was between us.

"George Thorogood," I said. "Now you funny, too."

"Anastasia," he said. I nodded. I handed the heavy bags of food across to him.

"Take these then. It's my thank-you."

He took the bags.

"Oh yeah, the clothes I left here—I can see how tonight is bad, but bring them to work for me, okay?"

"Sure."

We kept looking at each other, and neither of us was smiling. It was the first time that he had not done right by me. I couldn't understand it, why he wouldn't let me in to his apartment, not even for a minute. Lynanne didn't hate me that much.

"Later," I said.

"Yeah, good-bye," he said.

2 9

I got back on the train and went right into the city. But I was dressed up, not down. I sat in an empty car and I couldn't decide where to sleep. I could not bother my brother, because then I'd have to explain why I couldn't go home. Wyt didn't need me around. Me and Luz weren't anywhere near straight. I had a little over $900 in cash in my front pocket. Where to sleep? A midtown hotel with clean sheets and the smell of the midwest all around me? That would be blowing money on nothing but unpleasantness. A ten-dollar Bowery dive with cardboard walls and rats in the beds? No. The career bums would call me a drug dealer and take everything I owned while I slept.

I ended up staying in the subway, flying downtown and then back up, dead asleep for most of it. Sometimes I woke and looked at teenagers who were looking at me, but that's all they did. I was still thick, and I looked more like an undercover cop than what I was, which was one of them. Around five I thought of going to the all-night porn theaters still struggling to exist around the edges of the awful new Times Square. But by then it was too early to bother.

I woke for real at seven on the 2 train, headed downtown. We were passing Eighty-sixth Street, doing about forty, when I sat up and looked around. The car was warm. I gripped in my pockets and found my money. My good shoes were still on my feet. On all sides of me, the super-early-morning commuters dozed on their way to work. And it had been so long since I'd kept my eyes closed and pretended to sleep on the trip down to Miracle. I looked at them and thought, You are all still in it. And me? I am fallen outside of it, where there's no good reason for me to be on this early-morning train. I dusted myself off and stamped my feet and waved my arms to get the kinks out.

After I ate some breakfast I went and bought a new beeper and a cellular phone. I left messages about my new numbers with Wyt and I told him to forget the old ones. I called Isaac and he said to come in the next day, that there was work. I called Dini, and her office said my keys would be with the doorman that Friday. I did not think about Lynanne and Felix. Because there was nothing else I needed to do, and the day was empty and mine, I started looking for open service entrances.

I headed over to Sutton Place and took a closer look at the buildings you never hear about, the buildings with simple, grand names, The Towers, River House, United Nations Place. A doorman stepped out of a building and took a look at me.

"You here about the Grunbergs' computer system?" He pointed his chin at the plastic bag I was carrying that held my phone and beeper and said 47th Street Electronics Warehouse on the side.

"Yes," I said, "that's why I'm here."

The Grunbergs had nearly $4,000 in cash, a velvet box that held seven big watches, and a tiny framed drawing of a bald man with a long beard that looked like it was done hundreds of years ago. I prayed like crazy that the little picture wasn't another Rembrandt or some awful thing, because that was so just asking for trouble. But I did take it, that and the rest of the stuff, and packed it all in a computer box that was sitting in their foyer.

"I've got to take it back," I said, when I got downstairs.

"Computers are a mystery," the doorman said.

"To me more than anybody," I said.

We laughed together, and I went out. I left the stuff with my new doorman, Todd. He showed me my basement storage space. He swore up and down that my things would be safe until I got my keys. I told him I believed him, and went to the movies.

I saw a French movie about how classical music drives a guy with a big nose insane. The movie was at the Paris Theater off Fifth Avenue, next to the Plaza Hotel. Inside it was warm and smelled really nice.

That guy in the movie ranted like a madman! He had problems with these sexy young women, and with his father. He kept yelling and throwing his head back in a way that made me dizzy, so I focused in on that crazy music. They played it loud in the theater when it overtook him and it was beautiful, with lots of harp. Every time the guy got into some frenetic sex or an argument, the harp went up and up until I could see the pulsing red blood vessels on the guy's nose. He was quite a performer.

And I thought, I am like that guy, the great divide between rich and poor is driving me insane. But that didn't work—it wasn't the truth. So then I was happy, even as I was confused, because it turned out I wasn't so sure what was driving me nuts after all. During a slow moment in the movie I went to the bathroom and splashed myself with water, which got a little messy, but when I was done my face and hair were clean. I decided that my clothes looked lived in and relaxed, rather than sleeping-in-the-subway dirty.

It was six o'clock when the movie was over. I came out into a mass of holiday shoppers going up and down Fifth Avenue. I leaned against a Bergdorf's wall and watched them. They looked happy.

And I didn't hate them for having so much stuff. How could I? Who knew them? I didn't. I wanted just as much as they did, and I wanted to be with them. I was with them, like them. If anything, my desires were more finely tuned. So I wondered what kind of madness I was in, where I just felt like everybody else. I was hungry and I knew I would have to eat alone. Felix didn't want me near him. He'd made that much clear. And if he didn't want me, and I didn't dare go anywhere near Luz? I was alone and I could eat anywhere. That's how I knew I was fusing with all of those people, because I kept thinking how I could eat what I wanted, how I could have anything I wanted. I was sure that was the most important thing to so many of those shoppers, and now, to me, too.

Catty-corner from me, across the park with the golden statue, was a restaurant. I crossed over and looked in the window. It was a beautiful place, called Harry's, and the bar was crowded but the tables were empty, because it was still early. The walls and furniture were all done up in pale yellows and white, so I knew the place was four-star. I went in and the people there were nice enough. They gave me a table way in the back, all to myself. I ordered tiny ravioli stuffed with lobster and then I had a "Steak à la Cipriani." I drank a glass of wine the waiter recommended.

I shook my head, no. Because I was lying. I wasn't someone who tried make things more fair if that was where I chose to eat my dinner. I sipped my wine and watched the restaurant slowly fill with assholes. And I acknowledged that—that yes, sure, those people were assholes. No doubt about it. But those people and their money were not what kept my hands gripped hard on either side of the table and my eyes wide open, unblinking and fearful. It was something about Luz. I drank the wine and even as I drank, the idea of her unfolded and re-created and disappeared in front of me: a thought as difficult to hold tight as it was to know the amount of honesty it takes to create trust. And I thought, but I do want to understand, about her. Unfortunately, there was a lot of work that I had to do first, that I had no choice but to do.

I ate a painfully sweet and smooth chocolate dessert and I thought, You love her. She's driving you mad and you don't know her and you run from her. Who do you love? You love Luz. The waiter saw me sitting, staring.

"Would you like a port?" he said. "A nice after-dinner port?" I thought, What am I doing here?

"Yes, I'd like that," I said.

The pounds of me stayed in that comfortable chair, my belly full, my molten weight stirred by the very beginning of understanding.

If you love her, what are you doing here? Why did you run?

Isaac had me on a moke move, an office move where there was no chance of a tip. The company we were moving did something where each employee had to have at least one and sometimes three computers. They were moving from Tribeca to this warehouse area in Chelsea and there were boxes and boxes, all considered delicate.

There was a crowd of us, everybody except Dennis and Felix. I figured Dennis had overheard Isaac get the phone call for the job two days before and called in sick. Dennis probably called Felix and he would have called me, I thought, except I wasn't where I was supposed to be.

I barely felt like a Miracle man anyway, since I'd worked so little. I'd pretty much fallen off the ladder.

Teddy came over to me. There was nowhere to sit, and I'd sunk to the floor. I guess I had my head in my hands.

"Lemme talk to you over here," Teddy said.

I followed him around the corner and through a door, into a concrete stairwell. When the big metal door creaked and closed behind us I swear to God it sounded just like a woman sobbing, like a tape of that noise—on and then off. I opened the door and let it shut.

The woman cried out. A really painful sob—nothing in the world would heal her pain. I did it again, short, and the noise was quicker, more like a bleat.

"You wanna play with the door or talk to me?" Teddy said.

"Uh-huh, I'm here." He was flexing up, getting ready for me, twisting his neck and shoulders and arms.

"I ran into Jimmy Charny the other night at Hooligans."

"Yeah, what were you doing way up there?" I tried leaning against the wall, I tried folded arms, nothing worked. I was a wreck, with sweat in a thin sheen under my arms. A cold breeze made its way up the staircase and I shivered.

"I get around, Kelly. I'm old but I can still drink. He says you met with him a while back—you know, let me stop here. Do you know what he's been up to?"

I shook my head, no. Teddy rubbed his temples with his left hand. The skin on top of his head went up and down.

"He's talking some shit about you. He says that you're the sucker. You don't want that problem. You should know better than to hang around with a loser like that, like you could ever trust that guy. Speaking of which, trust is a bitch. When it falls apart, you can't put it back together."

"I guess I know that," I said. But I didn't really. I just wanted him to hurry up. "What's your point?" I asked.

"My point? Miracle doesn't trust you anymore, 'cause we've heard too much, so this is your last job for us."

A door opened below us and I looked down the shaft and watched a meaty hand hold onto the banister and move down the stairs. My chin trembled a bit.

"You're not firing me for stealing, are you? 'Cause you have no proof, you never saw me take anything off a job."

He watched me. His black eyes were sad. He tapped me, hard, on the chest.

"Yeah. This isn't court, stupid, this is the working world. Felix is gone, too."

"You have to tell him. I won't."

"I already did."

"He's got a family, Ted."

"We all got families."

You don't, I thought.

"He knew it was coming," Teddy said. "He didn't say anything, but if I was him, I'd be pissed at you. He was here before you, and he was fine, you both were, before you got to acting like you do now."

"So, this is over right? I'm fired. Our conversation is done?"

"Yeah, it's done. I just wish—you could be such a good guy, Kelly Minter, you got good in you." He reached up and hugged me, but I couldn't hug him back.

"If you need anything, I can help you, stay at my place if you want, if that's what you need—only you got to understand, the world doesn't owe you shit, you got to get that."

He let go of me then, but I hadn't heard him. All I could think was that he'd fired me. He turned from me, opened that crying door. I wondered why everybody who was older than me, who I looked up to, turned out so cowardly in the end.

"That's fine," I said. "Every time one of you bastards pushes me away, that only frees me up a little more, to do what I have to do."

"Yeah, that's generally what guys like you say," Teddy said. He went out in front of me, and didn't try to look at me again. But for me it was true. He fired me. I was that much more free.

Truly, I was worried about Felix a whole lot more than I was worried about me. His only other job prospect was through Lynanne, who knew of a job shoveling coal for a school in her district. I'd heard them talk about it one night when they thought I was asleep. The job sounded like pure pain, like a punishment worthy of Greek myth or the Old Testament. There was a coal delivery once a month, and you spent each day eating away at the mountain, filling the furnace, with ten-minute breaks every three hours. It was a job from a hundred years ago and they couldn't find anyone who would do it, but it had benefits and health insurance and a retirement plan.

Lynanne wanted him to take it. I believed that it would kill Felix long before he made it to forty.

I was fired, so there was no need to wait around. But there was also nowhere I had to be. The apartment wouldn't be ready until the next day. There was nowhere . . . It was an amazing feeling, not having a perch in Manhattan, owning up to having nowhere. I walked some downtown blocks in the cold and then bought a copy of *Time Out*, which was supposed to tell me what was going on in New York. I read it on the subway. It was cold in that subway. You could breathe and see your breath.

And then I thought of the money and all that I needed to do way uptown. I was just upset enough to go back. I thought how it wasn't fair that I couldn't be at my perch. That money was still there. I believed it was there the same way you believe, no matter how far you go from where you grew up, your house is still standing, and your family still lives there, and they're waiting for you to come home.

I got out and switched to the uptown 2, to the shuttle at Forty-second, to the 6. All the time I kept thinking, Bad day is gonna feel better now, over and over till it was a chant. If I had a musical bone in my body it would have been a song and I would have sung it aloud on the train. Only it would have sounded terrible, 'cause of my lack of a musical bone.

I fingered my keys as I walked over to my building. There was nobody around, it was five in the afternoon and plenty cold enough to keep everybody who had the option inside, and besides them, the schoolkids were home and those who worked were still at it. I kept at my chant. I did a very for-real jackrabbit up the stairs and got to my door and had my keys in and the door opened before I caught my breath. I wanted to look at that view, to check for that yellow light and to look at all that was forbidden one more time before I embraced it, lived in it, took my very own piece of the action.

My apartment was empty. No answering machine, phone, chairs, card table, bed, bookshelf, photo of Cass, clothes, fridge, twenty-five thousand in the ceiling, nothing. All that was left was dust balls, toilet paper, a shower curtain mussed with soap scum, the scuffs on the windowsill where I'd spent a year with my feet up—that's it. I'd seen loads of apartments and this had always been the fun part for me, where Teddy would say, "Go check around," and me and Felix would go up and make sure that the place looked exactly like this, filled with nothing that could conceivably be worth anything and we'd get the satisfaction that came with knowing that we had sucked the very life out of a room. I had been moved out.

I stepped out into the hallway. The very last of the day's sunlight came down through the open doorway that led to the roof, and so did the cold wind, so it was easy to feel sucked out, frozen out. I could hear people come and go on the lower floors. I stepped across the hall—not stepped really, since there was only three feet of space—but moved. I knocked hard on my neighbors' door. My neighbor was some kind of electrician-handyman with two tiny kids whose limbs were only as thick as baby bamboo trees and a wife who always smiled, spoke no English, and was home nearly every hour of the day. I knocked hard on that door and it was the same door as I had and I felt it give. He answered it.

"What happened, where's all my stuff? You, goddamnit! You're supposed to protect me! What happened!"

The guy looked up at me and I could see how this was not a brand-new scenario for him, commiseration after an injustice being as common an act as prayer.

"It must have happened fast, 'cause I never saw anything. My family, they never saw anything, either."

"They had to make noise, you didn't hear all the noise?"

The guy just looked at me. His eyes said, I'm gonna put my ass on the line for your stuff? You've done so much for me, I'm gonna mess with some thieves when you haven't been around, when for all I know you could be dead? I nodded. We understood each other. I looked back into my place and wondered at that empty room, at a site I'd seen so many times before.

"Must have happened fast," he said.

I took a step back inside and opened my freezer. Empty.

I told him I was sorry I banged on his door.

"And I am sorry for your loss."

We shrugged at each other. This was what the world was like. You could expect no different.

"Only I was going to give it all away, all my stuff," I said.

He only shook his head. What did it matter? Right. Someday, we were all going to give all of our things away. Quiet, he stepped away from me and back into his apartment. I knew he would not invite me in, he did not want the stench of my loss on his things.

I stood in the doorway of my apartment and swung that door back and forth, back and forth, and listened to the ho-hum sound the door made, so different from the crying woman I'd met earlier. I wished I'd taken the time to get the money out of the ceiling and put it somewhere, anywhere else. But I hadn't.

I thought of Jimmy Charny, of his cheap contrivance, of the incredible lack of human dignity that allowed him to stand around on those streets, watch those people, and wait and wait, in the hopes of spying prey. It was clearly his work, what with dragging away the clock radio and every other bit of garbage . . . I had no doubt that he'd gotten the keys from a friend of his mom's. He knew all the damn supers. He knew everything, that I was staying with Felix, that I had money stashed, every damn thing. He'd even bragged about getting over on me to Teddy.

I went back in and looked out the window and there was a helicopter that looked like nothing so much as a massive fly. It hovered and then it did an incredible thing. It landed on the yellow light and blotted it right out, so the sky was only the deep blue of an early December dusk. This made a lot of sense, suddenly, since the light came from a helicopter pad on top of Metropolitan Hospital, which was just six blocks down from where I stood. Yeah, I'd never seen a helicopter land there before, or maybe, before, there was just no great benefit in looking. Fuck this place, I thought, hand-me-down dreams and all. I slipped down those stairs as quickly as I could. I made no noise, had nothing to carry. I said silent good-byes to the worn steel balls at the end of each banister. I stopped on Luz's floor, and put my hand on the wall of her apartment. I could feel her family in there, and her, and I wanted to go in so bad, but I did not want them to see me like I was then. And I knew Ocides was not going to understand me. I kept going down.

Of course Luz was on the street, coming toward her building with a bag full of groceries and a knapsack on her back. She was still in her life, doing her routines. The only wrong illogical surprise thing for her was me. I stared at this young woman on the street and I thought, Did you ruin me? I came toward her, moving fast. Maybe I had tears in my eyes. I was certainly in my moving outfit, and I looked the same, but I was far gone, where my life of only a few weeks before felt like a strange place I'd visited on a day trip in high school.

"You can't be here now!" she said. Her voice was fast and urgent.

"Did you help him? You did this to me?" I asked, and I ran.

And I was afraid and I prayed that I was wrong. I was desperate and just a little too far from believing what I hoped was the truth, that she only loved me, and when she looked after me, as I continued to run, as I looked at her face again, her eyes were only wide with love and desperation and shock. How would we ever be together, if each time we found each other was a bad surprise? She could not have helped him. But her building reeked of betrayal and I ran away from her. A white man running through the streets of Spanish Harlem at dusk. Only the smallest children turned to watch me go.

3 0

I looked for Jimmy Charny. No one had seen him. His mother wouldn't answer the door. I spent the early morning asleep on the subway and I woke up in the train yards in Queens. I got up and went back down to where I could find him, to the Upper East Side bars.

In Hooligans I told the bartender who I wanted. In the Wicked Wolf I did the same. Neither of them said much about it. Probably a lot of people were looking for people, and what's more, quite a few were looking for old Jimmy Charny, the wanna-be thief, the messy mover, the rotten motherfucker. I walked out of the Wolf and over to Lexington. And then, suddenly, I saw the back of his head. A little dented in maybe, under a Mighty Ducks hat, with his keys swinging at his waist and his bad-fitting greasy jeans ending up all rumpled at the top of his fake Timberlands. Jimmy Charny. He was headed up Lexington and I fell into step behind him. It was bright out; winter sun bleached the street. I wanted him inside, where we wouldn't be blinking, fighting against anything but each other. He had a lot of money that he needed to admit he owed me, and I also thought it would be good if a bunch of people saw that. So I followed him up to Hooligans nice and slow, and I took some small savor in watching him perform his snarling love affair with women, only to have them ease away without focusing on him. If they perceived him at all it was only with disgust.

He stepped into Hooligans and I followed him. The room was dark. I stopped for a moment to wait for my eyes to adjust, and for my pulse to cool. Then I came up behind him and put my hand on his shoulder. I used a firm grip, a confidence hold. He turned slowly, saw me, and still told the bartender he wanted beer—a prelunch Budweiser—said, "Make it two." I kept my hand on him.

"Hey, hey, Martin Kelly Minter, the young gentleman," he said. Not concerned to see me in the least. I figured he was high, or had simply forgotten who he'd stolen from, what, when, where.

"How you been?" he asked.

"You're a thief." I kept my voice down low. My brow felt thick above my eyes.

"No shit. We all are, and you, you, too, right?" He laughed.

"But you ripped me off, you emptied my place."

Jimmy Charny only smiled.

"News to me. I didn't do it," he said.

We had moved from the bar itself to the middle of the floor. We watched each other: Him all thick wire covered with scruffy cat skin, eyes like dirty nickels. I had my hands at my sides, my bottle of beer twitching. He gripped my wrist, stared at me hard, and took the bottle from me.

"You—" I said.

"Let me tell you a story," he said. "Sit down over here." He guided me over to a booth in the way-back, where only the full-form regulars were allowed to sit. He turned on his side and put his feet up, and I could hear his breathing level off, the pain that his body had begun to give him.

"Make it quick, I got—"

"You got nothing, Kelly, nothing just now, okay? No places to be or nothing. What if we fought and I shot you? There's guns in this city, like anywhere, and some of them are pointed at you. I know this. Things go bad you'll be two blocks up in Mount Sinai on a gurney, so relax, 'cause we're just talking, and you're in no rush. 'Course I understand that being who you are you don't like to stay in one place for a long time, but here you're okay. For a little while, anyway," and he laughed. "Who stole from you? Kelly, you tell me."

I felt pinprick itches on my ribs, but I did not touch them.

"Who else had the keys, dick?"

"Don't you talk to me—"

"Come on, Kelly, you're a bright boy, who could go right in and take? I didn't know you had anything at home. You live on the sixth floor, that's a lot of work for an old guy like me." He stopped and looked around the bar. I watched him, like he was going to point a bad guy out.

"This is sad, watching you deny what you know. It's like when women get hit. You know who does it. Not strangers, it's always the guys they love. Same thing with theft. People steal from who they know. That's how they get caught. Which is also why you've had a good run below the borderline, 'cause you're white, but you're such a complete fucking stranger. Now who did you?"

"You're not saying Luz did this to me."

"Who's Luz? Your woman? I don't even know her. What guy would have done this to you? Come on, boy, think."

I ran my fingers along the grooves in the old table. He was in no rush. I was only an added attraction, some extra heartbeats in an otherwise dead quiet midday.

"Felix," he said. "And maybe this Luz, she helped him. Somebody had to. That's the way things work, simple like that."

"He didn't do this to me, he wouldn't. I know him. And forget Luz. She didn't do it, either."

"Oh, you know them so well? You're the authority on people, I didn't know that. I'm telling you facts here."

"You're a fucking liar," I said. I grabbed the bottle and moved to punch him with it, but he moved, and then all I did was smash that bottle against the other side of the booth. Immediately—it was like gripping noise, wild loud music, old metal, Led Zeppelin in my palm—I felt the glass. Three guys were on me, pulling me out of the booth. Jimmy helped.

Then it was like in a movie. The whole bar was screaming. Everything was funny, gaping throats, jaws stretching out to me, Jimmy Charny getting nothing but laughs off what I'd done, even as I was walked and back-stepped out of Hooligans. I called Jimmy a fucking liar again. In the chaos of blurry streetlight, I believed myself. My hand was bleeding, still filled with unspeakable music, blood all over the front of my coat, and there I was, unable to use my eyes to see, in the freezing cold.

Jimmy came up in front of me.

He said, "You go find your old friend, ask him what he did. You're getting to be a good story, Kelly. I can't wait to find Teddy and tell him about this."

I looked up at him.

"You're bleeding," he said. "You're a mess."

"Just you wait and see," I said.

I cradled my screaming icy hand and walked downtown. I looked around and then I knew one more thing: It was Friday, and my apartment was ready.

I went to a sports store and bought myself a sleeping bag and a plastic pillow, jeans, some T-shirts that said Fila on them. I'd chosen the ones with the brightest colored designs.

"Should I bring up the things you stored in the basement?" Todd asked. He kept looking at my hand. It was wrapped in a new shirt, but it was painful and ugly-looking and I knew I had to deal with it.

"Just leave everything down there for now," I said. "I'm not ready for any of that yet." Todd shrugged and I went upstairs.

I fumbled with the keys and when I finally got that big solid wood door open it was . . . weird. Again, again I felt like a visitor, an interloper! I gnashed my teeth against the feeling, pulled off the shirt, and put my hand against the wall, left a warm mark there, a smudge, and I was still a stranger. The day wasn't bright and I couldn't find the light switch and I walked about in the dark and measured shadows. The carpet in the bedroom felt so soft I thought it was alive. I spread out my sleeping bag, and finally found the lights—they were all on dimmers and I turned them on and kept them way down low.

I crept upstairs and that fat empty belly was an exhibition space, a vacant museum hall that happened to contain a kitchen area. I noticed a smell that was entirely new to me. It was the smell of a room without dust, of cleaning products used so effectively that attention is drawn only to whatever in the room is actually meant to smell. I thought, If I bring in some flowers, that would do something cool. I looked down at my clothes and I knew I had to be out of them. I took them all off. I threw them on the floor and they lay there, all heaped up and looking like dung. A small white plastic garbage can underneath the sink slid out on rollers when I opened the door. I threw those rotten clothes away.

I turned off all the lights and touched every part of that place in the dark. It had begun to rain. I looked up through the skylights and watched the lit-up drops as they came down and hit, and then I crept out to the balcony overlooking all those gardens and I lay out on the point and felt the rain hit my skin. It was freezing out there, though, and I was back inside in five seconds. I washed my hand in the sink and wrapped a sock around it. Even I could tell that I had to get it sewn up. So, though I didn't want to, I called my brother, Kevin.

"Hello, Kevin? Yeah, it's me. Listen, I hurt my hand, and I need to come and see you, okay?"

"Yeah, I've only been fucking calling you for weeks! Your answering machine is broken, did you know that? And you don't work for any real estate company, either—what the hell?"

"Yeah, I'll tell you about it. Listen, I'll meet you at the hospital tomorrow. You gotta clean up my hand."

Then I called Wyt. I left a message on his voice mail and did my best to keep it in some garbled code.

I said, "So I'm all set up and you can call me at that number and I'd be psyched to see you."

"You got any menus down here?" I was with Todd, downstairs, and it was late enough for dinner, but just as I was afraid to be in the building, I was afraid to leave it.

"I got this one, Ah Unataka."

"What?"

"Japanese—it's good. Get the zensai, some other stuff. Only you got to order a lot to get full. It's not like regular food."

I took the menu.

"You have to sample, like, I used to be a busboy at Cafe des Artistes, on the West Side? Investment guys would come in there, order five, seven entrees, each, and then just taste them, a couple bites of each, until they were full." He cocked his head. I could see him thinking about that, a tough image of excess lodged in his head.

"What did they do with the rest?"

"Send it back. We'd eat it sometimes, steak, liver, fish, from the other side of the plate. It always made me a little bleary, though, to do that."

"I'll bet. But really, they didn't mind all the waste?"

"Are you kidding?" He laughed. "I thought you'd be into that story," he said. He still didn't know who I was really, or what I was doing there. And we hadn't become friends. He was an operator, who I could tell was not alert because of his job but because he was thinking of all sorts of other things.

"You want anything?" I asked.

"Nah, I bring meatball heroes from home that my mom makes me."

I was on the phone. "Give me, just give me one of everything on the menu. Except no repeats, nothing that's the same."

"Yes?"

"Yeah, tasters plate or something, one of everything. Don't hold back. I'm having a party."

They confirmed my address. I sat on the floor then, waited the twenty minutes. I was so fucking hungry I could barely think. I mean—I had to get so full. I looked around the belly, and up, at the shining dark blue sky that was above me. I was so hungry and lonely.

The food arrived in white cake boxes, light, square balloons. Todd helped the delivery guy bring it all up.

"You must be having quite a party," Todd said.

"Uh-huh. You want any pieces before I get started?"

He shook his head, gave me half a smile, and went back down.

There was a step stool in a cabinet next to the sink. I got it out and put it in the middle of the room. I opened up each box and the dishes had little tags on them. Oshokuji, sashimi, Spanish mackerel, sakizuke, the zensai, sunomono, matsutake, roasted duck, jellyfish and shark fin, lobster, abalone, giant clam, squid, marinated beef tongue, quail, and then, in its own wooden box, Kobe beef. The beef did taste good—it was worth the eighty dollars. Assorted little extras, shumai, satay, kukiwakame, some vegetables. Plus tip, a $950 meal. I stared at it all and it was like good art, hypnotic, fresh, rich, intense.

I closed my eyes and opened my mouth, took deep breaths. I am not afraid. I can take all of this in.

I sat on the stool and the stuff was spread out in front of me, each thing on top of its white pillow box. I got down, grabbed something, and got back on the stool to eat it, like Cass's seal. I ate the big clam first, because it was the scariest thing I'd ever seen. Then I varied: duck, fish, meat, meat, fish fish fish . . . It kept going and I drank Sapporo beer and came down off the stool to snag something, and then climbed back up. Time got a little slow and funny. I'm gonna get fucking full now, I thought. I won't be so hungry anymore. The colors on the white were brighter than oil paint, the pinks, yellows, deep red and brown meat, shining translucent green seaweed, oily doughy shumai, and so clean! The food I ate was always dirty. This food was so clean that I could look at it in the bright light. As I moved along I began to hold it up to my eyes before I put it in me.

I ate fat pieces of bright red toro belly tuna with my fingers. I kept eating. And then the light white boxes were cascading around in front of me and the beer bottles all fell over and the phone rang and I did what I'd been looking for. I fell off the stool.

I don't know how long I lay there, but it couldn't have been too long. The phone stopped. I stood up. There were still some big mushrooms on one of the boxes and I shoved those in, along with some jellyfish that I didn't really like, and a bit of tongue, which was so good. Everything was done—fourteen main courses and who knew how much else. I got some warm clothes on and walked out of there.

"You okay?" Todd asked.

"Oh, fuck yeah! That shit was good! Thank you!" My belly was jerking me around, through the front door, down the steps.

"You're sure you're okay?"

But I was already gone, stumbling around out on the street, headed toward the park. It was all in me then, so now I knew what that was like and that was good. My eyes were brimming with it, all that perfect color and texture brought from the sea and the whole world over, all of it in me. I never did go in the park and throw all that shit up! I never did!

3 1

Kevin hustled me in through a back entrance at St. Vincent's, so I wouldn't have to pay for treatment. We went into a white room with a sink and a bed with a piece of white paper over it. He had to spend some time cleaning out the cut. It wasn't good. He sewed stitches from the bottom line in my palm that the fortune tellers read all the way to the base of my thumb. He kept dabbing at me. He kept saying it'd be over in a second, just like they trained him to do.

"So how ya been?" he asked.

I didn't say anything. My brother's face was close to me, closer than it'd been since I could remember.

"You want to tell me what's going on?" he asked.

"You look lousy," I said.

His eyes were bleary and he hadn't shaved, so the normal expanse of his face was even larger, what with all the stuff to look at.

"Yeah, out last night with my fellas to this place on Amsterdam Avenue, drinking all these pints of Pilsener, then was up straight through the night getting better acquainted with this cute Fordham law student." He laughed a little, but he still didn't look comfortable. He went and found a white pad and put it on my palm, and then he got some gauze, and started to wrap it around my hand.

"Thanks," I said. The bandage was the same color as my skin.

"Yeah. Listen, I called the movers but they said your butt was gone, so I called Sutherland Properties, 'cause I figured you actually got that job, but they said I had it wrong, that you'd rented some place from them. That doesn't make sense to me. They're a high-class operation. What are you doing, Kelly?"

"Well . . ."

"What?"

"Promise you won't get pissed at me?" And I couldn't believe I'd said that! Like we were children together and I'd stolen his latest *Playboy* and then forgotten it somewhere, left it out, and it had disappeared, been confiscated by our parents. Promise? What the hell were promises?

"I fixed your fucking hand for free, I'm your brother, aren't I? I'm not gonna get pissed at you."

He was washing his hands in the steel sink, slowly, with that smelly medicine soap they use in hospitals. I was still sitting on the bed, my bandaged hand in the air.

"I—look, just listen and don't get pissed. I stole a bunch of money—not stole—I took some stuff and made some deals and now there's a whole bunch of money that's being held in my name. I could get some of it and you could invest it for me! It's a chunk, I swear! I did it in a safe way, though, I'm not gonna get caught, and you should see this place I got. We could have dinner there! I like all that shit you like, Kevin, I swear, I could take you to Harry's! They know me there, I think. That's what you like, right?"

"Where? What are you talking about?" He turned off the water. I watched him slap his cold hands on his neck. He still looked a little off. But he was my brother!

"Don't fuck with your fat old brother," he said. "I must be much too hung to be hearing you clearly."

"I'm not! I did some stuff, and I thought it was, that I was gonna share some money, and I am, but also, I mean, I've got money now, I'm okay now!"

I had his attention. He went and pushed the door, made absolutely sure it was closed.

"Who knows about this?" he asked.

"Well, nobody, really."

"Does Felix know?"

"Yeah, I mean, me and him—"

"Fuck. Just like when you were kids. What a shit influence!"

"Hey, it wasn't him. It was me, I swear!"

"Fuck!" He was shaking his head back and forth. "You should never have been allowed to drop out of school, fucking Mom and Dad, letting you do what you like!"

"You don't think it's cool?" I asked. I didn't mean that, though, exactly, I just meant, you know, that I was trying. I flexed my fingers back and forth. When I did that, I could still feel ice-cold pain in my palm.

"Don't move. And don't move your hand, either, you messed up some nerves in there—they'll heal, but just leave them be. I'm going to go take a piss. Then I'm gonna call Mark Festinger. He's in the DA's office now. Maybe you remember him from Bridgehampton, this summer, the guy who wore a bandanna all the time. I'll call him. Don't tell me anything else! Don't tell me what you did!"

"You don't think it's cool?"

He only stared at me.

"No. No, I don't think it's cool. I never thought you and Felix hanging around together in the forest for two summers was cool and I didn't like watching Cass drop your ass out of school and I don't think this is cool, either. Give me about thirty seconds now."

Yeah, I thought, thirty seconds to speed out the back door.

I found Felix at a playground hard by his house, Frazier playground, recently rebuilt by the city. It was afternoon and forty-four degrees, the way New York gets sometimes in December, where it almost feels like the city will skip winter, and then there's snow that night, and warmth again the next day. In New York, even the weather doesn't have proper control over itself. I came up and sat down next to him and he looked me over without showing his face. He was hunched a little bit, with his arms folded.

"What did you do to your hand?" he asked. We looked at my bandage.

"I got all upset, Felix, when I heard some stuff. I broke a bottle."

"What did you hear?"

"You tell me," I said. "You tell me what I heard."

But he only spat down on the concrete and didn't say anything. Anastasia played on a slide in front of us. There must have been twenty kids on the slides and cheap jungle gyms, and around the perimeter of the park there were benches. We sat next to the teenagers with their pit bulls and cigarettes, lots of leather on them, expensive sneakers, and headphones not on their ears but on their temples, so beat pulsed on their heads. They had babies in carriages with them. Old people were there, too, old faces pointed toward the sun, talking quietly to each other, backing away when the children came too near.

"You come any closer to that janitor job?" I asked.

"You mean down in a basement? Shoveling coal into a furnace?" Felix looked at me.

"Yeah, right, that one."

"That's a job I would never take," Felix said.

In a corner of the park, near a fence, an Asian woman went through a series of stretching exercises that might have been tai chi: slow, methodical, oblivious to those around her.

"You think she gets exercise doing that?" I asked.

"You think I'm a fucking dummy?"

"Wha-at?" That's just how I said it, too, with broken syllables. Felix turned to me and he had on a real scowl, a narrow-eyed expression, teeth bared.

"You think I'm so stupid I'm gonna shovel coal? I'm gonna do a job that's fit for a beast?"

"No, Felix, I just—"

"Listen, just 'cause you made yourself disappear into the middle of the East Side so you can be the master thief doesn't mean—"

"Hey—"

"Doesn't mean I'm gonna rot without your dumb ass. I'm not stupid. You think I am, but not so, not so—I took my piece of the deal and now I'm finished. You're headed bad, and I'm finished with you."

I watched him. I saw his eyes flash out at me, their brown all of a sudden alive, as if there were an electric current in him, like I'd shorted him, shocked him. I couldn't remember really seeing his eyes since we'd battled in the woods, a dozen years before. His face was ugly, and, I think, so were his eyes, all tired and angry and hooded. It was amazing that Anastasia had turned out so cute and normal-looking. He had stolen from me. He had. He had emptied my apartment and now he felt free to look at me, to stare. I'd come to him to be sure the way a lover says, "I know you hit me, I know. But if I come back, are you sure you will not hit me again?"

"Kelly, it's time to stop thinking you're the shit, you missed out on a lesson or two already, my friend, you missed a couple steps along the way. So don't tell me about some prehistoric coal shoveling job. I took my piece and I'm done. I know you're going big, but I got all I need. Me and Lynanne are going to start our own school, a kindergarten. I already signed up for college classes for the fall, long-term goals, man, I got them, you don't. You think you can steal forever?"

"I—how did you get so angry with me?" My voice was all dropped down.

"Because I kept thinking on what we were doing, and I finally saw how this wasn't about me and you. You got to clear up some shit. Man, you were just using me. It wasn't ever about doing right, and still that's the way I'm going. Not you, though. You're just one of them."

We were both quiet then, on the bench.

"You bastard," I said.

"Yes, I am," Felix said. "Yes, I am a bastard. And you fucked that up for me, too. You did a big ruining thing to me, and then you hid it away."

"You knew about that?"

"Sure, I knew for years and years."

"I'm so much more than sorry for that," I said. I put my hands on my face. A mistake like that—my mother changing her mind, and Felix cheated out of a long life with me in Rantipole Farms—it was so huge, and it had all gone wrong because I wanted to be a thief in the night.

"Yeah, it's late for apologies and I don't need them anyway. That's not what went wrong between us. If anybody taught me to steal, it was you, and all I'm getting is payback. My family will get strong, my daughter, my wife. We're getting stronger. Anastasia wants to keep playing, I can see that, why don't you go?"

"You did it alone?" I asked.

"Me and Dennis. I told him the deal. That money was all I wanted. Get yourself straight, try not to hurt anybody while you're at it."

Faces are their own until they've done some years of hard work, and then soon after that, they are what the owner makes of them. So older people, people who have seen a few things and have expressions that are all wrapped up in anger and hatred? Those people really are that way. I looked at Felix's face and that is what I saw, all that hungry anger, turned around and punched into me, every cynical bit and tragic understanding that I had somehow refused to take in, had come and settled with him. I looked at him and thought, Why shouldn't he steal from me? I would.

But he had not mentioned Luz. I was afraid to ask if she knew about what he did. I'd run from her, neglected her. It was possible that she knew, that she helped him. I didn't move.

"How can we be brothers?"

Felix looked up at me, and again he stared. For so many years he'd looked away when I looked at him. But now things were changed, he could stare me down, and he did, he looked at me hard and I looked away, across the playground to Anastasia, who was deep in play with two other girls.

"I watch you get so tempted by money. You took the tiny few lessons we learned together and turned them all twisted and wrong. I'm not your brother. Kelly, here's how I see it. We shake hands and it's all dead serious, but we shake across a table, see, a table that's all beautifully set up in some restaurant. We have to reach across to shake. I look away, you grip my hand so much tighter, and you pull and you flip me onto the table. There's wineglasses there, forks, knives—all that shit breaks and rips right into me, into my ribs, and you're strong, you pull me back and forth, breaking more shit, all of it, the food, the plates, the fucking water glasses, all breaking and sticking me, tearing my belly, my neck, and I'm screaming and you won't fucking let go! You show up at my house with food and I see the worst devil at my door. You want to take me down with you, just like when we were kids. I'm not going to let it happen. We are not brothers."

We weren't looking at each other, were both just looking into the dirt, with our arms around ourselves and our hands holding our sides, holding ourselves together, but apart from each other.

"You know what they say?" I asked.

"What's that?"

"The way you see others is—that's the way you see yourself. What you would do to me?"

A bus pulled away and its exhaust shot up and cut across the cold blue sky. The kids kept playing, concentrating on their fun.

"Maybe so," Felix said.

"'Bye, Ana!" I yelled. She looked up and smiled, waved to me. I jingled my keys in my trousers pocket.

"Don't hurt that girl," Felix said.

"Luz?"

"She's your heart now, all you'll ever have. You been warned." He was already looking away, watching his beautiful daughter.

"Teddy will rehire you," I said.

"He already did. He just needed to cut us in half. It's me he cares about, not you."

I stood up.

"If it weren't for my child and my wife"—he dropped his voice—"I'd kill you myself. That's how much I hate what you've become."

"You'll see. You're afraid, just like my parents. I'm going to make things good and I'm only half the way there."

"I thank God your parents sent me away. They taught you wrong and they know it. Maybe Luz can save you. Maybe not. But I'm finished. If your family taught me anything, it was when to go."

I left the playground and made sure to stay on the cobblestone walk so the dirt and sand didn't scuff my brown suede shoes.

———————

Felix with my father in our garden, dusk on a hot day in the middle of July. Felix helped pick vegetables for dinner while me and my brother lay out on the floor in the living room and played Nintendo. That first summer Felix was real quiet except for when he asked why things were the way they were.

"How do you know when tomatoes are ripe to pick?" he asked my dad.

"Well, there's the color, when they're a good red, or just before that, because they can get too ripe if you leave them off the vine . . . after a while you just know, like you know the difference between right and wrong." This was the kind of thing my father loved to say, real general, not too helpful, and subject to wide interpretation.

"I don't understand your dad," Felix said, when we got ready to go to sleep.

"Nobody does. He doesn't even."

"If you go with what he says, the whole world knows what's right, but most of the whole world only does what's wrong."

"I dunno," I said. "Me and him don't go out in the garden together."

I didn't understand my father or Felix then, and I don't now.

Of course, a lot had happened since then. I'd stopped talking to my dad, and I hadn't eaten fresh vegetables since me and Cass cooked together in Brooklyn before the days of margaritas and no dinner at all.

But my dad had said it, and me and Felix were still trying to get it right. How do you know the difference between right and wrong? You just know. And if you don't know? Everything becomes less than fair. Everything goes wrong.

3 2

I walked down the street and I thought: You don't see straight. You miss things. You don't pay attention. I thought, You have that vision problem where there's black rectangles that block the parts of life you need to understand. I thought, Fix this problem. Find Luz.

I beeped Jahaira from a pay phone. This time, she called back.

"Don't come anywhere near here. It's a bad time now," she said. It was the first time I'd ever heard tension in her voice.

"We know about your apartment, everybody does. And they think it's about payback and drugs and all that. So if you come back here—everybody wants to hurt you."

"Why?" I asked.

"Because my father and everybody, they say you brought disrespect on the building."

· "What does Luz say?"

"I don't know."

"Tell her I'll send for her."

"I don't know if she'll come to you anymore. All I can say is you have to stay away from here, for now. And you should know—they're looking for you."

So there was nowhere I could be in New York. It was not yet time for the theft, and I didn't feel safe lying low in that apartment. It felt like that was a place that people knew about, where I could be found. I knew that Cass was in Vermont, and that she'd take me in. No one would ever think to look for me there.

So I went down to Port Authority. I called Cass and bought a bus ticket. I went to Manganaro's Hero Boy, where I had a couple of beers and some rice balls, and an eggplant parmesan hero. I ate until my head was buzzed, dulled with food and beer and heavier than just drunk. I thought: Weigh yourself down, make yourself heavy, so you can't think.

I saw this Greek or Turkish store, where they had all these troughs, or round bins, all filled with different dried goods. That's what it was, a dried goods store, all bins of dried rice, beans, pasta, spices, fruit, anything that would sift through your fingers and was dry, they had it. It all looked exotic as hell, and I went in and breathed, all those combating smells like some crazed jungle torn out of heaven, and I bought pounds of everything. Dates, almonds, white rice, chocolate-covered peanuts, cumin, pepper, thick sugar-coated lengths of pineapple, pumpkin seeds, salted green peas, lentils.

I was full. But I was still so incredibly hungry. I was buying, I couldn't stop buying. I bought soap, too, Greek soap that was sea green and felt like sandstone, and a bag of short pencils that was on the counter and on sale, $2.95. There was dried beef to my right—I bought five pounds. The man at the counter was bald and he wore a greasy blue shirt and a colorless vest that had once been velvet. He did all the adding, all the plastic bags of different-colored stuff piled up between us, and he came up with a round number, $220, shrugged at me, and smiled. I paid him and went out onto Ninth Avenue, really weighed down now, both arms dragging everything in the world I didn't need. There was the sharp burning city sunlight that did nothing to warm me. I thought, That's okay. I'll be gone for a while.

I stood, struck dumb under the big overpass that services Port Authority. I looked in at the homeless drop-in center that always feels like the real waiting room for the bus station.

I went in there and some old lady said, "Can I help you?" I reached into my big bag.

"No—I just bought too much groceries. Let me give some to you."

She was the kind of lady who knew that it was easier to just let me do what I had to do than to point out that we were not in a dona-tion center, that they didn't accept donations, even. She probably had kids of her own, and she told them the same thing I got told, always help out others, no matter what, otherwise you go bad quick. So she understood. I scrambled through the big brown paper shop-ping bag filled with different pounds and I came to the rice and pulled it out, got back up, handed the pound to her.

"Thank you," she said.

"Take this, too." I handed her a pound of gold foil–covered chocolates.

"These are very nice," she said. I got out of there really fast, pushed on the grimy glass door and ran out and across Ninth Avenue. It was a rush situation, is what I'm saying. If I couldn't see Luz, I needed to leave town very badly.

There were only five or six people in line for the Vermont Peter Pan bus, and I waited with them. Hippies, a few of them, and some older people. A few others came up and then the Peter Pan people boarded us, easiest thing in the world, and it felt like a big deal, like we'd all been served a pardon.

The driver got up and made some announcements: Don't smoke. Cram your Walkman headphones up your butt, like that. Those old white drivers with their glasses and their sand-colored hair always look like the president of the United States. It's the oddest thing. We rolled out, up Tenth Avenue, along a strip of street that no president had ever seen and that I was sure I'd never miss.

Cass was waiting when I got out at Brattleboro. She was all beautiful and windblown and calm, the kind of woman who would look right at home at the Hi-Life, sipping red wine on a Sunday after a weekend in the country. Among my first thoughts was that she'd make a fantastic cover for a crime. Among my first thoughts was the realization that I had broken up with her, and I had sounded desperate and needy on the phone, and now I was interrupting the daily flow of her life, that, as opposed to me, she was placed there. I was entering her place.

"Hey, Kelly," she said.

"Cass."

I handed over all the pounds of food I'd bought.

"So heavy," she said.

She put the bags in the backseat, without looking to see what they all were. She didn't really care about what I had to give her.

I wondered if I was so handsome, or had been, when I'd first met her. If she was a perfect picture, a photo layout in a fashion magazine of what the great woman artist should be, then what was I? I stepped up to her, where she leaned against her car, one foot up, arms folded loosely, and I kissed her in the correct place, half on, half off the lips, intimate and friendly, soft red lips, warm skin. She smelled clean, scrubbed pure in a way that is impossible in Manhattan. We hugged each other and we were like a perfect thing, same height, proportions, a solid silhouette on strong shoulders, the kind of couple I'd moved and envied and robbed and hated. Her car was a Volvo station wagon from the mideighties that smelled of cut flowers and turpentine. When we were settled inside she tugged at me, unzipped my jacket.

"I missed you," I said.

"That's sweet of you to say," she said, and she smiled.

We moved through town at her pensive pace while other cars moved around us. It was a perfectly decent town, without major chain stores, but also not intentionally quaint. There were teenagers around, punked-out kids on skateboards doing everything they could to reject the 1840s converted farmhouses they'd been raised in. They were stoned and bored, those kids, not like me when I was their age. Where they were jaded, I was bewildered. Maybe I caught my breath then, as I watched them. Maybe I thought, It is too bad I met Felix. It is too bad my parents raised me like I was an experiment in civic duty. It is too bad, Cass, that I left school when you did, all because I was looking for something to hang on to.

"So you are in trouble?" she asked.

"Why do you say that?"

"You said you were in trouble when you called."

She turned and looked at me. We were at a red light, at the end of her town.

"I only meant that I needed to get away for a while, not that I was really in trouble."

"Oh. You're not in trouble then, it's okay. You look good."

"I don't know. I wasn't chased onto the bus. My rent is paid up. My money is safe . . ." I thought: You never, never tell yourself the truth. Why not be honest? I thought of Luz, lying on her bed, up against her window, looking out into the night.

"Kelly, what have you done?"

I was gripping the dashboard then, thick black vinyl over hard sponge, hot because of the sun through the windshield, but constructed as a forgiving substance. I thought: I have done nothing. Hold on to the dashboard.

"I haven't done anything. I did have some trouble though, with Felix."

"Felix . . ."

"My friend."

"Oh yes. I remember." But I could hear how she just enjoyed saying the phrase, how her dusky voice wrapped around words, made them mean less somehow, because so much depended on the fact that they sounded slow and beautiful. I thought, This is why I dropped everything for her the first time, because she is unrecognizable, because I could not know how much she understands. Because she was as remote as my parents.

"He robbed me. We had a partnership and he stole from me."

"What did he take?"

"Somebody else's money, and my bed, my clothes, like that."

"Do you care?"

"Not about the stuff, but him robbing me, it hurts."

"Theft. So much stayed green this winter, I don't know why . . ."

I did not turn to look at her. If she hadn't been listening, that would have made me feel impossible sad. I put my hand on her thigh and rubbed up and down, until I was close to the heat between her legs and I looked up at her and she was smiling.

We pulled off the main road and began to climb up a silent hill. There were low stone walls and old houses spaced far apart. You couldn't see their windows from the road, and this was so different than living just beyond the Rantipole Farms gatehouse in a cheap plywood-and-glass ski chalet that waved a limp hello to all the weekenders.

After a mile of climbing we arrived at a field that overlooked the town and the valley. There were three buildings sided with white wood, each with a roof made of vertical steel panels, so the snow could slide off. The panels meant that the buildings reflected light. For so much of the day, they glowed.

The kitchen had a big old table in the middle of it, with a bunch of chairs. We sat down. Cass had all the right stuff: wood cabinets, marble slab counters, a great variety of plates, pots and pans hanging from a rack over a big old Wolf stove, garlic and peppers swinging from hooks, and beyond all that there were pictures by other artists who loved Cass. Each picture was good, little thoughts, pirouettes on paper. Look at me! Look at what I can do! We stood there, watching each other, and being in the house didn't feel right at all.

She said, "Do you want to take a walk?"

I nodded yes and we went into the mudroom and put our coats on.

"What we'll do is take the path up the mountain, and when we get there you'll be able to see two valleys, then the walk down is nice, too, the sun should be just going down then, it takes about two hours. Really, it's beautiful."

"That sounds like it will feel good," I said. We went out of the house.

"What happened was, I tried to do a lot of things at once, and then I fell hard for this girl—"

"Oh yes?" she asked. Then I didn't see how I could tell her about Luz. I didn't want to talk about Luz with her. But Luz wasn't leaving my head. She pounded at me like she was the answer to a question I didn't have the fucking guts to ask. I kept thinking: You have taken so many chances! Go back to her! You love her! She will take care of you! Make things right. But I wasn't with her and I didn't understand that, how I was walking up a mountain in Vermont when I wanted to be with a woman in Manhattan.

I walked up the path behind Cass and felt the cold wind around us. I watched her step, not one foot in front of the other, but one foot around the other, Indian style? Smoother anyway, fleet foot.

"Not too cold?"

"Oh no," I said. But I was cold. The sky was heavy with dark streaks and clouds. In an hour it would be dusk and worse than freezing.

We kept climbing, another half mile to the top. Nature is nothing like New York. There is a real chaos to it, the way rocks roll under your feet and branches dip down low. We arrived at the top just as the sun dipped and hit mountains across from us and got all fiery and strong. It was beautiful up there, and it made the views of Manhattan I had in my head look like a cheap postcard, a flashy proposition.

"Do you know the Balthus painting, the mountain landscape?" I could only shake my head. I had long since sweated out any memory of art history.

"Well, this is like that," she said, "where you sit up here for just a little while and you feel like one of the chosen ones."

I thought, I have never felt that way. I have only ever felt the opposite of that. The pure privilege in such a feeling soaked into me like the sun itself, and I dabbled in it, and I did not like what I saw. Imagine us, though, imagine us just slightly above the rocks in a Vermont landscape in winter. I was desperate, sick with trying to understand why I was up there with Cass, when I didn't want to be there, like there was still something she needed to tell me, some question she needed to answer. We went back down the mountain and into the house and we stood, again, in the kitchen.

"Do you want to have dinner soon?" I asked. "Are you really hungry?" I stared at her. I'd been with her for so long, for so many nights, and I went to her and she held me. That house was so quiet, and in that way, not so unlike where I grew up.

"No, let's go upstairs," she said.

We went and climbed into her great big warm bed with its down blankets and quilts and sheets made of combed cotton. We took off our clothes and I still wasn't thinking straight or clear and I kept grabbing her, hugging her, and she was doing that, too, hugging, but then, it didn't stay that way.

"Come on, you can do it," she said.

"You want me to do it?" I asked.

Then it turned into something different, sex, a horse fuck, where I felt my whole midsection slide right up into her and the sweat under all that expensive bedding was slick to the touch. I did it and she was damned glad, she said, because she hadn't had any sex in quite a while, since the goddamned visiting poetry professor at Middlebury had gone back to New York. When we were finished she had a phone call in the other room that she had to take. I wanted dinner. I fucked her and I was still hungry and I wanted to get out of there and I loved Luz and that was that.

We ate chicken pot pies. We talked about art. She said things about her work that I could not follow. After I helped clean up the dishes from dinner we went into the living room and I built a fire. There were two big stuffed chairs and a green corduroy couch, arranged around a table in front of the fireplace. Lots of framed pictures on the walls—mostly drawings she'd traded for—and thick dark rugs on the floor.

Cass went out to warm up some apple cider.

"To complete the picture," I said.

I closed my eyes when she was gone. I put my fingertips on my eyelids and I felt warm, not tired, but burning. I got up and went to a tiny drawing she'd done of a man holding a lipstick, which was framed and not on the wall, and half hidden behind another picture. I tore the brown paper back of the frame with my thumbnail and worked the picture out of there. It was so small, signed, and it was me in the picture, a reproduction of one of the old sketches she used to do of me while I cooked for her. I went to the mudroom and slipped the little picture into the breast pocket of my coat.

Back in the living room I heard her say, "Listen real careful, okay?"

"Huh?"

We sat down close to each other on the couch. She had my hands in hers.

"I know, I know. I'll go back to New York in the morning."

"Yes, that's part of it, but—I feel so bad. I am sorry that your friend stole from you. I do remember how important he is to you."

Maybe the fire crackled a little bit. The cider was on the table in front of us. Cookies there, cinnamon sticks in the deep blue mugs.

"Maybe he was right to do it. I mean, I was good there, for a time, I had it all figured out. Then nothing I did worked."

"Nothing?"

"I think I'm in love with somebody. I don't know what's happening."

We watched the fire. She pressed her fingertips together.

"Kelly, listen, what happened earlier—sometimes when it's not love, what we were doing, repeating something, like our old intimacy. Well, sex gets that way, where that's all it is, is fucking."

"I didn't know," I said. But I looked at her and the moment she said it, then, I did know.

"I'm sorry. But I did need you to come here, to see you."

"It's more than that. I'm in trouble. I needed someplace to hide," I said. Her jaw set and I felt very bad. It was a hurtful thing to say. But it was so difficult to tell if she really cared.

"That's okay," she said, "that's okay. After all, I used you the same way."

"Is that what people do?" I asked.

"Some do, yes. But when somebody really loves you, they don't do that sort of thing to you, you should know that."

"That also. I didn't know that, either," I said.

"Maybe, maybe you don't know 'cause you never had anybody love you like that before, in that good way."

"You didn't?"

"Maybe I didn't, no."

Cass looked away. I knew enough to see that it wasn't me she was thinking about, but it was her, thinking over the way she knew how to love.

"I'm not in a position to give you any advice," she said. "I'm not going to give you any advice."

Then she was quiet and it didn't matter, because our visit was over. Luz was for me in my heart. I had to leave. I would have a child with Luz. Alfredo would grow older. He would have a younger sister or brother. We would be the finest family.

Cass went upstairs to sleep. I stayed by the fire until the morning, when she brought me back to the bus.

3 3

Then I had to be in my new apartment, because there really was nowhere else to go. I stayed there and waited. Felix's betrayal woke with me each morning and then stuck around for the day, like an unwanted and particularly vicious animal, like looking in the mirror and finding a nasty scratch on your face that only serves as a reminder that the other day somebody tore into you. I promised myself that I wouldn't think of him and that didn't work. I found that I thought most about what I wanted to forget.

I walked by that store, Decency, on Madison. I looked in and it was the place where my brother had wanted me to feel the nap. They had big winter coats in the window, now that it was December and freezing, and they were obviously at their price peak. But I went in anyway. I was still in Felix's army jacket. The salesman was less than comfortable until I took the thing off and showed how I was in a blazer and tie, just like everybody else. I finally settled on a full-length black cashmere coat.

When I was in it I disappeared. I looked darker than a shadow in an alley at night, outside a jazz club, with the smell of cool beats in the air, and somebody inside singing "Can't Help Lovin' That Man" while the shadow (me) pulls on a little reefer and holds it in, gripping an oily black gun, waiting for the manager who did my lady wrong to come out, so I can kill him. It was that kind of coat, rich, but with a black-leather sexiness to it, cut with a softness that made you want to strip naked and wear it inside out. I tried a new walk that was my own version of the pimp shuffle, a sauntering drag-step. In my new coat, it was fun. I bought it and went back out to the street. I felt great—lonely, but great. After a while I got tired of carrying around Felix's old army jacket, so I tossed it in a garbage can. And then I began to walk uptown, but I stopped.

Instead, I circled around the place on Park Avenue where the party had been, where the job was supposed to be. The day doorman was young, my age even, and he watched the street as if it were a game; that is, he was interested, he looked like he cared what was happening. The service entrance was on the side street, like normal, but there were three gates that I could see, and they were all buzzed gates. You had to say your name to somebody and they listened and you had to spell it out and then they checked you off a list and then and only then would they buzz you in. I watched a guy with a flower arrangement get buzzed in and buzzed out, and those buzzes were short. I felt an alertness around me, as if that street had had just about enough of me standing about watching. I remember walking away, head down and moving in a buglike scuttle, rushing to the noise and mess of First Avenue, nervous and alarmed at the idea that I had been asked to do a thing that perhaps I could not do.

The job was too difficult. It needed more than me. Serendipity and fortuitousness. I felt myself begin to depend on a forced luck. I realized that Wyt must know someone who could open the doors. But then, why would he need me?

After another day passed, when I couldn't stand it anymore, I went down to the Bar Boudoir to try to talk to Wyt, to get him to explain the crime to me, and hopefully, to speed it up, but he wasn't there. Nobody was. The hostess refused to tell me where Wyt and everybody else went; in fact, she got quite upset when I suggested that everybody actually had gone somewhere. Out of embarrassment, I ended up at the bar, where I ordered an eight-dollar glass of beer and looked at a copy of the *Post* that the busboy lent me.

It was afternoon, and the back windows let in gray slats of light that made the place look old. I could see particles of dust in the air and small rents in the fabric of the fat armchairs and I wondered about how much, just how much we deluded ourselves, as we stepped in and out of artificially lit spaces and convinced ourselves that yes, here, now, this was happening.

The newspaper had an article about a rich young girl who had a really good time at a new restaurant called O'Hara's the night before. She'd been dancing on the table when a waiter asked her to get down. She got upset and ran after the man with a steak knife. He had to wrestle the knife away from her. During the conflict, she slipped and broke her ankle. So she planned to sue. Another article told about a brothel that had just been shut down in Princeton, New Jersey. Some former real estate agent had been importing women from every corner of the world. But in that bar, it was quiet. I thought that perhaps all the rich kids, the new pimps, and the old real estate executives, maybe they were all asleep upstairs, phones ringing at their bedsides, while the people of the world rushed to give them more money.

"Phone for you, sir."

The bartender held out a black cordless phone. I pointed to my own chest, in that classic idiot move.

"For me?"

He nodded, all patient and long-suffering. I reached across and took the phone from him, and I couldn't help it, I looked sideways down through the bar doors, toward the street entrance, because I was afraid Ocides or somebody was going to come through that door and shoot me. The long look was nothing but nice, just a hotel lobby in the afternoon, transient and light as an A train gone express from Fifty-ninth to 125th Street.

"I'm here," the phone said.

"But Wyt—how did you know I was here?"

"I'm upstairs. They call me if anybody asks. Come up, room 808. But go to the bathroom first, please, let them forget your face."

So I tipped four on top of the eight, drained the glass, and went and pissed onto the wall of water they have in their bathroom. It's an astonishing thing, that wall of water. There were tons of articles about it at one point. We'd laugh about it in the back of the truck, about how drunks would walk into the trough at the bottom or lean their heads against the water, when really you were only supposed to pee on the wall. An eight-foot-tall black granite wall with water streaming down it. That's enough to make any buzzed guy take the plunge. I took my time, pissed in long streams against that fantastic piece of ingenuity.

Wyt had a room, not a suite. The walls were pale dove gray, so the room felt cloudy and nice. I looked around and everything was cleaned and polished and fluffed and untouched to the point where it looked as if Wyt had let the maid do her job around him and then hadn't moved. We sat across from each other in armchairs, with a low-slung steel table between us. Wyt poured us each a whiskey from a small bottle on the table and we sat there, both of us in suits, the fine light pink curtains drawn against the sun.

"You have been good?" he asked.

"Bad."

"Bad?"

"Lousy, I've been lousy. I'm stuck waiting to do a crime—"

"That last word is not a word that we use."

"Right, right. I'm sorry. I haven't been talking enough lately to remember . . . anyway, what about you?"

"My clients have hacked down my percentage to a tenth of whatever the piece did at auction, when it was last at auction, which has been both unbearable and untenable. I live here now."

"Cousin kicked you out?"

"Yeah."

"What about the TV and your stuff?"

"My things are stored. Your short bald foreman broke the set. Swore it was an accident, but I saw him drop it. 'Darn' was what he said. I'm finished with your company."

"So am I."

"And it is the holiday season."

"Don't mention it."

We sat there, and though we were both down, I know that we thought we looked pretty cool, so we didn't move. That is, two guys in suits, slumped in easy chairs with drinks in front of them, curtain as backdrop, both capable of moving large sums of money, where a stylist had looked us over and we could only have this conversation if we looked just exactly right. And what was at our base? I still didn't dare sniff and find out.

"You do realize that this job is a bit different?"

"Yeah, like impossible," I said.

"No. Never that," he said.

I could hear the sound of a vacuum cleaner in the hallway. That seemed so incongruous, like the maid should have known that now was talking time. I sipped the whiskey and felt a little high. Since leaving Vermont, I'd neglected to feed myself right. I'd eaten in sudden fits, but then I'd forget to eat after that, and this was frustrating, since I never felt full. So I'd grown thinner.

I jingled my keys in my pocket.

"I've got a problem," I said. "I'm in love and—"

"Don't talk to me about your love," he said.

"What?"

"It is enough. You work for me. I am not interested in your love. Go, wait for my call."

I got up from the chair. I'd forgotten that we were doing business. I'd forgotten that all over again.

"Remember—we do good work together. I am always thinking of what a useful partnership this is. I am pleased with it."

"Thank you," I said. He nodded at me and I walked out. In the hall I listened, because I wanted to hear what he would do now that I was gone. How does heartlessness behave? Does it turn on the TV? Yawn? Lie down on the bed? Do all that and then masturbate? But I couldn't hear anything and I didn't know what he was doing. Maybe the same as me, stock-still, silent, and afraid in the oddest sense, where you've forgotten what real fear is and something more like dread sets in, when you're not quite ready for the next thing to happen.

3 4

I was walking home the next night from a trip to buy soap and shaving cream on First Avenue. I looked up the length of my fine block and there was Luz. I moved faster toward her and she watched me. She didn't move at all.

If I could only have said then what I felt. There was an incredible, a true heartrending tug inside me, thankful, sexual, all overcome by unnameable fear.

She chewed gum and blew a round pink bubble, snapped it. She was dressed simply, in blue jeans and a black down coat. She had the collar turned up so it hid her jaw. The way she smiled fast, I was so sure she'd allowed her heart to speed up when she saw me, so though we were both still, and right up close to each other, we were moving.

I glanced up to my door and saw Nat, the night doorman. His cap was tipped way back and he watched the sky.

"You found me," I said.

She took my hand and then I embraced her, felt her waist, her ease with me.

"It took a while. I had to walk around until I saw you, then I followed you."

"How long—"

"A few days. But it's a little neighborhood. I knew where you'd be. Invite me up, I want to look at the view from here."

She went up the stairs ahead of me.

"Any mail for me?" I asked.

"No, sir," Nat said.

"Huh." There had been no communication from Tuck Golden's office that week. I meant to call, but it was so much easier to wait a day, and then another.

"'Night," we said, when the elevator came. Nat nodded at us. She was the first visitor I'd had. I believe he was pleased to know that I was suddenly not quite so alone in the world.

We went up together in the little elevator and I stood behind her.

"I'm sorry I ran from you," I said.

She turned around, looked serious. "Now I think it's best that you ran, you can't come into my neighborhood. You know that. What happened with your place showed my father he was right to do what he did with you."

"I understand."

We got out and I opened the door. We went into the bedroom. My sleeping bag was there, some folded clothes, some dirty things piled together on the floor, that was all. We stood and looked at each other.

"You spent days looking for me—so, have you been working?"

"They fired me, for stealing, took so much stuff I owed them back pay." She smiled. And I could imagine her, calculating her hourly wage, stealing twice that every day. Blaming shoplifters when it was part of her job to catch them. The management scratching their heads, then having to watch her as she watched, realizing how little point there was in that.

I stared at her, at her fine skin and determination, and I was so happy that she had found me.

"Kiss me?" I asked.

"You're acting really strange, Kelly, all wisdom, like you know something. How long have you been here?"

Her eyes were a little big, not like fear was in them, but alertness, cat's eyes. She took her gum out, stood up, and went to the bathroom to throw it away. The light went on.

"Not long. I went to see my ex-girlfriend for a little while."

"Why?" Her voice was muffled, but she was not worried. Cass was no threat to her. She knew that.

"So she could forget me, I guess. So we could forget each other. But no. I don't know anything." I had not raised my voice.

I imagined her looking at herself, at the sharp makeup outlines around her eyes. She spoke slowly, and I could just hear her.

"I knew you were okay, that you had your heart in a good place, did the right thing, knew who needed help, but then, when you went big—"

"But I'm not good anymore."

And I was sure about that. If I was good, we'd be somewhere else. Felix would be with us. Wyt would be a stranger. Kevin would not be my real brother.

"Forget all that. I still want you," she said.

My friends and brothers spun away even as Luz came back into the room and sat down in front of me again. I watched as she flexed her arms, dug into the carpet, tested it, her body moving up and down through her fingers. I thought, I ran from her, she followed me home. And I knew that right then it was dangerous for us to be anywhere near each other. And if I told her that I loved her? Soon, she would have to go home. In her house, our love would hurt her.

"What are you doing now anyway?" she asked.

"Waiting. Do you want to wait with me?"

"I'd rather do with you whatever it is you're waiting to do."

"That's good," I said. "That's nice."

I leaned forward and kissed her once. We were careful not to lose our balance.

We went up and stood in the middle of the big empty room with the skylight showing a strip of moon and a lot of the glowing dark blue night. We stood there and we undressed each other.

I found a red blanket in a corner and I laid it out. We had never been really naked together. Always her bra and panties were just off or just on, always things were nervous, rushed, poor. I found myself pushing all around her, biting at her as she lay back, eyes closed. Her body had swelled a bit since I'd been with her, her breasts were larger, nipples thick and straining against my mouth, her belly rounder, all of her somehow more sure, more predator. I listened to her breathing as I kissed down a line from her nose, to chin, between her breasts, and then down, between her legs, until she began to quiver and we were both burning—I could feel the heat all through her body, so it didn't matter that the room was cold.

"Let me show you the balcony."

"Isn't it too cold?"

"It's okay."

We took the blanket out there and laid it on top of the old snow that covered the point and oval that was my perfect balcony. She lay down on the blanket but she did not shiver and I got on top of her. Maybe some people in the surrounding buildings came to their windows. I can only hope the sanctity of the rich night was compromised for just one second by our noise. Steam came off us. The faded red of the blanket turned crimson when the snow melted into the wool.

I hope all those fucking bastards saw me on top of her, me all white and pale, my bare white ass moving on top of her. I hope a lot of people saw us, were scared, or afraid, or fascinated and jacking away, wishing that they could ever make love so hard in the snow. I remember going inside and crying quite a lot, afterward. But outside had been a beautiful picture.

She was curled up in front of me with the wet blanket over her. There was steam around her, an impossible cloud. I was naked, down on the floor, leaned against a wall. There was beer in the fridge, and food, but I didn't want anything.

She said, "You've changed since the fall. You're older now, more sure."

"Well, you have to harden up sometime. I've lost so much, and so even when you show me love—"

"You need to take it. I give you love. And you need to accept it, to understand that." She spoke so clear but it was wet and cold all around us and maybe it was not so easy to understand such a simple thing.

"Listen, when everything was stolen from me, my apartment, you know, and the money, that messed me up—you have to see how hard it is to trust—"

"I went to him. I begged him to give it back. I went to his house. He told me, 'Stay the fuck away.' That's what he said."

"You talked to him? You knew about it?"

"Yeah. Your fake brother. He said it was an all-secret thing. Came up in a rented van with some big black guy and they took everything in half an hour. Nobody was gonna speak to either of them and ask what's up. You'd been gone a month. Everybody thought you were dealing drugs anyway, was why you acted guilty and tried to give away food, and that move out was the payoff. Funny thing though, Kelly, at first, at the beginning my father didn't think that. He was the only one who believed you, and you messed that up. Those guys showed, then he believed all the drug talk. You should see him, how sad he is. He wanted us to get married. And that's when I got upset and went after Felix. He said he didn't even know where you were."

"Staying with him was where. Out buying food for his family."

And then I wasn't crying anymore.

I said, "Married, huh? So now I'm not waiting."

"For what?"

"What I said before, I'm not waiting, I'm gonna do this thing myself. I want you to apologize to your father from me. He's a good man."

"If my father knew I saw you he'd throw me out the window."

"I can change that."

"No," she said, "you can't."

"I can try," I said. "We don't have to be dangerous forever."

I got up off the floor and went to the fridge and got out some beer. The cans were cold and I touched them to the muscles in my stomach. I opened two cans and gave one to Luz. We sipped the beer.

"It is true," she said. "You would think it would not be so impossible for us to be together. You would think it would be easier."

She got up and took off the towel, and stood before me. She flexed her toes. The nakedness of the room must have had that effect, where she felt comfortable undressed in that space. She had never stood before me this way in Spanish Harlem.

I felt my balls pull up a bit and I was hard again, staring at her. I looked up at her, at her big naked body as she stretched in front of me and relaxed, showed herself to me. She pulled me up, and even after I was standing she held me, so I was hard between her legs and completely hers.

"Let's go downstairs," I said. We went down and got in the sleeping bag. It was such a perfect place, and I had been showing it no respect at all. We were very slow with each other, and we did the dream thing, where we said I love you back and forth to each other, all through our sex. Afterward, I knew I was still trying to rid myself of a fact, to shake off a nasty punch. My blood brother Felix ripped me off.

"He was my brother," I said.

"No," she said. "He was not."

She held me to her and I rested my head there, in her curve of neck and shoulder.

"It's a strange place we're in, to be so sad," she said.

And then later she must have gotten too scared, about us, because she was gone.

3 5

I stood in the vestibule of my building with Todd. He smoked a forbidden on-duty cigarette that he held too close to him, so the smoke moved into the wide sleeve of his coat. If I watched carefully, I could see thin lines of smoke come up out of his jacket and circle his neck. Together, we stared at some dumb middle-aged lady in a fur coat the color of a Bronx Zoo panda. She sat in the passenger seat of a Jaguar and screamed instructions at her husband, while he proved that old and rich as he was, he'd never learned to parallel park.

It was ten A.M. and freezing. We were into the bitter cold of dead, unforgiving winter. People hurried down the street, their heads angled down against the wind. I was in my long coat and a suit, because I was dressed for the crime and because I could no longer figure out how to dress casually, without a suit. Nothing was easy.

Everything, everything! It was all difficult. It had been three days since I'd seen Luz and that time was weighing on me, like days without food, where the hunger of loneliness gnawed at my resolve.

"Should I go out and help them?" Todd asked.

"No," I said, "it's freezing. What did they ever do for you?"

"True," Todd said. Ashes fell from his sleeve.

The guy did a few bumper taps with the green Lexus behind him. My phone rang. I pulled it out of my breast pocket.

"Now is perfect," Wyt said. He cut off the call. I opened the big door.

"Have a good day, sir," Todd said, back in his doorman role. By then I'd learned it was better to just nod and mutter thanks, better than telling people not to say terrible things like *sir,* which was just—it was like when those bastards suddenly parked that car, when the man got out and jerked his thumb up at Todd, "Get over here, we got packages, we're here to see Mrs. Hartwig, now move it!"—all so far beyond my control.

I walked along and ran my fingers around my eyelids, which were puffed out and ridged from too much anxious sleep. I kept making up little sayings, as if I was the star of some easy-to-follow action flick: soon we'll be together; after this, baby, we'll fly far away where they can't catch us; oh, we'll be okay, we'll be fine. It's just you and me till the end.

I came up to the right building and I knew it, like greeting a familiar opponent. I knew its lines, its tempo. I knew the invisible cage of space on the street where the doorman paced.

I walked up to the black iron gate and I pushed the buzzer. There was silence. I touched the door and it was open. A freshly cut wire hung loose above my head. I went through that door and the next two. The alarm system had been killed. For me? I found a door and crept up some stairs slow enough so that my breathing didn't change. The staircase had the clean and brisk air of good maintenance, where dirt was not tolerated, where people paid to maintain a true high standard. I pulled at the air, hard, took deep money breaths.

A fat little maid went down past me, and she was carrying a big winter coat, a plastic bag, and her sneakers. I looked and saw that her eyes were closed and after she passed I listened to the tiny noise of her stocking feet. I was sure she was keeping track of my steps even though I was in my superquiet Barneys burglar shoes. I know I heard her whispering all sorts of prayers.

The landing on the right floor was deserted and the door to that apartment was not closed. I watched the edge of the door as it wavered slightly with the force of inner and outer air. By then I knew that if a door is hung right, perfectly, it will quiver in wind like a sheet of paper, even if it weighs more than a man.

"Hello everyone," I said. I was on the inside, and I tried to sound like I belonged. I had fitted hooks into the back of my overcoat and I planned to hang the paintings there, just hang them off me. And if they bulged when I left the building, so what? There were stranger things.

I got ready to move fast but I turned in, in too far—the staggering beauty of the apartment. The slowdown happened. I slipped off my overcoat. The little picture of the sick man was right where it was supposed to be. I walked, waded into all that perfect furniture. The other picture, of the dark red spot fixed high in the black background, was in the dining room. I stood in there and leaned up against the sideboard, listened to the clicking shivers of the silver tea set, crossed my ankles. I thought: It has never yet been my intention to get caught up in desire, to get busted by all this money. I thought: I am twenty-one years old and I have never yet dealt with the truth.

"Things have been hard," I said, "very hard." But the dining room snubbed me and didn't answer.

In the living room, I sat down where I'd sat with Cass just a few weeks before and I let my head roll back. Of course there were mints on the side table. There were always mints in these fucking places. Like the garbage bags of rice in the Acevedo apartment, these mints were a message: We have food; there's food here. No need to feel anything but good here. As if you fucking already couldn't tell. I flipped the bowl onto the floor. Falling onto untold yardage of Oriental rug, there was no noise.

I folded my arms over my chest and it was as if I were waiting.

"What have I been up to?" I asked aloud.

"Well, maybe I haven't made good yet, but I will—I shall. Uh . . ." I had to fight to keep my voice down. "I'm sorry about this, these little misunderstandings that have happened, these mistakes." But maybe all that wasn't so important. I felt heat under my shirt, sudden sweat at my eyebrows, my palms.

"You don't mind if I sit here a while do you? It's just I haven't had the time to get the right couch for my own apartment."

I stretched out.

There was so much to that fabric! A brocade of pink inlaid with creamy white, all so thick that I could literally dig my fingers in and the fabric fought up against me, pressed me to it. I dug into the design and the cheeks of my ass pressed down into the bottom cushions and I could feel my spine settle in, find its way in all that perfect rhythm and slip in and jibe. I needed to have more of my skin touch the fabric and even as I pushed my face into the wonderful thick pink smell, I was opening my shirt, my jacket, my pants. I purred maybe, a lot. The whole room was the dead silent of complete safety. The quiet of the caves of the rich.

"You are so good," I said, "you are so good to me." I fumbled with my clothes, tried to get as much of my skin as possible laid out there, so I could just feel real sexy and comfortable. I was laid out full then, on the most beautiful couch in the world—a wonderful trusting thickness against my skin. I was welcomed there, where I was supposed to be, beyond doubt.

"Would you hurry up?"

My face was buried deep in the warm furry gap between back

and seat. I had heard something that was not me. I felt my lips curl, a needle not of fear but of some awful frustration. The message always the same: you won't get what you need here. And I was interrupted.

I knew that voice. I got up and tucked myself back into my suit. The room was still beautifully silent, but there had been that voice, unmistakable. A loud male sigh. I walked down twenty feet of hall into a massive and yet completely anonymous spare bedroom that the maid must have dusted ten minutes before. Wyt. He was sitting on the bed, his legs crossed, one hand propping himself up. He had the other in front of him—he was literally looking at his nails.

"What are you doing here?"

"I asked you to hurry up," he said.

There was one of those useless embroidered incidental chairs next to a blue marble dressing table. I sat down.

"Look, guy, listen to me, the customer was concerned that other items would be stolen. Apparently you overdid your task on the first job. Of course, I can't walk out with these things myself, since I am so known, but I am here to make sure you take only what was agreed upon." And then he hummed, "I love to love you."

Did he even know my name? I was staring, not relaxed, a feeling not in but *on* my stomach, something blunt and painful pushing at me. It—whatever it was—it hurt. I couldn't focus, I could only look at his clothes, the way he was dressed like a fashion designer, in a double-breasted suit and a turtleneck sweater. He looked—he looked like such an asshole, all invited, all worthy of the bed.

Why does that matter?"

"You don't know?"

"What are we really doing here?" I almost said, you are—you have ruined the whole thing for me, the goodness of it.

"Look, who do you think my clients are? These people. The owners are my clients. I steal their art and sell it back to them, plus they get the insurance settlement—I'm like a hack shop, you understand? Illegal hack shop, take things apart, put them back together, make more money—but there has to be some real criminal involved, you, a thief—"

But he saw how I was staring.

"Listen, guy," he said. "I will get some large sum of money for this work, of which as much as—tens of thousands, fifty even, might go to you. That's, for you, stupendous, unreal money."

"You should not exist."

"Ah, ah! The money does exist! I'm working on that! The account with Tucker Golden, I know, there are some problems there—"

"No, you—"

"Yes, it will exist. Now, you want to sleaze off on the couch, that is fine, you leave your mark, like an animal. Pathetic, really. But so what? We will not give that evidence to the police, and my clients know that they have to endure a certain amount of, of—"

"Sleaze?"

"Sure, like I said, yes. If they want to work with me, get their cash flow high again—"

I stood up. I used the arms of the chair to steady myself. I got over to him.

He waved his hands around, like, let's save a lot of time, this is how the whole rest of this conversation will go. I saw his face harden, saw how I was only an employee. And I couldn't be that anymore. What good were we doing anyway? An insurance scam? Like mixing baby milk with rancid water to make it last longer—nothing but hurt. The sort of awful thing my parents had taught me was wrong, the very worst kind of crime. In that second I was amazed: How could I have moved so far from what was good?

"Listen, little thief, just do what I say."

So everything I'd done with him was helping nobody. The rich never got poorer. I would never fill up. The poor, they never got the money. I never gave it to them, anyway. And I was a known thief.

I hit him. What else could I do? I hit him backhanded, hard like I was in the back of the truck and I was slamming a box into place. I put my shoulders into it. He'd probably been hit before, back where ever he was from, because he flipped right off the bed and rolled away. He didn't get up. You could see it in his whole body, the cringing, how he wouldn't fight, didn't want to get hit again. And yet he'd been hurting people for years. He was a minus, a negative suck, helping nobody.

"Now what the hell?" he asked, and he pronounced the *the* weird, like a *z*. So I hit him again, and then again, in the chest, and he was bigger than me and he stood up and I hit him again, lower, and even as he reached for me I stepped back and punched him.

"You fuck me up!" I yelled. A little maniac—I was crying. I kicked him in the shin, punched him to the floor, punched his head when he was down. I heard the soft plodding noise of my hand punching him, the same as when my brother Kevin hit me. There was that descent into cold water, Felix knocking me into a stream without hesitation, us both asking, Is this for real?

Is this brotherhood for real?

Wyt rolled into a rounder ball, and when I was ready to hit him a second time, he reached up and grabbed my fist, held it. He must have thought I was some kind of idiot animal.

"You are acting so wrong," he said. "You should go." And he meant, You are making a mess of things.

"Is there cash here, have you got some?"

"No," he said.

I looked around. There was a black leather bag on another chair. I went over, picked it up. There were a lot of ATM twenty-dollar bills in the bag, what seemed like hundreds of them.

"I'm going to take this," I said.

"Sure. I was just going to split it with you," he said.

"Well"—I shrugged—"I'll take it, and we'll forget all this."

"It's all forgotten. Stupid criminal, poor boy. Greedy bastard, you want it all to yourself."

"I don't."

"You do. Dumb righteous bastard. You are the worst of them all. Serves me just right, that I pick a little know-nothing fall-down thief. I should have been more careful, but you always need the expendable element of the plan . . ." He kept going, whispered to himself, muttered curses. I turned to go, but then all I saw was Felix, walking away with everything I owned, stealing from me, telling my neighbors it was okay. I was sorry that I thought of Felix. I saw how it would be, me and Felix, always poor, fighting each other, gaining nothing.

A brotherhood built on mistrust and theft. A philosophy built on nothing but an insurance scam. All along I had no idea. Maybe I did know. Wyt was still rolled up, faced away from me. A panting ball, waiting.

"I'm going now," I said. "I don't know you. We never heard of each other."

I walked out. I took that thin man painting with me. It was mine.

The swift walk back, one thought, Luz was in me, learned me. I thought about her body, the tension rods, the hardness when I touched her. Luz was the place where I was from, where I truly belonged. But it wasn't safe there. And I was afraid.

I gave Todd my keys.

"I don't exist, now come with me," I said.

"Okay." He followed me into the elevator. In my apartment, I gave him $2,000.

"Call the cleaning service. Tell them I moved out. Have them clean up and they can take it from there, throw away all this stuff, take what you want."

"You going on a trip?"

"Yeah."

The little picture banged against my back. Todd helped me pack a suitcase full of only the good clothes, the things I'd bought when my money was no longer my own.

"I got a cousin who would like this sleeping bag," Todd said.

"Take it, take it all."

There were dark clouds above us. As we packed me up, I was sad that the empty belly lacked its usual sun-strengthened color.

"Nobody ever stays in this apartment too long," Todd said. "I guess all the sunlight drives them crazy."

"It's not the light, it's all the people looking in at you."

"But there's shades!"

Todd went over to the kitchen area and pressed two buttons that I had somehow thought were for a garbage disposal that didn't exist. Incredible sheets of white silk slid over all of the skylights and then other shades went down over the windows on either side of the room. When all the shades were down, the room glowed softly. It was nice in there. It was not the onslaught of money that it had been. It did not feel so empty, after all.

"I guess I missed out on that—insulation. It never occurred to me to look for it. Too bad."

"Too bad." Todd laughed. I took out the painting.

"Take my bag and this picture—store them with my other stuff in the basement. My girlfriend will pick it all up. You'll know her because she'll say she's my girlfriend, okay?"

"No problem," Todd said.

I packed bills into the pockets of my overcoat. I was gone from there in three minutes.

I went to Port Authority. I planned to go home. I would
lay low, and set up a life for me and Luz. Before I bought the ticket,
I beeped Jahaira, but Luz must have taken her beeper because she
called me back, fast, at my pay phone.

"It will be okay," I said. "You can meet me up at Rantipole. I think
my parents will put us up for a while. You can bring Alfredo up
there, too. They'll be cool with that."

"I don't know, Kelly. It's more than my father who's looking for
you now—the police came and asked about your apartment. My
father talked to them. He said they, they're putting things together.
Look, leaving here—it may have to be that way. But if you're wanted
for real, you can't bring me into it."

"I won't. I'll fix all of this, and I miss you—we'll be together soon."

"Please think it through—what you decide," she said. I promised her that I would.

Then it was early afternoon, and I thought, I should call my mother first, just to make sure. I had not been home in three years. I was thinking I'd stay for a while, maybe pick up some odd-job work, do a night watchman gig on a construction site or some such thing, then me and Luz would be together, there. See if we couldn't work it out, get a place together. We could enroll Alfredo in a school. He could be in my parents' classes.

"Hello, Mom?"

"Marty!" I looked around. What the fuck? Marty. That's what my parents called me. My name is Kelly. My name is MKM. My name is Mickey. But Marty? That's not my name. It still felt like there was someone to my left or my right that my mother was talking to. I could not conjure her up. All I could see was that fishbone barrette, a smock dress with a faded print, L. L. Bean duck boots over quarter-inch-thick blue wool stockings.

"Marty, Kevy has been—he's been worried. He said he can't find you, that's he's been trying. He said he even called Felix! But Felix said he didn't know where you were—he said he didn't know anything about you. Marty, what have you been doing?"

I tried to imagine her, standing in the kitchen. To conserve, they would only have lights on in there. My father would be standing, watching my mother on the phone. I imagined his half wave in the background. Tell the boy I say hello. I looked at the newly worn bottoms of my pants, at the dirty edges of my dreamy black coat. I could not press myself upon them. They'd brought me up right. I was grown up and I had to go to where I was supposed to be.

"Marty? Where are you now?"

Truly, she'd never done anything bad to me, not ever. It was wrong to force them to protect me. I could not hide there.

There wasn't nothing wrong with them, my parents. Only, I couldn't go to them now. I looked out at Ninth Avenue. The sky was ice clear, but still that same terrible northern gray. An impossible, violent lack of color.

"Marty, what can we do for you?"

"I'm going to be fine."

"What?"

"You never went back home, did you, Mom? The two of you never went back."

"What does that matter to—"

"It's okay, I'm glad to talk to you. I'm going to go uptown now."

I could just hear my father in the background. "What the hell?" he yelled.

"Is it true, what you've been doing?" my mother said.

The noise and all the light from the street needed to stop.

"Wait," my mother said.

But why? Why wait? There was nothing wrong with my mom. She knew just what I was doing. There was nothing she could do about it, and probably, she would not protect me. But it didn't matter. I had been claimed elsewhere, by Luz. I was no longer stuck through with the elaborate lies and pacts of childhood.

"Tell Dad I love him, and Kevin, tell him that, too, and you, too, Mom. I love you. I just wanted to give you a call." I had been wrong so often, about so many things, that one more step toward a misguided trip on the way to my real home—that was nothing. I was grown up enough to know that I was going to be wrong most of the time and wrong was not always the worst thing to be. The only thing I knew that was right was Luz, and I knew that for sure because she'd told me so.

It was weird, how they couldn't understand. You got to focus. You got to choose just a slim few people, give them your love. I got off the phone. I could feel the two of them looking at each other, wondering, turning their radio back up. So now, if there was going to be an interruption, if I was going to have to see the police before I could keep on going and making things right, that was not such an impossible thing to do, if it would clean things up.

I could have gone to my parents and they could have told me, all over again, all the things they thought they'd made me understand. They would have done that and then I would still have to come back, to go uptown. But to take such a long trip? There wasn't time. You got to focus. Give only a slim few people your love. When she sent Felix back to New York, she sent me there, too. But it was only a small mistake, and it was not their mistake. It was mine. I'd been grown up good and well enough, the best that I could hope for anyway. So it was time not to run.

I stepped out into the street and it was freezing and dusk.

I called Felix. He was home. Him, too, my parents, all in their warm homes. Me, outside.

"I need to come see you," I said.

"My brother, no. Please forget me."

I thought, My brother? My brother. We were fixed then, I thought.

"Why?"

I listened as Lynanne, the same Irish as my mother, yelled in the background. She wanted him off the phone. I listened to Anastasia cry. I watched the people stream into Port Authority, now that it was the end of the day.

"We don't know each other anymore. If you ever want to do right, you'll forget we ever knew each other. Take the blame on yourself."

"My brother—"

"Now, I can't even lie. Don't call me your brother. I won't do it again. Be glad I took that money, that'll be your mark, the good you did. My family thanks you."

"Felix—"

"I figure, five years, seven, I'll become a teacher. So long as you don't give me up. You hear me?"

"I do," I said. "That's . . . that's good—"

"It's you who should get that job, feeding the furnace, the coal job. Then you could get some time to think. Promise that you'll forget you knew me."

"That's all you want?" I asked. I knew I could do that. I had done him wrong so many years ago, and now, I could remember to say nothing about him. Instead, I would talk to the police about Wyt. That was fair.

"I'm going to go see Luz now," I said.

"Then no doubt that's where they will find you," he said.

Felix was often right. I had always liked to listen to him. I went and took two trains, arrived uptown.

When it is freezing, the uptown streets go empty. Perhaps weather is given too much power there, too much respect. I turned the corner on to what used to be my block. Across the street, I watched as the door to the social club opened. There was no light behind the door. Ocides came out. He was twenty feet from me, not smiling, a huge black coat over his work clothes, a ski hat on his head. He turned around and yelled into the social club. Then he turned to me.

I crossed the street. There was no traffic, not a car in sight. Though it was dusk, there was an incredible late-night feel to the dark.

"Ocides," I said.

"For you, I think it's over," he said.

"I know, but I wanted to see Luz."

He stepped forward.

"You won't see anybody. Don't move," he said.

"What?"

He jumped forward and grabbed me, got behind my back and locked me down and I could not move. I struggled free of him and turned. But he'd made a hammer with his two hands and even as I moved to meet them, he knocked me to the ground. I wasn't laid out, but I wasn't up, either. I was down on my knees. I looked up at the night sky.

"Now we wait for the police," he said.

Luz came out of the building.

"You say good-bye from there," Ocides said. "You don't come near him."

"I'll miss you," I said.

She ran out and stood between me and her father. She held her hands out and I let her pull me up, but after that I didn't move.

"He won't run, Daddy, let him go." And Ocides looked at her and then I heard him breathing and he did. He nodded. He let me go.

"What do you want to do?" she asked. I stood there, looking at her.

"Let's just—we can sit together for a moment, before they come. I know we can do that," I said. I started to walk, slow, toward the White Castle around the corner. Luz walked next to me. But she turned back to her father.

"It's okay," she said. "You can have them find him in the parking lot. He knows it's over. I know it's over, too, for now. Nobody here is going to run anymore."

We walked together, just like we had in the early fall. And I wasn't hungry, but I wanted to sit with her, for just a little while, in all that bright honest light. We got there and walked in and there were only a few other people sitting there, eating. Behind the Plexiglas, they watched us, because we sat down on one side of a booth and didn't order. I kissed her.

"It just took me so long to figure out how to get to you," I said. "I know I messed that up bad, getting clear, but at least now I know."

She smiled and then she almost laughed. I looked at her incredible face, at her big black eyes and her mouth. She shook her head, the both of us knowing that if we were ever going to make it, now, it was going to be a few more years.

"When you leave here, you take my coat. There's money in it, for you. And there are a couple of pictures and some other stuff in my basement. You need to go get it all from the doorman and then hold on to it. We'll sell the pictures, when I get out. In the meantime . . ."

"Yeah," she said. "In the meantime, I'm going to be so angry at you."

"You've certainly got the right," I said.

"I know it. Inside, I'm furious with you. But in a while—maybe we'll be together, if I'm not upset anymore and if you get smarter when you're in. And you don't forget me."

"That's good," I said. "That's enough for me to go on."

She pushed her head at my neck then and all I could do was hold her and say nothing. I thought about how you have to stay with those who claim you for their own. You must trust someone, sometime. Focus. Give only a slim few people your love. I looked around and people were watching us, and they couldn't stop, and I don't think they even knew why. But nobody made a move.

"I love you," she said. And I whispered it back to her. Then I felt really good and not so young, anymore.

"Let's go outside," I said. We walked into the parking lot. I picked her up and spun her around. I held her and she laughed and so did I and I took off my big black coat and she put it on.

"I'm going now. I need to not be here when they come. I'll tell Alfredo you'll see him soon, okay?"

"Yeah. I do love you so much. All I'm ever going to be about is you now. You know that, don't you?"

"I do. Listen, Kelly, don't forget. I'm not sorry about any of the things you did, not any of them."

We heard the police cars coming. So then it was time for me to go, and for Luz to walk away from me.

Acknowledgments

Thanks to Jennifer Braunschweiger, Fran Gaitanaros, Jillian Medoff, April Lamm, Linda Schrank, Built to Spill, Faith Childs, Harris Schrank, The Blue Mountain Center, The MacDowell Colony, Ann Treistman for her excellent work, and, for her awesome will, Jennifer Carlson.